This page has been intentionally left blank

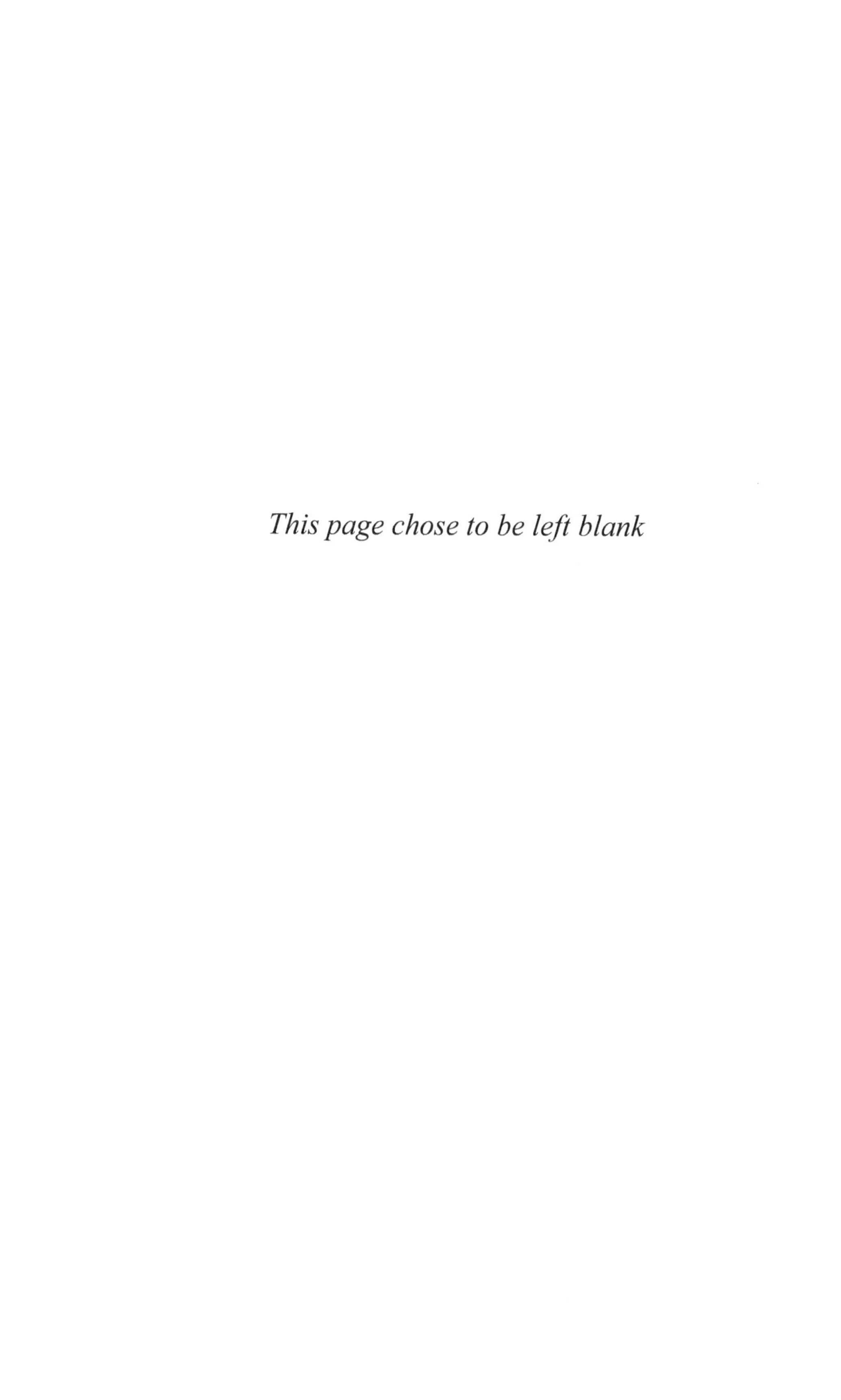

This page chose to be left blank

Opus Two B:
Sammy's Funereal Adventure

One novella and
Two novelettes
Two essays
and
Five short stories

by

Doug Miller

Edited by D. Schulek-Miller

This page is dedicated to Mel Blanc.

Second Edition

*The author confesses that due to unprofessional format errors in the
first edition and the creation of another essay that he did not wish to
keep from publication until Opus V (already WIP), this new edition was
necessary.*

That's all folks.

9 August, 2020

This book is dedicated to He who is everything,
Kate, Miles, Pascale, Adam,
and
Mary and Jerry of blessed memory.

Table of Contents

ACKNOWLEDGEMENTS 6

SAMMY'S FUNEREAL ADVENTURE 10

TIME FLIES LIKE AN ARROW... 125

ISAAC MEETS NEOGEORGIAN 134

HE AND SHE POINTLESS 156

LADIES, LADIES, ON THE WALL 166

BODACIOUS BOB'S BOUTIQUE BLESSINGS 176

HE KNEW HE WAS STANDING THERE 215

BERTRAND MEETS VENUS 233

COME FLY WITH ME... 241

LIMITATIONS OF BRAIN RESEARCH 273

Acknowledgements

First we have to declare that nobody in this book is modelled on or resembles anyone living or dead. Think about that for a moment. How many people do you know that are 120 years old, eh? But no character in the fiction stories is anything but a product of the author's turgid imagination... excepting Rabbi Moshe Aishich, Rabbi Isaac Luria, and Rabbi Chaim Vital and their blessed memory, who were all very real and immensely spiritual and holy men of the 16th century. But the author is not so old that he knew them so they are historical characters. The author is hopeful that any light treatment of these significant figures in Hebrew history is not taken as disrespect.

And Chapter 5 of Sammy's story is dedicated to personal and electronic colleagues who've had to tolerate the worst of government incompetence and corruption for decades.

And as the author is not aware of any of his lives being led as insects or pilots, those and anyone or companies referenced in these stories except for the previously mentioned historic figures are obvious inventions of the author's distressed imagination... however much you think it resembles your late departed cousin from the old country or a company that used to be famous, it isn't.

And anyone's guess as to why Isaac has no demons would be of interest to the author as he knows, but do you?

Admittedly, some of these brief stores are but silliness....
but have you watched what passes for "news" lately? We
live in a strange age when the political fabrications of
purported adults are less believable than the small stories
printed herein. The incredulous fabrications of hysterical
dimensions are designed to look like facts...when facts are
delivered aloof and cold. Curious, isn't it? And they
expect you to believe them and not this? Balderdash!

And the author thoroughly thanks his poor children who
have endured late dinners and an apparently non-listening
father in preparation of this volume and its stories.

Comments and questions may be submitted the author at:
sammy@spongebrain.ca .

Sammy's Funereal Adventure

So, what would you do at a funeral if the corpse suddenly sat up and began talking? While 'run like mad' may be the initial thought that comes to mind, but in this day of videoing the sinking of the Titanic before climbing into the lifeboats, maybe not. A witness to the oblivious people with "buds" in their ears walking along aurally blindly, having forsaken the audio warning channel for "their music", might wonder how many would survive if a danger that only presented itself aurally might appear. Few, unfortunately.

If the eugenicists want to wipe out one third of the population of the planet, as many say they do, all they really need to do is hand out incredible smart phones for free along with ear buds and let the Darwin Awards take their course.

Chapter 1 - We're all going to Sammy Silver's Funeral.

It was nothing unusual, just an ordinary Jewish funeral. Sammy Silver was lying there in his kittel in a pine box on the dais while a portly Rabbi Goldbaum was standing over him, twittering off all those well-known phrases and hackneyed sentiments typical of Jewish funerals before the serious prayers began. Now, seasoned funeral-goers observed that this was a serious diversion from routine but the Rabbi was stalling to be sure all the mourners arrived, as there was a last minute change of venue.   The dais was in the centre of an amphitheatre style auditorium encompassing fully 270 degrees of seats around where the Bimah usually stood during services, with seven levels of seating stretching from the base of the two-level raised dais, rising to much higher elevations at the back of the sanctuary with a wide aisle running around the top and five evenly distributed stair-stepped aisles coming down from the back to the central dais. The Ark was discretely covered by a curtain and not as visible as it is during the services that this shul[1] hosted three times daily for the surrounding congregants as it was one of the larger and more splendid orthodox shuls in Ottawa.

The ceremonies had been moved from Sammy's respectable shul to this larger and grander synagogue because the volume of mourners kept growing and growing as they heard of the untimely, but never unexpected demise of the 120 year old man. After all, he was a real outlier in the age demographics even amongst Jews.

It wasn't that Sammy was famous or even all that popular. He was making a fair living for his family these days as a writer of short stories, whose combined books did

---

[1] Shul is the casual Orthodox Jewish term for Synagogue.

middling well. He was also sufficiently entertaining to be
able to promote them on local and national radio shows and
the odd television appearance here and there. But much of
that was, Sammy thought, because he was blessed with his
ever youthful thinking and a quick mind that had not
slowed despite the years. It was not that he believed that he
was so entertaining, but he thought he was something of a
sideshow freak, one of those strange but true individuals
that people do not see or hear very often. And, to Sammy's
mind, it just became more obvious after he had reached and
surpassed 110. The attention was nice, his wife and
children didn't mind, that level of exploitation was not
harmful and it paid well...so why not?

The mourners later generally agreed that the Rabbi
had just used that old line about the one exclamation
everyone wants to hear at their funeral: "Oh my G-d, he's
breathing!" when Sammy popped out a snore so loud and
nasally resonant that his present and former wives
immediately recognised the source of it - whereupon they
both screamed softly, slapped their hands to their faces, and
fainted in their seats.

"NO," loudly yelled the Rabbi, now staring down at
Sammy, "HE IS BREATHING!"

And that was loud enough that it woke Sammy up
like a start, he sat up, leaned his forearms on the side of the
box, looked around and, not as loud as the Rabbi, said,
"what the heck am I doing here and do you have some
Alka-Seltzer and Excedrin, please?" clutching his forehead
with his left hand.

Whereupon half the female audience joined
Sammy's wives in a screaming swoon, some just screamed,
and a few shrieked "Dybbuk!" in the midst of near hysteria.
The ones that thought Sammy a Dybbuk[2] got up and ran for

---

[2] A *dybbuk* is a demon that takes over dead bodies and generally has a
malevolent intention or is possessing to alleviate a responsibility not

the exit. Some people phoned friends, others pulled out
their phones and began recording. Strangely, no one
phoned 9-1-1 to get ambulances to help the women that had
fainted; but one of the telephoned friends had the presence
of mind to do so, thankfully.

But that was not Sammy's primary concern at that
time, as the pain in his head was absolutely monumental.
At the screaming, Sammy covered his ears.

"Please, please, not so loud, my head is pounding,"
he said softly, not even realising the source of the
screaming, but then he began to be aware of where he was
and how he was dressed.

"And what am I doing in my kittel in a box,
anyway?" he inquired.

And at that point the Rabbi swooned, and plopped
across on the chairs on the dais.

But being Sammy's children, Rachel, Moshe,
Joshua, Joseph, Sarah, and Margaux ran to the dais and
hugged or tried to hug Sammy, saying, "Oh Daddy, you
aren't dead."

"We're so happy."

"Baruch Hashem."

"This is wonderful. Are you really alive?"

"Can we go home now?"

"Does this mean we don't get cake for dinner?"

As painful as it was, Sammy thought for a
moment.... what do you mean I'm not dead?

Did they think I was dead? Kittel?.... oh.... OY!...
OY VEY ES MIR!

But as Sammy was overjoyed to see the children,
his pounding head felt like 20 miles of bad pavement on a
130-degree day.... and the kittel does not allow for much
modesty. So Sammy was torn between embarrassing

completed when alive. Beneficially, an *ibbur* confers positive traits on
the possessed and was often spiritually engineered to help the recipient.

himself in trying to get out of the box so he could get changed.... or waiting for a dozen aspirin because he really was in serious, serious pain. The full size of the audience and where he was had not really sunk in, yet and the pain was enough that he didn't care one iota if it was Rockefeller Centre because the Rockettes were loudly tap-dancing in his head, going to one ear then shuffling back to the other.

The reason Sammy was in such pain and what may have brought on what appears to have been a cataleptic episode is that to celebrate the holidays and get in the proper and joyful mentality he and a friend were drinking Vodka Gimlets using a lovely smooth kosher for Pesach Vodka and Lime cordial rather than lime juice.... and the lime cordial was 70 proof! So after three of them, Sammy's friend retired to a large comfy chair to sleep it off, but Sammy thought them very tasty and had a few, maybe four or more, more, whereupon he not only passed out but was so becalmed that he was diagnosed as having passed on! Therefore, when he awoke, it was not a headache from returning from the dead and confronting He who would judge him, but a monumental, once in a lifetime hangover from a really, really, really mean chorus line of Vodka Gimlets that gave him this cranium splitting headache.

And while we've been explaining Sammy's torturous pain, the mourners were sort of flummoxed as to what to do. With Sammy's lovely wife visibly unconscious, they didn't know if the post funereal party...er... mourning was still on or not. Obviously, the drive to the cemetery was off, so many wondered if they should go back to work as surely this would be a news story somewhere that their colleagues would see and wonder why they didn't return.

Some people have no soul. Really, the thought of witnessing a Lazarus event and just calmly sashaying back to the office is entirely dehumanised and implies an absolutely lame sense of eventing. However, the professionals on hand could see the basis for an excellent party building here with lots of food, wine, booze, long minutes of media coverage, radio, TV, press... and potential international crews, as well. This was going to be a long party event with a lot of publicity angles. Sammy's literary agent, Sid, was sitting in the third row but currently on the phone with New York, and was quickly trying to figure the breadth of the coverage he could get to promote Sammy's books with this new angle.

Sammy's Rabbi, having turned over the ceremonial and Halachic details to Rabbi Goldbaum, was having mixed feelings now such as (1) what kind of aliyah could his gabbai create for a man that had just come back from the dead? and, (2), gee it must be drafty in that kittel - ah! Sammy needs a long coat! So, the Rabbi fetched his raincoat for Sammy and held it behind him, a la Noah's sons, as Sammy clambered out of the pine box with a level of difficulty that one would rightly expect from a thoroughly hung-over man of 120, trying to negotiate the exit of a pine box perched on a couple of supports and from which people are NEVER expected to leave under their own power. Ouch, the splinters! Cheap pine! Now that demure placement of the raincoat was supremely considerate for it solved multiple problems for Sammy and gave him more than a little relief.... but his head was still throbbing like the bass speakers in a boy-racer car.

Then, thanking his Rabbi profusely, wrapping the raincoat around him and having his children gathered round as though they weren't going to see him again, Sammy regained a bit of composure. He went behind the coffin, carefully stepped around the dazed form of Rabbi Goldbaum, stepped up to the microphone, and said, "Ladies and Gentlemen... Ladies and Gentlemen... if you'll calm down for a moment and savour one of the few times in known history that the corpse actually directly addressed the mourners..."

And he waited for that to sink in -- or for them to listen as there was still an audible babble - as one might expect when the dead gets out of the coffin and people were paying more attention to their phones than to him. He wanted to say a few things before the medical crews got there to attend to those that had blacked out in shock as he could faintly hear the sirens approaching, so to speak.

"Before the paramedics arrive, might I just thank all of you for coming to my expected going away party. Sorry, I'm sort of at a loss for words as this is not one of the things one expects in their life, but surely no one else here has spoken at his own funeral. I'll get better when we get back to the house and I can get dressed -- and thank you Rabbi Blum for the discrete loan of your coat. So, if someone would please call the caterers at my house and tell them we'll be a bit early, I'd appreciate it as I don't seem to have my phone with me and my wife is currently indisposed. We'll be along when we get her up and ambulatory and are sure everyone else is fine. But, by the way, has anyone seen my car keys?"

And there was a slight titter through the crowd, indicating that the initial shock was beginning to wear off.

Chapter 2 - The Painful Joys of Returning to Life.

     The cacophony was head splitting for Sammy. He was beginning to think that it would have been better being dead for the pain. Sirens from paramedics and ambulances on the one hand and loud "Mazel Tov's" from all the people in the shul who were filing past him on their way out if their wives were walking already... so many had fainted you'd have thought it was a 1963 Beatles concert. The ones that weren't walking were being attended by paramedics and their husbands and children in some cases - Sammy was not sure if he knew all these people or they were coming to witness the side show of an old man's burial.

     Gee, he thought, I'd never imagined being dead. Do I remember anything that seems like death? Sammy quickly mulled that over and dismissed it as any thought beyond trying to talk was far too painful, still. The pain was not allowing any deliberate thought, trying to make a sufficient impression on him that he would never drink so many of those ever again! OY!

     Sammy and the children shuffled down off the dais and over to his poor wife, apparently trying to regain consciousness and straighten part of her decorum, her dress, her hat and veil in the chair, as spread legs and a flopped over head were never very stylish or comfortable. Sammy and the children arrived at her side about the same time as a paramedic and his medical case. He took out an ammonia inhalant, broke it in half and shoved it under Sammy's wife's nose and her head came up FAST! Sammy was impressed.... but remembered his pain and asked the paramedic if he had anything to relieve his throbbing head.

The guy looked at Sammy, a guy in a white dress in a raincoat, and thought: this guy looks as though he wishes he were dead... and then the children then told him that their father had been in the coffin but had woken up and gotten out - "wasn't it Hashem's miracle?"

Paramedics are used to all sorts of stories, most you don't want to hear, but this was a new one - so, okay, he thought, let's play along, "okay, mister will you sit down and let me take your vital signs?" Perhaps this is the default routine in confronting anything you don't understand in the Paramedic world. Imagine coming face to face with a man that you've been told has just risen up out of his coffin. In the Paramedic world, what do you do? Ask who called for the medic? Nahhhh, what next? Oh, yeah, vital signs, of course. Right. Sure.

At the same time, people were still streaming past Sammy yelling "Mazel Tov" and a few wives were trying to comfort a now fully awake Serah and she was still not fully cognizant of the new Sammy she had and telling them that she'd talk to them at the house. Put them off, put them off, and put them off so I can regain what used to be my composure she was thinking. "Gee, how does a nice Jewish girl get into these things? What have I done to deserve this?" was also going through her mind in the profusion of strange and sudden images confronting her.

Simultaneously, Sammy was trying to convince the paramedic to give him painkillers the size of Godzilla because the hangover was not getting any better.

"Look," he whined, "just a little Morphine, not a lot, I just have to get rid of this pain." Sammy had not had a headache like that since he had suddenly decided to give up caffeine cold turkey 50 years ago and experienced a headache like someone driving a railroad spike through the frontal lobe of his brain without anaesthesia. It had lasted for hours! And nobody could give him anything to relieve the pain. He couldn't understand that at the time and it made just as much sense now. It was so bad he almost could not bear to open his eyes!

"Look," finally said the Paramedic, "sit still for a minute and let me take these readings and I'll give you something to relieve the pain, ok?"

"Anything," Sammy whined, "anything, please."

After a few minutes, the medic wrapped up his equipment and said, "okay, you're fine... BP a little high, but for a guy wearing a dress and a raincoat, I guess it is ok. Now what has caused your headache, do you know?"

Sammy groaned, "yeah it was those Vodka and Lime Cordial Gimlets day before yesterday. Never again never, never, never again," groaned Sammy gently swaying his head.

"Ah. You don't need Morphine, but this might help." And the Medic grinned wryly, took out a syringe and a vial, pulled about 15 cc's into the syringe, bared Sammy's arm and injected it into his upper arm, after using a sterile wipe to swab the area.

"Give that about 20 to 30 minutes and you will be right as rain," said the medic, smiling knowledgably. He packed up his bag and moved to the next faint woman as many were in the process of rousing themselves but needed a bit of a whiff to come fully around.

Curiously, the Paramedic had not asked anything as to why all these people had developed fainting spells...was a thought that did not enter Sammy's head as he was waiting for the miracle pain reliever to work. But before that happened, two of Ottawa's finest ambled down the aisle stairs toward Sammy, Serah, and the children.

"Are you Sammy Silver? " the first of them inquired of Sammy.

Sammy, feeling a little better, ventured, "Don't I look like a dead man?"

Now, cops are used to hearing almost every kind of response you can imagine, all the way from wheedling whines and incomprehensible idiocies to life-threatening hostilities totally out of proportion to the apparent situation. After a while even the attempts of drunks to be creative and original become just so much more tiring, boring, and "here we go again" predictable, but getting a wisecrack from a stiff is just a bit beyond the ordinary, even to Francis Patrick, 20 year veteran of the force.

Before Francis could respond and remove the wry look from his face, Sammy piped up, "pretty vocal for a stiff, aren't I? I wasn't really dead, but I was pronounced so and it is one of those situations where seeing who is disappointed at my resurrection will be highly interesting, no?" Sammy was flicking back and forth between slightly hysterical and comatose, so his verbal acuity was less than usual.

"Sir, we are just here to investigate why so many ambulances were summoned to a funeral, nothing more, really. We see now that many people were overcome, let us say, with your sudden and miraculous recovery. Frankly, we get very few calls to funerals and none where the deceased talks to us, so we're a bit plussed (Francis had always wanted to use that word but rarely had the context presented for it, but here it was, even though it wasn't actually a word), particularly by a guy in a dress covered by a raincoat. So, if you don't mind, could you tell us your address and phone number so that once we figure out if there is any investigation we need to do, we'll call you?"

Sammy was sufficiently composed now that he repressed the urge to ask if there was a charge for living while dead or being dead while living, as he thought better of it since it soon turns into Parliament jokes. The cops might just figure that the folks attending needed a good funeral of which Sammy had deprived them. So Sammy meekly gave them his address and phone number and watched them scribble them down in those ubiquitous little notebooks cops always seem to have. How do they know one note from another he thought... but surely they transfer the information to another form later... yeah, of course.

As the cops plodded back up the stairs, here still was Sammy in his Kittel and Rabbi Blum's raincoat, standing next to Serah who had pretty much come "to" and was just getting up, straightening her dress and hat and standing fairly steadily for a woman whose dead husband had just revived in front of her and a shul full of mourners. Again, it is not a scene one expects in this or the next life, actually. She wasn't sure whether to hug and kiss him or scold him for ruining a perfectly good funeral, as the arrangements had been a right pain, having to change shuls in the middle of things. The children were still literally hanging on to him as Serah finally said, "I guess we better go home so you can change and we can have a celebration rather than mourning party.... and I'd forgotten!" she brightened, "now I don't have to sit Shiva[3]! That is great! Oh..." and the mood seemed to change, "but I'd best call the caterers as we'll need more wine, booze, and food, now as everyone will be partying and we'll likely get people in that weren't even here. After all, there are very few Lazarus acts in this day and age. Sammy, Sammy, Sammy", she said, turning to him directly, ".... you are always such a surprise," shaking her head slightly from side to side.

As Serah took Sammy's arm, motioning that they climb the stairs to leave, "you can now write a few more stories as there aren't many who get to write about waking up at their own funeral, eh," she said almost brightly, planting a peck of a kiss on his cheek as she did. The children followed as Sammy surveyed the scene in the sanctuary, observing that most people had already left and the Medics were with just a few, now... and even Rabbi

---

[3] "Sitting Shiva" is a Hebrew mourning practice (that includes a lot of other traditional routines) where the close relatives of the deceased sit on low chairs and receive visitors to commiserate - though the polite practice is to let the mourning relatives initiate any conversations.

Goldbaum had recovered on his own and was cautiously making his way up a different aisle. So everything was back to normal as soon as he could get changed and remember to refrain from Lime Cordial Vodka Gimlets...forever.

Or so he thought. But nobody does a Lazarus Act in this day and age without attracting far more attention than they expect and probably not the kind of attention they want, either. Sammy was to discover that painful reality soon.

Chapter 3 - Sammy and his Life.

Serah was sufficiently recovered to drive them all home. Remember, Sammy had no ID or license or shoes and imagine explaining the reality of that morning to a traffic cop if they'd been stopped. It wasn't a long drive across town, but it was punctuated by a very peculiar conversation on Serah's phone between Sammy and the caterer at their house. Phillip the Caterer was a robust man, not usually given to excitement as the food business generally teaches you that anything can and will happen in catering a party, dinner, wedding, or mourning luncheon, but he was not prepared for this. Nobody was prepared for this.

At least they were able to get up their drive and into the garage, though the street was filling with cars and people walking to their house. The family was able to exit the garage through a side door and into the house by a back door so that the crowds out front would not see them. Once inside, Sammy went through the kitchen, greeted Philip and his crew, turned to the centre hallway, then to the front entry hall, then up the curved stairs to the landing and then into their bedroom to change and was thoroughly relieved that his wife hadn't thrown his clothes away, yet. The children actually followed him and went to their rooms to change out of their formal clothing. When he had put on a pair of khaki's, a blue striped shirt, socks and penny loafers, and hung up Rabbi Blum's raincoat and his Kittel... he reconsidered and added a blue blazer as a stiff has to look properly respectful and thankful for recovering, no?

Serah had gone to the kitchen and spoke with Phillip, trying to figure how they were going to handle the mourners and sift out the interlopers. Then, while the caterer had called for more prepared food and dishes to be delivered from his kitchens, the truck wasn't there yet and he was worried it would get stuck in the increasing crowds of people and cars. Serah needed some ideas as she was still slightly reeling from having to rearrange her life yet again within 48 hours. Phillip's people were hustling about, mostly near the wine bar, adding a few Whiskies, Rye, Bourbon, Gin, and mixers and adopting the idea that this could be a far longer party then they had expected. A few had to call to cancel later plans or put them on hold... what an inconvenient guy, this Sammy; what did he think he was doing, ruining a perfectly planned funeral?

So, let's take a moment and look at Sammy, perhaps - for there may be some explanation needed. Sammy Silver was not like the old people many see trotted out on the news for sideshow value. He actually had been exercising for years to keep himself limber - as he needed to be with his wife of the last 20+ years. She was fully 40.... or was it 50... or maybe 60 years younger than Sammy? She was lots younger anyway and years earlier everyone thought the wedding peculiar as Sammy never had enough money to attract a Black Widow or Trophy wife. So why did she marry him when she was a real looker and could have pulled off a marriage to a number of far better financially well-off spouses? Why, indeed?

Then, if that level of derision was not enough, the talk of irresponsible parenthood was quite the rage amongst almost everyone within and outside the Tribe when Sammy and Serah began having children (AT HIS AGE! WHAT ARE THEY THINKING?) - but the Silvers didn't care. This was their life and no one else's. If Hashem was to give them children, surely there was a good reason for it as He did nothing without a purpose. When asked, as he often was and usually in a tone that dripped condescension and gushed moral pre-judgement, as to why he had children, Sammy always had two answers. One was to wax eloquently about Avraham and Sarah, the scions of Hebrew life, who did not have Isaac until Avraham was 100.... and this got a lot of hubris-laden huffs of tangentially-self-righteous blowback from the conveniently secular Jews and non-Jews, i.e., people who did not relate to a Torah based life. Sammy and Serah didn't care. This was their life. The other standard response was to simply note that they have done nothing but the usual marriage sanctioned relations and if Hashem wanted the result of that to be children, there were children, period. Sammy often wryly said he was merely the instrument of Hashem's will, so to speak.

Sammy became inured to this kind of derisive attention when he used to help manage businesses and change decades before he began to write stories. In earlier years, he was one of those "road warriors" who lived in airports, hotels, on client premises, and on the roads in-between all of them, trying to make a living for his family in the many years before his age and a new wife caught up to him. He had four children while doing that work and Sammy wasn't sure whether it was the work or his self-centred attitude that separated him from his early children and then his wife of the time.

Sammy was never the outgoing type, the sales type, the leader type, but was always the solution developer, the analyst, the process and methods engineer. So when he had to be the leader, and this started years before the road-warrior stage, he simply disassociated and did whatever was necessary, not really relating to himself or the role, but focusing on what had to be done, the epitome of the cynics of long ago. The problem with disassociation is that it generalises to everything and, sooner or later, nothing you do is "you" but the role you believe you are supposed to be playing. In fact, when it fully takes over you have no idea what you really feel, what you think, what you are, or what you should be doing if the role you know or imagine does not specify it. The essence of "you" is well and truly lost. You have no idea what you want even to the point of companionship. It is a heavy price one pays for offsetting anxiety and not being comfortable in the skin one has chosen or has to adopt for work or life. Eventually, if one is really fortunate or blessed, they realise the imaginary reality one's anxieties have scripted to cope with the activities one could not handle for whatever reason. And they take measures to correct the insensitivity, if they can.

But if one is not that blessed, it often becomes that moment nearing retirement, that instant on vacation after years of doing what one does, that immeasurably small thought space where one realises or begins to realise that everything is a sham. Everything one does, everyone one knows, everything you thought you wanted is all a show that is not you - and you are absolutely unsure of what 'you' are; lost, confused, vague, muddled, and sometimes emotionally panicked after losing your grip on what you thought you had been for decades.

This is an awakening that appropriately frightens the dickens and sometimes the life out of people. Imagine discovering in one swell foop that all you've been doing for decades has been for reasons that only some disconnected eidolon understands. What happened to you? For many, these are the nightmares of retirement - and we speak of this as appearing at the time when those pressures and schedules cease, a time when the thoughts and fears lurking behind them can come out, once again, to see the light of day they've been denied for decades. And when they come out, as they are sure to do if one stops work and pushing them back into the recesses of one's life and mind, how many activities can you take on to ward off the realisation?

Sammy faced that question when he had to stop travelling. Laughingly, the realisation he also faced was that ordinary companies do not hire people in to direct and manage their executives most of the time - and certainly not as permanent employees. Ah. What he had been doing for years qualified him only to do what he had been doing, having little generalising ability in the real world and certainly not at this point in his life and with the lack of a local network because he had virtually no contacts or established relationships locally. How could he, as he had always been on the road? It was not one of those things one plans when they are busy playing a role designated by the circumstances in which they find themselves.

Sigh.... so what to do? This was all in the years before he had met and married Serah, so there were few demands on him other than living expenses and he had some cash flow from foreign investments that could support him for now... as long as the foreign exchange rates did not go too far astray. But what to do? There was not enough money to jet-set around the world and sitting at home on the computer was like watching paint dry.

He tried some hourly wage work he could find... then he began posting on social platforms, both news articles and short opinion pieces. He began writing a few short fantasias, very short stories, 10,000 words or less, and they found an appreciative audience. It occurred to him that the return to literacy in the current electronic culture should be in small steps as people weren't going to dig into Tolstoy without a lot of preparation for longer works. So, thus began Sammy's vignettes. It would take 8, 10, or 12 of them to fill a proper sized book, so that is where he went. And it worked. There was never a title that reached those best-seller lists, but enough to provide a little income that was better than hourly wage-slave rates. And all it took was ideas, inspiration, some discipline to sit and write, and a developed reputation as a storywriter. He finished a couple of longer short stories into novella length books but, as he expected, he did not have the touch to keep people interested for those long haul ventures.

And that was Sammy's routine life: wake-up, daven[4], exercise, write, the occasional outside meeting, an odd radio or TV interview very infrequently, and events at the shul. And, oh, did we mention parenting his children from the last marriage? When we started all this the reason Sammy had to stop travelling was that he became a single father when his former wife decided to seek "outside interests" and the children were left with him while they were still in high and elementary school. Okay... another, but delightful challenge Sammy thought. Sammy had not brought up teen-agers directly before as he was always on the road before. It was a learning experience and taught Sammy the value of patience, the levels of which he was not aware he could surmount. More than once the phrase "old dog, new tricks" came to mind.

But with the advent of Sammy's search and discovery of new patience resources, there was also that issue of returning to life and trying to find it when you've spent 30, 35 years actively avoiding the anxieties the tasks in front of you always presented. For example, if you are not an outgoing sales kind of personality, how do you convince a recalcitrant potential client that they want and need the project for which they signed up? Sammy rarely gave up those challenges, as with one company it was his job to overcome expected client reluctance, an almost persistent routine with every project opening.

There was the time, however, that during the conversation the recalcitrant client took out a loaded .357 magnum 6" barrelled pistol from the bottom drawer of his desk and placed it on the desktop saying that he wanted Sammy to understand just how serious his reluctance to go ahead with the contracted work was. Momentarily Sammy thought about discretion and corporate valour before agreeing that he could clearly see the seriousness of the client's objection. He turned around to ask his staff his

---

[4] Daven, for those non-Jews, is to complete the ritual morning (or afternoon or evening) prayers.

opinion, but his colleague had already vacated the small office, bent over, toddling down the hall, carrying all his papers folded hastily into the briefcase he had tried to close. With the client snickering at Sammy's colleague's instant departure, Sammy turned and noted to the client that the abrupt cancellation of the contract without payment would encumber actions of the group's team of legal experts. They would undoubtedly be in contact in due course. The highly reluctant client smiled and said, "Y'all just send them on down hcah and we'll give them a right warm welcome." Gathering his few papers, standing, and closing his briefcase as calmly as possible, "as you wish, sir," was Sammy's parting comment as he left the office and then the premises, collecting his colleague already walking toward the car.

Sammy was fortunate to have very few of those stories, but one can see why the disassociation would have been so important to enable work for that firm. In the longer run, other firms for which Sammy worked had no such experiences but the anxiety of performing in front of highly educated and informed executives never fully goes away. So, when the need for that disassociation vapourises, one is left with... what? Do you find real life or continue the charade? And if the former, how do you do that?

That was the question that vexed Sammy for months. It was almost the same as returning to the question that bridges adolescence to adulthood: "who am I" and "what am I?" And Sammy did what every other distracted person does, he put it in the back of his mind to work on while asleep and in the event of nothing to do.

Thc mind is a funny thing, We can focus and concentrate on an issue for hours or days, writing diagrams, processes, symbolic representations, charts, lists, and every other visual aid to come to grips with a solution that seems particularly elusive. But often, not always, but often when we relax our grip on trying to throttle every possible nuanced thought and bring it to bear, turn our attention to something else, and momentarily forget the bane of our intellectual existence, a solution often appears in the sleep, dreams, or sudden inspirations that arrive in the midst of the night or while doing something else. Sammy knew this process worked so he stuck the need to rediscover himself in the back of his mind and left it there. It might still be there for all we know, but Sammy no longer let that unanswered question dominate his thinking and he moved on to write and support and grow his children as best he could.

But we are prattling on telling part of his story while Sammy is hopping down the stairs to meet his guests, the mourners happy for a party rather than a quiet, hushed and dour visit to a Shiva House.

Chapter 4 - Life and the World Discovers Sammy.

Sammy joined Serah in a hasty welcoming and greeting line inside the front doors.

"Mazel Tov!" repeated as many times as there were people entering the house.

"Oh, this is sooooo wonderful, " she gushed. "We're so glad you didn't leave us," grasping Sammy's hand with hers that was cold enough to be in the grave itself.

"Sammy, you nearly tore my heart out of me... Please don't surprise me like that again?"

"Hehehehehe. I've never seen Goldbaum so flummoxed," snicker, snicker, "the surprise was worth that if nothing else."

"We're awfully glad you decided not to leave, old man."

"So, Sammy, are you going to write a story about dying?"

"Will you tell us what happened, please?"

"Did you see Hashem?"

"Was it dark, light, or were you conscious of anything?"

"That is one of the classiest ways to back out of a trip to the graveyard, yet, Sammy old boy."

"How did you do that?" asked an engineer.

"I'll talk with you later, right now I'm famished, " said the large woman as she headed for the tables, "funerals always gives me such an appetite!"

"So, have you yet asked if the almost event this morning invalidates any of your lifetime guarantees?" offered another engineer.

"Oh, Serah, isn't it nice that he's back?"

"Aren't your children happy? What about the ones overseas and elsewhere? Do they know?"

"Oh, they'll be here tomorrow remarked Serah, smiling - I think I'll let Sammy pick them up from the airport, " she said, giggling slightly.

"So, what kind of aliyah do you think this begets? That ought to keep the Rabbi and Gabbai busy. You at least get a Thanksgiving Blessing after tomorrow's Torah Aliyah[5], eh?" he said, chuckling.

And so it went with people coming in, the caterer panicking but more food and drink arriving from his stores and kitchens, for hours it seemed. Sammy and Serah were getting tired and left the children at the door to greet while they mingled and got something to eat. Sammy then realised it had been two days since he'd eaten or drunk anything and he was truly hungry. The house was never THAT large but it was filled almost to overflowing with people filling plates and making their way to the porch. Most all remarked that it had been exceptionally considerate of Sammy to pretend dying on such a nice day, eh? How different it would have been in winter, OY, not a good time to die... as if there was a good time?

Sammy had just filled a plate and got a glass of white wine when one of the children tapped his arm.

"Daddy, there are some people here to talk to you."

"Rachel, there are many here that want to talk to a dead man," smiled Sammy looking so fondly on his older daughter, "are these any different?"

"Yes, they're from the radio."

"OY, now this starts," sighed Sammy. "Okay, so, should I be nice to them Rachel?" queried Sammy.

---

[5] An Aliyah is one of a number of recognitions of Jews in the congregation that includes blessing the Torah reading, subject to a number of traditional requirements in the services.

"That depends. Do you want them to be nice to you and your books?"

"Rachel, such a smart girl I have. That is exactly right. Okay, lead me to the inquisition squad, then, please."

Standing near the front door was a nicely dressed, but poor man beset by questions from the children around him about broadcasting and if he was a "star". While he was amused and being charming, it was not a comfortable posture so Sammy put his plate and glass on a table in the entry hallway, thanked the children, and steered the man and himself out the front door, onto the front walk, and away from the porch and the many sets of curious ears.

"Mr. Silver," he began, "thank you and surely you understand that as word of your miraculous recovery has spread; the curiosity set, meaning the broadcasting world, wants to know if we have a miracle or just a remarkable set of circumstances. If we can do a few minutes' interview on this phenomenon, perhaps we can head off the seekers of a Lazarus Miracle because otherwise you'll have them camping out in your front yard just to be able to see or touch you or, worse, carry away part of your house, belongings, or anything attached to you including your family, I'm afraid. Two years ago we had someone in Eastern Europe portray their recovery during a funeral as a true miracle and people came from thousands of miles away to beleaguer them, stealing personal property, and almost their children. It was not pretty. There are some really desperate folks out there, sir."

"I hadn't realised so many are desperate for miracles."

"It used to be moderately crazy, if you recall the on-again-and-off-again guru and spiritualist phases of decades gone by, but as life has not gotten any easier anywhere in the last 30 or 40 years, the desperate seeking for answers and easy solutions has been getting worse. Surely at your age, you've witnessed the degeneration of the social fabric on an unprecedented scale."

"I see your point and I understand, but while we live in the same world as everyone else, we Jews are a bit separate, some of us far more than others, keeping to ourselves and occasionally not venturing out of the contact only with other Jews. Now I can't do that as I have books to write and publicise and they sell more outside the Hebrew community than in it, so I have interviews and most of my economic interactions are outside what might be referenced as a new geographic Shtetl community. But having said that I still wrap the cocoon of my family around us as I have to do to write. So while I am aware of these changes, I'm not as attentive as I was when I was keeping tabs on the political gang wars. Okay, what do you want?"

"By the way, my name is Paul Pundit and if I can get my sound man set up here we can talk here on your lawn."

"OK. Will this be taped or is it going live?"

"We rarely do live any more, sir. There are too many legal issues that can easily get past us, so we had to stop that. And let's do this before the TV truck I see coming down the street gets here."

With one of those sinking-in-your-stomach feelings, Sammy turned around to witness one of those TV vans with a dish on it rolling slowly down the street, avoiding some of the early leavers and late stragglers just arriving. Looking around for the children, he spied Rachel on the porch and motioned her to come over. When she got there he asked if she remembered where he put down his plate and drink. She nodded and he asked if she might retrieve it for him, as he was hungry and going to be out here for a little while. She smiled and went happily to do the errand, as she and the other children were so happy to have their father back... and to be able to watch him interviewed on radio and television, a chance they rarely had.

Paul Pundit set up, ran a couple level tests and began asking Sammy about returning from the dead. Sammy poo-poo'd the Lazarus business explaining his bibulous problems and an apparent cataleptic episode that was not detected during the washing or body preparation stages before the funeral - or obvious as Sammy lay in state overnight in the shul before the funeral the next morning accompanied by a Rabbi there to protect from superstitious events. Sammy went on to relate how overjoyed his wife and children had been at the mistaken condition - and how surprised his older children would be when they arrived tomorrow. He also talked about how a return to life party was much better than visiting a Shiva house. Sammy was asked if this would turn into a short story. "Of course! How can I let the opportunity pass - there are so many good puns to raise in a return story?"

Paul asked a few more questions and observed that the party was indeed still going on at the house and talking to a formerly dead person was not that strange after all.... even if he thought the conversation was a little stiff.

"Mr. Silver, do you mind if we use your wireless network to send this to the station?"

"Of course not," he offered and motioned for Moshe to come over.

"Moshe, will you please help these gentlemen access our wireless network so they can send the interview back to the station?"

"Wow, sure, yeah, absolutely.... neat," as Moshe gestured for the soundman to follow him inside to set it for him.

"Thank you, Mr. Silver. I hope your frank presentation will prevent a gathering of the crazies."

"Oh, I'm not so worried," noted Sammy wistfully, "Hashem has protected me a goodly number of times and this surely is another instance of His desire for me to stay around to do something. Thank you."

As Paul Pundit and his soundman were climbing back into their van in the driveway, the larger and more imposing TV van was waiting for them to leave so that they could pull in. Fortunately, all the food catering vans had come and gone and no more were needed this afternoon. Sammy took this moment to eat a bit more and refresh himself with a bit of white wine.... hmm... a pouilly fume, a curious choice he thought, but just right with the smoked fish.

Sammy waited on the lawn since the warning of the radio interviewer made him think that he didn't want any visibly distinguishing characteristics in any shot that anyone could interpret in order to find his house. In fact, maybe the TV van was the correct backdrop as it was thoroughly ubiquitous and identified the station for the commercial promulgation people. So, he walked over toward the van, asking the driver if the cameraman could talk to him, please.

"You got it, bud; we run an efficient operation, here. What can I do fer ya?"

"Ah, well, since I presume you are here to do an interview with me - and I'm Sammy Silver, by the way - could we do it so that the only background shown is the side of your van - even in your cut-aways of the interviewer, please?"

"Sure, bud, but why? We like to get a bit of visual interest in our videos and the side of this old rattletrap doesn't really do that, you know."

"Hmm," mulled Sammy, "are you tied to the van or can you move about?"

"I can go anywhere, bud. I tape or disc it all and them bring it back to transmit - we don't do live anymore unless it is an active story in progress."

"Okay, let me see how crowded the library is," Sammy added and ran off to check how many folks were still in his office, if any.

The talent had not really prepped Brad about this shoot so Brad sorta wondered what that old man was on about as Sammy went wheedling off toward the house.

When Sammy returned, Brad and his camera were next to the van along with the "talent", Rex Ravingcrass, one of the primary TV news reporters for the local stations and CBC when they needed him. Ravingcrass, thinking himself a wit, addressed Sammy on his return, "So, I have to confess you are one of the more lively stiffs I've ever seen, Sammy." Obviously Brad had mentioned who the old man was and Rex had been given the name from the assignment desk message.

"Sir?" queried Sammy, "I'm afraid you have the advantage of me, sir."

"I'm sorry, Sammy. Excuse me. I'm Rex Ravingcrass with whomever is going to broadcast this piece. You see we free-lance so much these days, we can't ID the station anymore but just leave them to tag it. But I came here to interview you about your remarkable recovery in front of almost hundreds at the Synagogue this morning. So Brad told me about your geolocation concerns, maybe we could do this inside?" Turning his head, Rex asked, "Brad do we have any lights for inside?"

"Sure, but let me check out the scene and see what it will take to pop it, OK?"

So, Sammy asked Rex and Brad to join him in his office, which was far more intimate and unidentifiable than the great outdoors. The professional partygoers knew the media would come but were disappointed that they'd not be included at least in background scenes. Upon seeing the famous Rex Ravingcrass go inside, the pro's still on the porch ambled their way inside to at least get a chance at being in a background shot.

Sammy showed them into the office - which was more a library as the walls next to his desk and around the rest of the room were covered with bookcases filled with all sorts of volumes of literature, history, politics, classics, books of Jewish life, religious tracts and so on - what Sammy called a normal Hebrew house library. In the centre of the room was a long leather sofa with an oversized leather chair at right angle to the sofa and a sure injury shin-banging oak coffee table in front of them.

Brad asked Sammy, "can I clamp some spots on the sides of the bookcases?"

"Sure, go ahead" agreed Sammy and he sat in the oversized leather chair, gesturing to the sofa for Rex.

They exchanged a bit of background as Rex was not familiar with Sammy's work but aware that he was a bit old, while Brad retrieved cameras, tripods, lighting, and set the lights. When they came on and Brad measured the light levels in front of both men, it was enough. After doing some scene shots of the library and bookcases, Brad put the cameras on tripods, each set to cover one of the speakers and interrupted, "we're set. Rex do you want to do the intro here and a wrap in the other part of the house?"

"But it is so nice and sunny outside..." began Rex.

"However, I want no visual or other information broadcast that might make our house identifiable in case the crazies take a shine to my story," Sammy interrupted.

"Oh... all right...I understand. Brad, we'll do a shot of me in the hallway in front of the living room crowd to wrap, OK?"

"Roger that, boss."

"I'll open sitting here. Let me know when you are ready."

Then Rex sat there, composing his thoughts, microphone in hand, waiting for Brad, who eventually said "Ready" and showed 3, then 2, then 1 finger to Rex, then pointed to him...

"Hello, this is Rex Ravingcrass with Sammy Silver, a one hundred twenty year old man that got up out of his coffin this morning when he suddenly woke up before being consigned involuntarily to a long sleep for which he was obviously not ready. In another room here, Sammy's family and friends have changed his mourning party into a celebration of his continuing life. Sammy, aside from your extreme age and vast history of experience, did you ever think you'd awake from the dead?"

"Rex," began Sammy, "I'd just want to note that there are others far older than I running around this planet - and "waking from the dead" has an awfully philosophical sound to it, you know. It is not one of those Lazarus events, but just a bit of catalepsy, an explosive centurion of a hangover, and a medical examiner that was not as careful as usual, perhaps. Nothing more. However," and Sammy began snickering, "for those folks that ran from the shul yelling 'Dybbuk', it was surely a memorable experience; none the less for me who would have been in big, big serious trouble had I slept for just a few hours more."

"Dybbuk?" asked Rex. "I don't know this term."

"Ah, a 'Dybbuk' is a Yiddish demon that tries to inhabit the body of the dead. Most of us left that superstition behind in the Stetl villages beyond the Pale. But to this day, Rabbi's still sit and pray over dead bodies overnight just in case."

"So, this was not a miracle? You didn't see G-d or that halo of light people say they've seen when they have near death experiences? Are you going to disappoint all those folks that seek to collect resurrection events?" asked Rex with a slight snicker of a smile as he turned toward the camera.

"Miracle? I wish. I need to have more conversations with Him, but not in the final judgement sense, please. And no, no white tunnels of light or anything

---

else I remember except a headache that was as bad as the one I got when I stopped caffeine years ago."

"And resurrection? Me? Are you nuts? Who in his right mind would want to come back, really come back from the dead in this day and age? Can you imagine what a life they wouldn't have any longer? Everyone would literally want a piece of them. Every major and minor religion would want to claim him or her as their own as proof of their credibility, denying validation to the others. Think about that for a second. Every religion would promise this poor schlemiel anything in order for him to shill for them because to be able to claim resurrection benefits as part of a religion is worth a lot of money, a lot of adherents, a lot of converts, and a lot more money and power. If you'll excuse the metaphor, it is the Holy Grail of the religion business."

"And worse, his life would be no longer his own as every media mogul and producer want him on their show so he'd have to get a roomful of agents to keep his schedule straight. And it isn't anything new they want - they all want the same story:

How was it?
Did you see G-d?
What did he look like?
Was it a He or a She?
What did it feel like?
Was it painful?
Is there a hell?
Did you review your entire life?
Who really shot JR?
What happened to Judge Crater?
Did it hurt?
Did you see Saint Peter?
Did you see heaven?
Did you see hell?
Did you see your dead relatives?

Did you see Elvis?

And besides that, the atheist groups will hound you mercilessly to admit there's no G-d and the religious groups will demand your allegiance so that they can claim resurrection as a benefit of their brand of belief."

"And for me, even worse, the Jews, my own tribe, won't believe it. Well, no, not entirely. We've been through the fake Messianic routine a few times already. The Reform and Conservative groups will deny the reality of it. The Orthodox will wait 100 years and generate a lot of Rabbinical opinions before trying to create the Halacha - that's Jewish Law - on the subject. And they might want to shun or excommunicate me for heresy in the meantime. Well, some might and others would be a bit more tolerant, the entertainment value of it all, you know. But the very, very orthodox would want to kill me just to see if it happened again as I certainly do not fit their definition of a Messiah. In fact, if the truth be known, I really don't fit my definition of a Messianic figure, either. So, why on earth would anyone want to be resurrected into the kind of society and cultures we have now? Given the Hebrew metaphysical belief in eventual reincarnation of souls into other bodies to accomplish the learning we did not do the last time, the gradual growth of our selves into the kind of person He envisions and loves is a lot more comfortable than the idea of being suddenly thrust back into this life when we were just looking forward to passing into something new, ya' know?"

Rex was having this "deer in the headlamps" moment when Sammy finished as he did not really expect a lesson on philosophy and life relative to modern culture from a 120-year-old- survivor of an almost death experience. He visibly shook himself into the present.

"Brad, do some take-aways with me looking pensive and thoughtful, please. Lose that last bit where I was almost gone. I'll try for that look and vary my position then I'll thank Sammy and we can do the wrap in the hallway." And that was it.

So, Sammy sat and watched Rex trying to look pensive and thoughtful in various poses. Sammy made faces at him and stuck out his tongue, trying to break him up. Brad snickered. Rex frowned at Sammy a couple of times.

A few minutes later, Brad declared, "Okay, we've got that... do the thank you, please. Ready and rolling... now."

Rex intoned in his best charming baritone, "Sammy, thank you for taking the time to share some of your extraordinary experience with us this afternoon. We know you do not call it a resurrection, but there are a lot of people out there who are really looking for one and a new Messiah, despite your denials of such a status. Thank you for sharing this momentous occasion with us." Rex waited fully three seconds before drawing his finger across his throat.

"Okay, let's do the tag in the hallway."

It took Sammy weeks to get the saccharine coating off the sofa. It was so sticky...

So, Brad took off one of the cameras and followed Rex into the hall to do the end scene. Fortunately, the party professionals were waiting in the sunken living room for this event, so Rex had an appreciative audience and decided to stand on one of the steps so that Brad's shot could pick up one of the art pieces above the mantle and over his shoulder, as well as the party pro's in the background.

"Blah, blah, blah, blah, bleet, bleet, bleer, blouh, blub, blub, rattle, rattle, shake, and roll" went Rex, talking more to the party audience than the camera and for which they clapped appreciatively when he finished. And Rex, don't you know, turned and bowed, acknowledging their applause. Brad caught it all on video for the entertainment of the rest of the studio, later.

Sammy watched, thanked Brad and Rex as they finished, asked if they wanted anything to eat or drink as there was plenty left, but Brad said, "we can't, sorry; we have a one-legged and paraplegic, Lesbian, Peruvian, Mountain Folk Mud Wrestling Team event to film, next. They are protesting that their management is selling their tickets dirt-cheap. They wanted to sue but their lawyer wasn't sure their case had a leg to stand on so they are having a mud pie throwing contest with the Bolivian Bolshi Bovine Butchers to raise money for legal proceedings."

So, while Brad gathered up the lights, tripods, cameras and put them in the van, Rex gathered in a glass of white wine and small talk with a soupcon of starry-eyed appreciation from the party-goers.

Chapter 5 - Life in the Dead Lane.

That night Diana Disector watched Rex Ravingcrass's story about Sammy Silver and was so seethingly angry she crushed her 'Old Milwaukee" can while it still had lots of beer in it, making a right mess on the living room carpet that wouldn't be cleaned up for months until the smell of stale beer drove her to get one of those Canadian Tyre carpet cleaning rentals to get rid of it. If that wasn't enough, she then threw the can at the fireplace where it rolled back and forth for a while on the bricks until it came to rest. She was HOT! Furious! Aggravated beyond the frustration any of those little plastic wrapped candies give you when they won't open easily by trying to gently tear the seams apart until you finally add Herculean strength, rip them apart and all the little candies fly onto the floor, all over the room, under chairs and tables, and you spend the next 20 minutes crawling around picking them up and throwing out all those on the floor, vowing never to buy them again.... but you do and try to remember to use a scissors next time.

Why? Why, you ask? She, no one else, but she of a perfectly embalmed profile was mortified across the broadcast public audience! She, referred to as "a medical examiner that was not as careful as usual", of all the insults! That scrawny little nothing old man dares to cast aspersions on her professional capability! The incredible nerve of the almost dead, sometimes! Diana was a professional embalmer that successfully sucked the very lifeblood out of the deceased, rich and poor alike. How dare this drunken old fart blaspheme her good name and reputation! She would have to have her retribution for this. Just because the Jews call in their own team to wash the body and prepare it for a simple burial without any of the modern conveniences that keep so many of the goyim dead virtually desiccated for decades, they have no right to disparage her honourable profession preserving expert illusions of permanence and immortality. 'Medical examiner', indeed! They were but amateurs compared to her learned expertise in the embalming arts, learned over many months of tortuous study at the Ajax Effendi School of Professional Embalmers and Death Dressers. That was followed by her graduate studies at the Erie Egyptian Necromancer School of the Esoteric and Occult Embalming Arts, which qualified her to dress Mummies, though that aspect of her talent was rarely used these days. However, the practice of pulling their brain through their nasal passages was a useful talent she was aching to try on a few federal politicians, dead or not.

To understand the context, though, Diana's frustration and anger have a long history that precedes her work in Ottawa. It goes back to her childhood in Kitschmetuchas, Alberta where her father, Darren, an unusually successful roto-rooter designer was able to evolve his craft into the invention that made the faltering oil sands businesses find their true profitability. This led to an amazingly prosperous youth for the young Diana and the Disector family. Unfortunately, the success of his invention attracted the attention of the endlessly envious and incompetently untalented Canadian federal government, which accused Diana's father of stealing a pre-existing government patent and took him to court. The judiciary system being what it is in corporate Canada, the government naturally won a clearly fabricated and false, malicious and malodorous fiction of a case and confiscated most of the earnings from the invention, leaving Diana's family poor and destitute. Diana's father had to return to designing solutions to free blocked-up toilets to earn just enough money for them to live.

Darren did get his own back on the government, though, when he was able to get the exclusive contract for cleaning out the toilets of Parliament and government executive offices some years later. In cahoots with a contractor that had his remote polar bear sexing invention stolen by the government, they tainted the food in the Parliamentary commissary with enough laxative to drive all of them onto the loo for hours. While they were ensconced on the Parliamentary thrones, Darren reversed the roto-rooter drives and impaled every one of them up to the tops of their heads, sort of a mechanical Vlad-the-Impaler retribution if you are familiar with his old methods.

It only took the crack Capital police three months to figure out how it was done. Actually, the figuring only took a few hours - it was cleaning up all the faecal matter that took the months of smelly effort before they could get to the toilets. That was amidst a union dispute about whose sh*t it was that had to be cleaned up because all the sh*t from one political party would not be touched by workers hired by the controlling party in power - so first they had to figure whose sh*t was whose before they could even begin getting the sh*t cleaned up. And mixed up in all that sh*t were various body parts of the hundreds of victims that had been impaled, so getting them cleaned up and identified was another sh*tty mess that took weeks. The citizenry, however, thought this just fine as the more sh*t that had to be cleaned up meant that less sh*t was being dumped on them by parts of the corrosive and corrupt government that was left after the debacle. There were calls for a special election, but nobody could get their sh*t together to make it happen, so everyone just left the sh*ts in office as they were.

When the police finally did figure out what happened, they tried to find and arrest Darren but he had slipped out under the cover of the sh*t and was nowhere to be found. He was actually a bit of a folk hero in Alberta where children grow up liking Cod Liver Oil Syrup and spankings more than the federal government. This all relates to the times back in the early 21st century when two incompetent governments, one provincial, one federal, nearly destroyed the entire economic infrastructure of the province and it took years to recover it. It was at that point when a young Diana decided to embark on a career that would not depend on government largesse for its survival - and dealing with the dead sounded like just such a venture, a necessary set of skills that hygiene, good taste, surviving children, and life insurance salesmen promote.

And Darren? What happened to him? Well, he ended up in California, changed his name, and made a fortune helping the State manage all the sh*t they'd not been able to handle for decades.

Many folks in Kitschmetuchas were quite surprised when Diana chose to go into the funereal arts rather than political consulting since her family seemed to have a real talent at stirring the sh*t.

However, back to the present, Diana was not going to forget the corrosive slight to her reputation inflicted by some yahoo that just happened to come back to consciousness in his coffin. Oh, no. She was going to find a way to make sure the newly alive Sammy Silver paid for his thoughtless insult broadcast to a wide spectrum of the public that besmirched her otherwise spotlessly bleached career record. She had no immediate plan, but because revenge is a dish best served cold, she would wait, think, formulate, plan, and slowly develop a way to repudiate the insult to her professional standing.

Chapter 6 - "...What do you do with a Drunken Sailor..."

Rabbi Dovid Goldbaum was not used to anything at Sammy Silver's disrupted funeral, nothing. It was almost treif[6], it was so unusual. The Rabbi had a slight shiver just thinking about it as he was usually a man who followed the Halacha strenuously, very orthodox and very observant. So, Sammy's lack of a cover on his coffin and his missing Tallis were very concerning. However, Sammy's wife explained that the coffin was open because the Tallis was due to arrive as Sammy couldn't be buried without it and the change of venue for the funeral just confused everything so the Tallis was momentarily displaced. Serah was asked about this by the _chevra kadisha_, who were similarly upset at not having the snipped Tallis in which to dress Sammy. However, this was all so sudden... many would say, "well, you know..." At least the prayers were said, the body prepared, and guarded through the night in the larger shul.

However, the events of this morning were extremely troubling to the Rabbi. It was not the cataleptic issue that bothered him so much, nor the surprise, nor the improprieties of the set-up as there were plausible reasons for them. It surely was not Sammy coming back to life as he was one of the more enjoyable Jews in the city. No, there was something the Rabbi sensed that was beyond the frantic and almost hysterical trappings of the day. It was nothing he actually saw, nothing he heard, nothing his direct senses measured; more, it was something he sensed

---

[6] Treif means unclean and is generally used to reference non-kosher food. A religious service like a funeral CANNOT be treif for the dead are deserving of great respect.

about Sammy and his preternatural reincarnation or resurrection or recovery, whichever you choose it to be.

Rabbi Goldbaum had never sensed this before so he was not sure what he was perceiving. He only knew it was not Kosher and Sammy's family had always kept Kosher, even to the point of being Shomer Shabbos[7]. No, there was something wrong. Perhaps he would ask Rabbi Rolf Helfenberg about anything that happened through the night to the body. Though he would be courting a grave disrespect just in asking the question, he felt it necessary, as the 'treif' feeling just wouldn't go away.

So, when Rabbi Goldbaum called Rabbi Helfenberg, Rolf immediately volunteered, "I was wondering if anyone would noticed what I felt. You are not alone Rabbi Goldbaum. There was something distinctly foreign and 'treif' about Sammy Silver and his recovery. I can't put my finger on it, but something is not right. Have you spoken with Rabbi Blum?"

"No, not yet because I thought I'd ask you first since you were there with Sammy overnight."

"But I only was with Sammy after he was delivered, open casket without Tallis, to the shul by the *chevra kadisha*. There may have been some time without someone there due to the change of venues at the last minute, you know. Maybe you want to check with Rabbi Rosenberg because I admit that I did not see any of them when I arrived."

Rabbi Goldberg was shaking his head. Oh, no, he was thinking; this should not happen to us, not to Sammy; why, oh, why to us? We've not seen this for decades. We

---

[7] Shomer Shabbos is a description of practices on Shabbat that perfectly respects not performing any of the 39 prohibited activities on Shabbos, along with a few others the Rabbinate had thought wise to add through the centuries. In brief, you don't cook, drive, turn any electrics on or off, ride bicycles, or do anything connected to your weekday work, even talk about it. It is a time for family and Him alone, mostly Him.

were so careful to avoid any time without spiritual guards. Why now?

"Thank you Rabbi Helfenberg for confirming the concern. I'll call Rabbi Rosenberg in a little while when I finish figuring the implications, here."

"Finish figuring the implications," Rabbi Helfenberg almost screamed, "Sammy may have been picked up by a Dybbuk, what other implication is there?"

"An Ibbur," noted Rabbi Goldbauum quietly in that tone of voice that implies more hope than the reality one does not want to acknowledge. "We'll see - there is something not right, but we cannot judge what it is just yet. That, unfortunately will take Sammy's help, whether he entertains the prospect or not."

"Agreed. So who is going to lead this inquiry?"

"It should be Sammy's Rabbi, not me, and not you, and not Rabbi Rosenberg, and hopefully we can do it without the Beis Din[8] butting their big interest into this because that will really bollocks things."

"Let me know later, please. I'll pray for Sammy's well being."

"Thank you. But remember his Hebrew name and understand those implications."

"Always, the original 'smelling like a Rose kid', he is."

"Baruch Hashem, what an interesting life he has. I'm glad it is him."

"Me. too. Shalom, Rabbi. Thank you for calling. I feel better for sharing this with someone."

---

[8] A Beis Din is a Hebrew court, the local authority for resolving Halachic (Jewish Law) and spiritual questions. Like shuls, they range from very orthodox to very reform.

Chapter 7 - Sammy goes forward, sort of.

So, here you are, back in your house, waking up next to your wife, hangover gone, alive again (still), children asleep in their rooms, and everything is back to normal... sort of. Sammy had gotten accustomed to awaking around 5:30 to 6, then watching the Sun rise, working, davening, or cuddling with his wife if she awoke, depending on the season. But there was something different this morning and Sammy couldn't figure what it was. Something was not quite right. It was not anything hugely wrong, nothing largely disturbing so much, but just one of those 5 degrees off feelings; so Sammy put on a robe and went downstairs to daven, figuring it was leftover guilt for not thanking Hashem sufficiently for a return to life.

Sammy washed, then went into his office to daven; and when he finished he sensed something still wasn't quite right, but it was time to awaken the children for school, so it would have to wait.

Sammy threw on some clothes and then initially woke children as usual, even Margaux whose pre-school wouldn't start until later this morning - but she liked to watch videos before she went. He always helped them prepare or get their breakfast organised until Serah came down to finish things. He and Serah had agreed on an education routine for their children quite different from that in either of their childhoods. Public school standards had finally sunk even lower than they were 40 years ago when it was recognised that the system was indoctrinating not educating, a problem that had existed from the middle of the 19th century but one which everyone chose to ignore. So the Silvers took their children to a Torah based Hebrew School for the morning, brought them home to lunch most often, then took them to a modified Trivium / Quadrivium approach tutelage where they and other Jewish parents wanting more firm secular education for their children paid for a few teachers and the small classrooms teaching grammar, logic, and rhetoric in the Trivium earlier level and music, astronomy, geometry, and arithmetic for the Quadrivium level courses. Obviously, various languages were part of the Trivium course load and advanced sciences and maths in the Quadrivium. However, this was education; and as often as The State tried to prove their approach ineffective, even the Trivium educated younger ones debated and defeated the best scholars the State could produce, mostly because the disciplines of logic and rhetoric were unknown in State education. The State still could not bring themselves to teach their students to think.

So, while Serah drove the children to school, Sammy exercised to try to stay limber and fit, not a painless or pleasant task at his age. Mostly the exercises were to maintain flexibility and physical stability as strength was not something he was trying to gain at this point. Heckfire, he felt blessed just to be able to get around as nimbly as he could, something for which he got almost endless ribbing from his younger colleagues. People asked him and he had no ready answer for his physical agility at his age. None. It was a blessing for which he could not account, but one for which he was forever thankful.

After the exercise, Sammy showered, dressed, and went down to the library to work. Work, yeah, what to write after yesterday's crazy events - it was as though nothing was normal anymore. Before his joyous celebration that turned to an event, he had been writing a short vignette about a fire hydrant that felt ignored and abused. "Yeah, only visit me when you want the water piped into here - I'm not even appreciated like my NYC cousins who get turned on to spray the locals in the hot summer days..." and so on like that, kvetching from a fire hydrant, who woulda' thought.

He'd turned on the computer and logged in. His hands were poised above his keyboard when he had the strange sensation of someone calling his name - a voice faint, far away, but clear, *"Sammy... Sammy"*. He looked around, got up and walked around, even going over to the doors to the porch, but the porch and yard were empty and there was no one else in the library.

Great, he thought. First I die, now I'm hearing things. And with that, his phone went off.

"Sammy here."

"Sammy, this is Sid and I need you to put some dates in your diary. Your sudden recovery has caught the imagination of your publisher and a few talk show producers who want to feature the resurrected Sammy Silver on their shows."

"Sid, now stop that.... please don't sell this as a resurrection. That just isn't true and it will only put me and my family in danger from the crazies out there. But how many and when - remember, I won't travel from Thursday to Saturday night."

"Okay, yeah, yeah, yeah... I get that. They are all early in the week and not long trips, so no sweat. I'll send you an e-mail with the details. Are you open for the next two to three weeks, Mondays through Wednesdays?"

Sammy looked over his diary for the next few weeks and there were no appointments or Holidays coming up, so he told Sid to send over the proposed schedule and he's get back to him as soon as he'd reviewed it.

"Thanks, Sammy. Speak soon, buddy."

Sammy hung up, turned back to his keyboard, trying to search for some kind of inspiration when he heard it again, *"Sammy... Sammy"*. Still faint, but clear, and it pulled all of Sammy's attention. It was not a voice he knew. It was not Serah, none of the children, no one he could remember - as if he was becoming paranormal or something...

He tried to shake it off as though it was just an illusion. Ignore it, it will go away. You had a very strenuous day yesterday and this is just a lingering after-effect, he thought, turning back to the keyboard.

"Sammy... Sammy... listen please..."

Now that sent shivers up Sammy's spine and down his legs, shivers he didn't understand. Creepy.

Sammy felt impelled to respond, but didn't want to because "hearing voices" was not one of those things that accompanies sound minds and thinking. Okay, yesterday may have unhinged him a bit, but not this badly, surely. Maybe it is just a delayed reaction to the shock.

"Sammy.... Sammy... listen, please..." faint, but still clear, the voice repeated.

Now, Sammy felt compelled to answer - simultaneously thinking, "what on earth am I doing?" - but answer he did.

"Who are you?" said Sammy in a normal, but tense voice.

"Sammy.... Sammy... listen, please... will you help me?"

Sammy stopped. He thought. Let's think about this for a minute. Here I am, 120 years old. I just had a near death experience and now I'm hearing voices... AND I'M TALKING TO THEM, he yelled at himself.

"Sammy.... Sammy... listen, please... will you help me?"

Okay, thought Sammy, for now let's treat this as reality and see what happens. I can always wake up later, right? There is no reason to get hysterical or panic, just explore a bit. You are safe in your house, in your library, Serah is in another room, nothing to fear, there are no visible hallucinations, just a voice.

"Sammy.... Sammy... listen, please... will you help me?" it said again, growing ever so slightly louder, but still faint compared to the vacuum cleaner he could hear in the

upstairs hallway, but it was sounding more like it was in his head, now.

"What do you want?" demanded Sammy, unnerved at this new feeling.

"I need your help, please."

"To do what? I'm only a writer."

"We need to rectify something. Something from long ago."

"Rectify? You need a Rabbi, not a writer." And now Sammy became quite unnerved with himself as he'd begun to talk to this voice as if it were real... {{{shudder}}}.

"Sammy... you are the one to help. We need to rectify something. You can help put things right. Please."

Sammy couldn't take it. He had become that combination of curious, frightened, anxious, and intimidated that causes people to disconnect, so he did. He got up, left the Library, and sought out Serah who was cleaning and straightening what wasn't completed last night after the party.

"Sammy, you look as though you've seen a ghost or been one," she said laughingly.

"Do I? I think there are some residual anxieties from yesterday that are just beginning to show up. Maybe I've a fright about being buried alive. Do you think I should stipulate that I get a fully charged mobile phone, a flashlight, and an oxygen tank when I'm next buried? Or do they still set up bells and strings for cataleptics?" Sammy said half-seriously.

"I think that when we are visited by this tragedy next time, we'll have our own embalmer or coroner check to be sure you're really gone, ok? But that will surely be sometime from now."

"Right. But I thought I should tell you Sid called and he has media appearances for me in the early parts of the next three weeks or so. It looks like I'll have to travel, but I've nothing in my diary for us or the children or Holidays, so it should be just normal stuff. I do hate the prison farm that air travel has become."

"Yes, dear, but the appearance money and book sales are what keep us going, remember."

It was a crestfallen "yes, I know - and I'll do it - and like every other time when I get into it, I'll probably enjoy it. It is the looking forward that has all the scenery of a bad road to it."

"If you are having trouble concentrating after yesterday, why don't you just think of ideas to develop and let your mind drift until I go get the children for lunch," Serah suggested brightly. "And, remember, you have to pick up the children from the airport, later."

"Okay, I'll try that. Thank you for reminding me. That will help even though it is a bit much after yesterday's debacle...no... celebration," and with that Sammy shuffled back into the library and closed the door.

Chapter 8 - Do we have to inform the Beis Din?

Early the next morning Rabbi Goldbaum, thinking this potential far too sensitive for the phone called, then drove over to Rabbi Blum's home to meet with him concerning his suspicions about Sammy.

After the usual perfunctory pleasantries, Rabbi Blum blurted out, "but I do wish he'd return my raincoat today."

"Sol, we have more to worry about than a raincoat, I'm afraid."

"Yeah, but it is my best one for shul and funerals and I need it back."

"Let me tell you about my concerns and conversation with Rabbi Helfenberg, please."

So, Rabbi Goldbaum explained his impressions of Sammy yesterday and Rabbi Helfenberg's corroboration.

"Did you talk with Rabbi Rosenberg?" inquired Rabbi Blum.

"Not yet. Because it should be you that discusses this with Sammy, so best you gather the data yourself."

"Do you think we should inform the Beis Din?"

"OY, only if it is proven and we have a physical manifestation should we talk to them. That would just throw a real pork chop into the cholent, get real."

"Are you sure it is a Dybbuk? Why not an Ibbur? And are you sure of your apprehension?"

"No. It could be either or, in fact, nothing, as we all get funny around the dead, don't we? That is why you, who know him best, should talk with him and see what you perceive - you could better sense something different about him. And if it is nothing then Rolf and I could be all wet."

Rabbi Blum thought for a moment. This is why I wanted to be a shul Rabbi, right? The people, right? Interactive human dynamics in the frying pan of life, right? Sitting Shiva and comforting the bereaved was all well and good, but this demonic stuff is a bit beyond preparations in Yeshiva and Theology Schools. Sigh....

"Okay, I'll call and see Rabbi Rosenberg and then I'll see Sammy. At least I can get my raincoat returned that way," said Sol in that resigned, dispirited voice that you get when you're anticipating doing something you don't want to do but you know you have to do it.

"Good. Glad to hear that. He is a member of your shul, after all. I'll be around to help if you need it or advice - though neither of us have ever dealt with this kind of thing before. That means you can be the lead author on any papers written for the Rabbinical Society... wait, if we don't get the Beis Din involved, we'll have our feet cut out from underneath us. We'll explore papers later. First, let's be sure Sammy is all right."

So, as soon as Rabbi Goldbaum had left, Sol looked up Rabbi Rosenberg's number.

"Isaac, this is Sol Blum. If you aren't busy right now, could I please hop over to talk briefly about Sammy Silver? And no, it isn't about his recovery as catalepsies are almost impossible to detect from what we do with a corpse."

"Thanks. I'll see you in about 5 to 10 minutes. Shalom."

Rabbi Blum had no sooner exited his car in Rabbi Rosenberg's driveway when Isaac Rosenberg came out of the front door to greet him.

"Sol, you don't know how glad I am to see you. I was not able to sleep last night thinking that we almost contributed to Sammy's death and but for his awakening.... I shudder to think of the consequences for him and for the entire *chevra kadisha* particularly for me as I was responsible for the turnover to Rolf Helfenberg, but the change of venues and my family schedule made things crazy. Sorry, come in, please come in," as Rabbi Rosenberg gestured toward the front door.

Rabbi Rosenberg led the way in and to a living room to the left strewn with child chairs, play pens and toys, books, rattles, and the odd pacifier on the coffee and side tables. The dining room to the right had a lovely formal table for 12 and books heaped in piles on most of it with a space or two in front of a couple chairs with just one or two books open.

"As you can see, life with triplets has its own script that we could not have imagined. Please come in," and Isaac cleared off a few things from a long and plush sofa for Rabbi Blum.

"Isaac, my wife and I cannot imagine having three at once. Our evenly spaced five were always enough to keep us helter-skelter."

"Can I get you some coffee or tea, Sol, maybe a soft drink?" Isaac inquired.

"No, no thank you, Isaac. I just need to know about the watching of Sammy's coffin as Rabbis Goldbaum and Helfenberg both sensed something strange about Sammy. To put it frankly, they are worried that something spiritually foreign may have attached itself to him when he was in a position of extraordinary vulnerability under your group's care and through the night. They perceived something not exactly...umm...'right', let's say. For some reason, in this day and age, they are worried that a Dybbuk or Ibbur inveigled its way into Sammy while he was or may have been teetering on the brink of death. I know it is wholly unreasonable and almost impossible, but if there was a palpable break in spiritual care and guardianship there are still those who believe the old superstitions and I'm just trying to put my head around what facts I can find so that if there is ever any inquiry, I can factually report on

what we did to ensure the integrity of Sammy's soul."
Looking directly at Isaac Rosenberg, now, Rabbi Blum
asked, "So was there any expanse of time when Sammy's
body was unwatched, alone, or over which no one was
saying prayers before you physically handed him over to
the care of Rabbi Hellfenberg?"

Rabbi Rosenberg could see his burgeoning
rabbinical career going up in black, black smoke in his
mind before he answered.

"It was my fault," he confessed, hanging his head
and shaking it slightly from side to side. "I had to get the
triplets from day-care because they were closing and my
wife was on the highway, getting back from work far later
than usual. Rabbi Helfenberg was not at the shul yet
because of the change of venue - he went to the old one
first - so he was late, too. So, because there was no one
there and it was going to take only 15 minutes, we put
Sammy on the dais in the coffin without a lid because his
Tallis was yet to arrive and after my colleagues left, so did
I. The shul secretary locked the shul and I went for 15,
maybe 20 minutes to get the children because that day-care
is not at all flexible and it is not far from there. So, even
though the secretary was in the office, there was no one
officially with Sammy until Rabbi Helfenberg arrived. He
arrived while I was gone and the shul secretary let him in.
When I got back, I went in and saw he was already sitting
by the coffin engaged in davening, so I didn't bother him. I
just left as the children were still in the car and I had to get
them home."

"There was nothing strange through our procedures
and none of us perceived anything wrong." Hanging his
head again, Rabbi Rosenberg was almost emotional, "if
anything happened it did while I was gone. It is my fault,
all my fault.... oh, what can I do?"

"Now Isaac," comforted Rabbi Blum, "we don't
know that anything is wrong. Please do not get upset."

And he gently patted Isaac's shoulder. "We know of nothing wrong for sure, only the perceptions of a couple of Rabbi's who, like I, do not like death and its ramifications just like everyone else. No matter how much we learn in yeshiva and seminary, we can never know death. It is just one of those things that makes some far more uncomfortable than others. Some people brag of avoiding taxes but I've not met one yet that has bragged about avoiding death - it comes to us all and Sammy, for some reason, is just a bit further out on that Bell curve than the rest of us might be. No wonder he gives people the creeps sometimes."

Isaac's head came up, looking at Rabbi Blum, "but if I caused Sammy to become demonically possessed, I'll not be able to forgive myself, ever..."

"Look Isaac, we don't know. I don't know. I haven't even seen Sammy yet since yesterday and I sensed nothing then. I have to continue my questioning - and it could well be absolutely nothing. Do not blame yourself for something you do not know, please. Just relax and surely there will be nothing. Really."

And with that Rabbi Blum had decided he could do little more - but he must remember to check back on Isaac later. As a father of three precious children he has larger problems to face than this even though he cannot see that right now. So, Sol stood up and made for the door with Isaac trailing behind.

Turning around at the door, Sol noted one last time, "Isaac, trust me, everything will be fine. Remember Sammy's Hebrew name and does he not appear to be blessed? You have far more to do to study and take care of those children, please. Okay?"

Isaac was weakly coming around and managed to erase the kiss of death look from his face, so Rabbi Blum figured it was time to visit Sammy. Whew! What a mess this could be.

As Sol got in his car and pulled out of Isaac's driveway, he called Sammy's house to make sure he was home. Serah answered. "yeah, sure, he's in the library. Please come on over. Do you want some coffee or tea, wine, whisky, or soft drinks? We have a lot left over."

"Great idea, Serah. Maybe prepare some coffee for Sammy too. This rejuvenation brings up things we have to discuss."

"Okay, we'll see you when you get here."

Chapter 9 - Well, does he or doesn't he?

Sammy was in the library when he heard the knock on the door.

"Sammy...I need your help. We have to make things right, please."

Sammy was getting annoyed at the voice in his head - as he had now isolated it to there and not outside him, but why he should have this he could not understand. Even on his worst drunks years ago... he never heard voices.

The knock came again and Sammy went to answer it.

He and Serah neared the door at the same time.

"It is Rabbi Blum," she said, "he wants to talk with you and I'm preparing some coffee for you both."

"Thank you dear. If you will open the door and show Rabbi into the library, I'll nip up and get his raincoat from my closet where I left it yesterday. Please?"

"Of course."

So, Sammy hopped up the stairs, taking them two at a time as was still his habit, while he heard the front door open and Serah greet Rabbi Blum. He retrieved the raincoat and nipped down to the library while Serah was coming out and heading to the kitchen.

"I'll be back in a few minutes," she reminded him.

"Thank you, darling."

Sammy went in the library - or his office as it really was - and laid the raincoat on the sofa next to where Rabbi Blum was sitting.

"Thank you immensely for the loan of your coat, Rabbi. Can I say it was a life saver?" said Sammy, grinning.

"I must admit, I'd never before had occasion to understand the discretion value of the example of Noah's sons the way I did yesterday, but it is my pleasure. But the reason for my visit is not just to retrieve my coat, Sammy. Rabbis Goldbaum and Helfenberg had some concerns coming off yesterday's events."

"Who is Rabbi Helfenberg?" asked Sammy as Serah brought in a tray with the coffee and some biscuits on it.

"The biscuits are pareve[9] by the way," noted Serah as she set down the tray on the shin-bruising coffee table between Rabbi Blum and Sammy.

"Ah, Rabbi Helfenberg is fairly new to our area and volunteered to watch over you night before last as you laid in the coffin in the shul. There was supposed to be a hand off from Rabbi Rosenberg to Helfenberg, but Isaac's children and schedules and untimely circumstances got in the way and the handover never happened. Oh, Isaac came back to the shul to be sure Helfenberg was there, but Rolf was already deep in prayers so he just left it. That is the problem.   There was a short period between when you were delivered to the shul where Rabbi Rosenberg had to leave for a little while and Rabbi Helfenberg had not yet arrived."

"So what?" queried Sammy. "It isn't as though I was about to get up, call a cab, and go out for a few drinks, you know."

"Sammy, you were lying there, wholly unconscious, dead to the world, and in what we might call a state of spiritual vulnerability where malevolent, or, maybe, even benevolent demons could come to control your Nefesh. It is not a certainty and it surely is an old superstition from the days when it was not so rare for people to awake in their coffins because medical science was not very advanced back in the Shtetls. You may not have paid attention to it, but when you sat up yesterday, a few women

---

[9] "pareve" is a relatively neutral food category that is neither milchig or fleishig, i.e., dairy or meat - as the separation of those categories is critical in orthodox homes.

ran screaming from the room, yelling 'Dybbuk'! Old superstitions are hard to eliminate and 'Dybbuk' is the name of the malevolent demon. So, Rabbis Goldbaum and Helfenberg thought they perceived something different about you and, if so, it is serious enough for me to question you because malefic Dybbuks can cause a lot of damage and harm, mostly to your self and people close to you. So I have to ask, have you experienced anything unusual, like being compelled to do something out of the ordinary or harmful that you would never think of doing?"

Sammy sort of laughed, "come on... I can't imagine that"

"Well has anything unusual happened to you since you got home?"

"Sammy... you dasn't tell him, please."

"Naw, nothing that returning from the dead couldn't explain."

"Are you sure?"

"Rabbi, wouldn't I feel it if something was trying to make me do things that are not like me? You know, something like the federal government," said Sammy with a snicker in his voice.

"Okay, Sammy. We cannot be certain until there are signs of extraordinary behaviour. So if you say there is nothing, we'll be happy with that. But I want you to be very self-aware for the next few weeks just in case, please?"

"Of course, Rabbi. Maybe you should ask Serah to watch me too cause these guys that get up from the dead are liable to do anything, ya' know?"

"Sammy, you really should take this seriously as the halachic consequences are severe and decades ago there was this movie about an exorcism that was not at all funny, as realistic as the portrayals were."

"But that was catholic stuff, Rabbi, not us."

"Yes, but we are so thoroughly bereft of His guidance today without prophets or anyone with the kind of wisdom of Akiva or Luria that we don't really know the extent of the forms out there to trap us."

And with the mention of Isaac Luria's name, Sammy got this strange chill that came on and passed just as quickly.

"Okay, then ask Serah to keep an eye on me, eh? But do I seem any different to you, Rabbi?"

"No, but I'm not very attuned to these things and my wife keeps reminding me that I'm an insensitive klahd[10], so I'm no test of spiritual purity. For a formerly dead man, you seem fine, but my experience with the dead is limited, you know. Anyway, thanks for the return of the coat and I'll speak to Serah on the way out," promised the Rabbi as he got up, scooped up the raincoat, and walked to the door.

"I think I'm recovering, Rabbi. But I do appreciate the concern," as Sammy tried to sound positive, rising from the chair and going back to his desk.

Rabbi Blum found Serah in the front entry hallway and explained the concerns voiced by the other rabbis. Serah thought a moment and reassured him, "Rabbi, I gotta tell you I see nothing really different in Sammy. He feels the same to me and acts the same with the children. If there was a serious derangement of his person, surely it would have come out and the children would sense it, don't you think?"

"Maybe. Just stay observant and let me know if there is anything unusual, please?"

"Okay, sure. And thank you for covering Sammy with your coat. He was really grateful to save some of his modesty."

"You're welcome. I'm glad I thought of it."

---

[10] See Robert Aspirin's Myth Adventures.

As Rabbi Blum turned and walked toward the front door, he remarked, "just be aware and let me know if there is anything, please. We can't let Sammy and the rest of the family down if there is an issue, no matter how remote it is, please?"

"Absolutely, Rabbi. I hope Sammy is going to be around for a good while more and we can't have him going off all weird and everything, can we?"

Rabbi Blum looked back as he went through the open door and gave that kind of wry half-grin that signifies "we'll try" while worrying that he'd not resolved anything at all.

Sitting at his desk, Sammy heard the front door open and close and was anxious that the voice would start again. But it didn't. Relieved, Sammy reviewed Sid's e-mail and began to plan for the interview tour for the next three weeks. They were not major events or network appearances - which was just as good as Sammy really wasn't up for that right now. Sammy, trying to recover his concentration, knew they'd ask what he was working on, what was in progress. The voice incident had so unnerved him that he was having a difficult time remembering what he was doing. Was it the fire hydrant's tale? He made a few pencil notes in his diary and was just beginning to get back into the swing and focus when the children came home for lunch. The trip to the airport later was similarly routine, though the shocked look on his children's faces was actually gratifying. It made the reunion all the more satisfying for the next few days. The voice did not return before the interview trips or immediately after, much to Sammy's relief.

Chapter 10 - Exploiting the Dead

There used to be a highly successful margarine commercial on television decades ago with the tag line, "it's not nice to fool Mother Nature!" From the first two radio shows and one of the local television appearances that week, Sammy was getting the idea that his coffin set piece recovery was running along those lines. The hosts and most of the call-ins on two shows were highly disappointed that he didn't have a "tunnel of light" and similar walking back from death story. Sammy was going to have to ask Sid what he had used to promo these appearances because so far it sounded like a Halloween special from the walking dead. The entertainment value of a 120-year-old survivor sitting up in his coffin was not sufficiently engaging to stimulate any of the first three stops. So, having done this before when he'd won book awards and made the various media stops for publicity, Sammy was expecting more of the same in the Cuyahoga Falls local radio station and was girding his disclaimer loins for another round of: "No, I did not beat the Reaper[11]," when the announcer surprised him with:

"Sammy, it is lovely to have you here and thank you for making the trip to visit us. We have a tradition on this show of trying to look at how life experiences can alter the operating principles of people's lives. So tell us please, has the experience of waking up in your kittel in a coffin changed your philosophy of life?"

"Chuck," replied Sammy, as that was the announcer's name, "thank you for the most original question on this tour and one that does not presume I had a 'return from the dead' experience. And I'm going to witter

---

[11] Firesign Theatre, "Waiting for the Electrician, or Someone Like Him", 1968.

on a bit as I'm a bit gob-smacked by that approach... but not
for long. Let's ask, then, how do we define our philosophy.
It either has to be so simple as to apply over all
circumstances we encounter in a blanket kind of guide or so
complex that the ramifications of every minuscule event or
incident are worked out with a set of guiding principles
with almost infinite variations based on the occurrence and
our analysis of it. For most people, the former amorphous
blanket is probably the minute-to-minute answer - because
life is far too complex for most to have to delve into
endless analyses and complexity for the day-to-day events
that drive 90% of our life. I suspect that is the reason the
pragmatism version of Thomas Dewey never really took
hold."

"But I've generally operated under a philosophy of
'It Depends' for most of my life, not paying much assiduous
attention to Aristotle, Plato or any of the well-known or
lesser philosophical schools except as what I think happens
to mirror their principles - and I do not think people in
general do much differently. You see, all of us grow up in
a culture that pretty much shapes our values, beliefs, habits,
and in family settings that mould our character into a fair
mirror of what observe our family to believe. Note that this
acknowledges not what people say, but what they do, for
the latter is what children take on as the practice of their
family, not the former even though they may learn to give
lip-service to ideals voiced by their parents."

"Sammy," requested Chuck, "could you explain this
philosophy a bit more, please. For example, what are its
principles, ethics, metaphysics, if it has any, operating
foundation, and so on."

"I'm more of a story teller than a philosopher, but
I'll try. 'It Depends' literally means that what people do
references most dimensions of their milieu at the time
decisions are made. That includes most of the situational
variables as one has to account for the various and

changing pressures in one's life, the familial circumstances, peers, employment, economic environment, the general politic, the security and comfort level of where one lives. And all of those factors at a minimum, but all of them in the larger perspective of the values imbued in the decision maker by the family in which he or she grew up and the principles, morals, ethics, and general behavioural perspicacity implied thereof. I tend to think it is very Existential but taking authenticity for granted because while we are a product of our environments, we are not solely that nor is that even predictable amongst those who choose to live contrary to their upbringing because the basis for all of it is the free well we were given as conscious, consciousness bearing beings capable of thought and reason. Therefore, the answer to most questions of 'what to do', 'what to be', 'what to choose', and decisions of that ilk is 'It Depends' - and it actually does depend on how those various dimensions are perceived in balance to the matter at hand."

"As to how one lives under this philosophy, well it is all rather Solomon like, don't you know. There is a time for this, a time for that, and a time to avoid both of them. It tends to be one of the earlier philosophies where the existence of G-d can be argued not so much from the direct argument as the classical philosophers did but from the clear existence of free will. The reining philosophy in what we are told is the educated world is materialism, where everything is determined, there is no free will, and every thing and every being is mechanical, a trait left over from Descartes' thinking, believe it or not. However, any thought by any person will demonstrate that there is more than enough free will as the fact that people behave outside the constraints of their operant conditioning family history betrays an ability to act outside the mechanical robot we are told we are. The argument for G-d and his *ex nihlo* creation of the universe flies in the face of the materialist mechanical philosophy which, even through the development of the big bang theory, could not give up the idea that the universe is eternally the same, so the constancy of everything is one of their rigid Dogma's. But I'm told Terence McKenna used to say that modern science was based on the principle of 'give us one free miracle and we'll explain the rest. And the one free miracle is the appearance of all the matter and energy in the universe and all the laws that govern it from nothing in a single instant'. Reliance on that one small miracle is the lynch pin of materialistic developmental cosmology and those of us less materialistic, less mechanical and far less constrained by such a rigid Dogma are keen to point out that the miracle is talking directly to the holders of such concepts."

Chuck responded, "well that all seems nicely universal, but what of it when cultural mores conflict? I'm thinking of the decades, nay, centuries old conflict between the Judeo-Christian world and the culturally immiscible fundamentalist Islamic world. In that context, adherents of both views could agree that 'It Depends' and still be at each others' throats for the differences in beliefs, no?"

"No. People who actually respect themselves and their humanity tend to respect others and so two individuals of highly different belief systems can easily allow the other to exist and go on without conflict. Life is like that in certain parts of the Middle East where the governance model stipulates such tolerance. The elements which foster conflict are those that are basically mentally unbalanced, where chiefs that are blatantly sociopathic or psychotic are driven by external politics and power greed to a frenetic state that is equivalent to that found in the gratuitously mentally unhinged, and do so without any belief system disparity. It is a mental health issue, not a philosophical one; and that there can be mass mental disturbances is not a new discovery, is it? Remember that religious nut that got hundreds to suicide down in Guinea decades ago? So often we find the drive of mental illness veiled under semi-religious disguises to the extent that there are even written case histories of such delusions in the psychiatric annals. Yet, 99% of the world's religious people are thoroughly happy to exist within the constraints of their belief system without becoming all violently hysterical. The difference, if there is one, is the ability of the individual to relate to the humanity within themselves, in a living culture, and around them, I would think. There you would find little conflict with this operational philosophy."

Chuck did not look convinced. "At a philosophical and mental level, I can see where that is correct, Sammy, but in day-to-day operation with some of the 'still crazy after all these years' examples we have in the Cleveland area, the discipline to make that approach work simply does not seem to exist at what we might call the street level. Then again, we are still dealing with a very combative stance from many culturally immiscible groups who seem to refuse to discard their Medieval Culture for the likes of any century after the 7th, much less the 21st. Their behaviour may be wholly maladaptive for this culture, thus bringing some veracity to your characterisation, but were they sequestered in an environment that did not expose them to the pressures and reality of this time, would they not be perfectly fit and 'normal'? Of course, but it is the 'fish out of water' issue, perhaps."

"Being a guy that recently escaped the grave, I'm not going to argue the point because like the philosophy denotes, 'It Depends'," smiled Sammy. "But to have a united country, there must be shared values and mores and without that you're just pumping the divisiveness that we've seen many demagogues try to emphasise for decades in order to split the country for their personal and political benefit, not for the country as a whole. However, that is another entire discussion, Chuck."

"Correct, Sammy and we're just about out of time for our show together, here. I want to thank you for journeying to Cuyahoga Falls, a lovely but not well known part of the Cleveland area."

"Not so for me, Chuck," replied Sammy in faux indignation, "because not only did I live down in Akron for a year a long time ago, but I knew a girl from Cuyahoga Falls that I might have married many years ago... but had I done that none of this would likely be true and I'd not be here. So life has a way of putting us where we should be, eh?"

"Now there is a huge Existential conclusion, Sammy - one I can appreciate and with that this is Chuck Bergeron signing off this session of 'Falls Talks' with Sammy Silver on WKRC[12], Cuyahoga Falls, Ohio. Stay tuned for Mindy Make-up and her hints for studying for those mid-term exams, right after the news with Les Nesmann."

Sammy signed a copy of one of his books for Chuck, said his good-byes, and departed, debating whether to try to drive home then or catch a night's sleep before doing the expected 12 hour drive. Yes, Sammy still could not stand air travel, a function perhaps of his years of living on airplanes, in hotels, on the road, in airports, and always in someone else's place / business / office, never his, so he drove to every appointment that was less than a 24 hour drive. He'd finished with two shows in Philadelphia and Lehigh, Pennsylvania before driving across Pennsylvania to Cuyahoga Falls. It tired him more than it used to do. But, then again, he used to use tobacco to help keep him awake for the drive - Gee that was a long time ago. Maybe he'd just find a cheap and clean motel for overnight with a store nearby so he might find some food as keeping kosher on the road is lots of trouble and strange diets.

---

[12] Artistic license.... we moved it from Cincinnati, north.

Chapter 11 - Oh no, where are we now...

So, before getting on the freeway and looking for a motel there as they were always clustered by the airports and off freeways, Sammy found a large grocery chain and went in to find some fruit and maybe, just maybe they had a kosher section for cheese and crackers? Whoopee! Not only did they have a kosher section but had kosher baguettes, soft cheese, and packaged salami flavours.... with a bit of fruit it was far more than Sammy had expected. Now he was looking forward to finding the motel because breakfast had been many hours ago.

Sure enough, once Sammy got on the freeway, not 10 miles down the road was there one of those mid-range Hiltons, the kind Sammy used to frequent decades ago. Now, if it isn't full... Sammy was hoping. They weren't. The automatic check-in put him in a room on the second floor, issued the electronic door key, confirmed his credit card, announced that if Mr. Silver had any needs, the concierge was on extension 1080, and asked about a wake up call for the morning, noting that the self-serve breakfast bar would be up and running at 5:30 AM. Sammy wistfully missed the interpersonal aspect of travel that used to be - but that was long ago and before the thoroughly dehumanising discovery that human interaction is surplus to the requirements of completing small service contracts in the USA. Sigh....

Once in the room, Sammy unpacked his food, got out his handy-dandy Leatherman as well as his computer and called Serah and the children while eating a bit as he was famished. They always made such a fuss when he called, he thought. However, we might want to remember that Sammy still felt fairly active and vigorous, not at all fragile as many would think more appropriate for a man his age. He didn't even think of it, actually. He just was careful not to push himself too hard for too long, as his stamina was not the same as it was 50 or 60 years ago. Remember, here was a guy who was still allowed to have a driving license at his age when they usually removed it around age 95 or earlier.

He explained to Serah that the trip back was long enough that he thought he should get some sleep before trying it. She was happy to hear it as she was used to Sammy trying to do more than he could and veering close to serious trouble and exhaustion. She and the children told him to sleep well and they'd see him tomorrow.

Sammy looked for news to read while he was eating and it was always the same - the Circus was never ending and so many of the people out there seemed to dance to the self-destructive tune of the Big Top. Very strange he thought. Why don't they catch on?

Sammy finished, cleaned up, and changed for bed, brushed his teeth, ensured the door was double bolted, moved the pillows all over to his side, and lay down to sleep. He was tired, as he had gotten up early to finish the drive into Cuyahoga Falls for the radio show. The only nice thing about road travel these days was that he could more or less set his own schedule, as long as he showed up for his designated interviews on time. It was infinitely more relaxing than the pressure-cooker schedule he'd had years before.

Falling asleep was easy, even in this strange bed. Sammy was soon deep in dreams in places he did not know. He tried to control them, but was led from ancient libraries to caves to a town to a graveyard, all in Israel! He'd never been to Israel but knew it was so by the Hebrew on the signs. More strangely, he was not an observer in these dreams but an active participant, driven, purposeful, manipulating ancient manuscript covers with gloves, on some kind of mission not clear to him. It was so vivid and he was interacting with what seemed to be real people through it all. Finally, it finished, he was released, and he drifted off into a deeper sleep of peace.

But when he awoke...just in time for the breakfast bar to open... he remembered most of the dream and wondered about it all through his shower and getting dressed. It was still on his mind when he went down to the breakfast bar, the first assault on the daily perceptions of the road warrior. It was always that usual assortment of too liquid but drying scrambled eggs, bacon-looking artificial meat, maybe boiled eggs, mini sweet rolls, likely non-kosher bagels, breads of different colours and textures that taste the same with a toaster to heat both bagels and breads, various commercial cereals, yogurts, a few fruits, juices, assorted jams, jellies, and cream cheese individual portions, coffee, teas, and the ever harried attendant that not only was supposed to fulfil special orders but pour coffee, clear tables, reset, and provide gracious instructions to people who acted as though they had never travelled outside their home neighbourhoods before. If the joint thought itself really swank or was regularly full, the attendant had an assistant whose job it was to make pancakes and waffles, nothing else.   If it was in Europe, it also had sliced sausages and smoked meats, smoked fish, herring, hard and soft cheeses, plain and flavoured yogurts, perhaps a quiche or two, quarter melons, half grapefruits, various berries, crepes with fruit or chocolate sauces and powdered sugar, and incredible fresh bread rolls and croissants. But this was Northeast Ohio so forget that, as Sammy awoke from a bit of a reverie from his days of European business travel. And none of it looked kosher. Sammy asked the attendant if the bagels were kosher while she was clearing a table and the look he got was one more like the pain filled one you get when berating a puppy than a verbal answer. Sammy just waived his hand and moved on, getting some black coffee in a polystyrene cup and returning to his room to finish what portion of the baguette was not hard as a publisher's heart. That and a little fruit with the coffee was enough to get him going. He picked up a couple of candy bars on his way out in case the journey was that bad.

Sammy loved driving, still, after all these years and the various changes that the governments tried in order to wrest mobility control from the drivers and car owners and pocket it in an autocratic government. The populace were having none of it and rebelled by destroying the very control stations the governments tried to establish. Countries outside the US and Canada were not so forthright and some caved in like spoiled children promised a treat... and became all the more autocratic and controlled for it, losing what little liberty and freedom they had before the Empire crushed them. But the war between the Empire and the US persisted for lo these many years after the initial rebuff of the patriot administrations decades ago. So, driving his old car was still a treat for hours on end because it gave Sammy time to think.

The dream still intrigued him because strange as it sounds, from amongst all his friends, he'd never been to Israel, not once. The reason was simple; there was never enough money because the foreign cash flow and publishing commissions were enough to live from day-to-day, but there was never enough for expensive vacations and holiday trips. The occasional summer cottage rental on a lake was about all they could manage. Remember, Serah now had a houseful of children to manage and did not work - plus she was getting a bit older - and if Sammy and Serah had not moved into Serah's far too big for her house years ago, even that would not have been possible on Sammy's income.

Sigh... it was one of those long sighs that shudders in every organ of your body, the kind that you feel to the tips of your toes. There were many things Sammy wanted to do for his family, to provide them, luxuries they could not afford and it was always a bother to him. But always following that thought was the gratitude that he could feed, clothe, and house them well... and Hashem was kind enough to keep this old gas chugging vehicle going without major hiccups; so it wasn't so bad - it was pretty good in fact. Thank you, he thought, once again.

Sammy was thankful for these times of solitary thoughts while cruising down a freeway under the speed control settings that kept him from getting speeding tickets. Just enough consciousness to pay attention to the road allowed the rest of him to think elsewhere. But Sammy was brought up sharply, suddenly, and without warning.

"Sammy, I still need your help, Sammy." There it was, again, back in my mind he thought. That woke him up! He was so surprised that he spoke to it directly. "Not while I'm driving," he snapped. And all was quiet after that except for the occasional music he tried to find on the radio outside of the C&W and immature pop that dominated the US airwaves. Sammy didn't like any of the three of them, pop, Country, or Western.

Chapter 12 - Who are you and what is it you want?

Sammy had been anticipating a 12-hour drive back home because the last time he drove from Cleveland to their home in Ontario, it took 8 hours and their new home was about 4 hours' drive further east. However, checking the Tom-Tom, there was an alternative route that was only 8 hours, staying mostly on US freeways. Whew! Sometimes the technology is a true benefit.

When he arrived the children paused their classes for a few minutes to greet him and Serah came out, giving the kind of hug and kiss he had missed for all those days away. After carrying his luggage upstairs, he returned to tell Serah a bit about the interviews that were almost always the same. After sincerely noting that she was grateful he was back, she excused to return to the kitchen where she was getting their dinner prepared.

Sammy carried his briefcase to the office and unpacked the storage drive and attached it to the main computer, switching it on and preparing to work on a few stories in progress, leaving the portable in the briefcase. He was sitting in his office chair at the desk awaiting the desktop to finish booting, loading all the privacy and anti-snoop programmes that one needed these days of wholesale cybertheft and electronic eavesdropping when *"he or it"* came back.

"Sammy, I need your help. You can do it and I need it. I'm sorry to approach you this way but I have no alternative, please."

Annoyed, frightened, anxious, and fearful of what was happening to him, Sammy felt compelled to ask, "Who are you, what do you want of me, and where on earth did you come from? Am I going daft? Are you invisible?

Where are you and why do I hear you? And why are you asking for my help when I'm just a nobody Jew?"

"I am the spirit of Rabbi Moshe Alshich. Nobody outside of a Yeshiva has heard of me for centuries, but I was renowned as one of the greatest darshanim of my time. I was a devoted student of Rabbi Yosef Caro and the Arizal. While Rabbi Caro thought enough of my work to make me part of his court in Safed, and even though I learned all my Kabbalah from the Arizal through his holy perception he thought me sanctified to rectify the homiletical interpretation of the Torah." The Spirit stopped. Then continued, "this isn't making any sense to you, is it, Sammy?"

"Frankly, no - and what do I call you?"

The concept of a face-palm in the spiritual world was unknown up to now, but..."You may call me Moshe, all right?"

Now the interaction was agreed, it seems.

"Let us say that I was the primary authority on service sermons in Eretz Israel at the time... though I was mostly in Safed... and I would have given up that expertise to have learned more of what the Arizal was teaching. I wanted to be his highest disciple but he would not have me. He made me fall asleep whenever I attended his classes. He insisted that my calling was in the speaking and lessons on Torah I would give through my sermons. Just as you have me as an ibbur, Sammy, I had the soul of Rabbi Shmuel bar Nachmeini, but my infusion was engineered, yours has been my initiation, not yours. Do you understand that?"

"Not really. I have been so busy in the material world that the things I should have been studying were ignored while I was on the road or helping with children. I live in a different world than you did Moshe."

"Yes, but only different in the mere materialistic dimensions through the myopic focus on that aspect since

the middle of your 19th century has severely constrained the intellectual and spiritual world-view of academia and the professions to the point of massive deception in order to eliminate the inherent spiritual dimension of mankind. It has gone so far as to reduce science from an investigation pursuit of intellect and creativity to an exercise merely confirming the Dogma of its construct. In many areas, we were actually far more advanced in the 16th century than you are now, at least in our approach. However, that is just an observation from outside the realm of life, for now."

"Okay, my purpose here. First, it is not really to add another dimension to your soul as despite your focus on the mundane, HE has more for you to do and you do not need that for this mitzvah. But you will need my 'ibbur' perception and will above the day-to-day if we are to do what I need you to help me do, please. Put bluntly, I need recognition by the spirit of the Arizal that I was actually worthy of his teaching. The only way I can do this is to help his transcriber, Rabbi Chaim Vital on a mission respecting his work and place it on the Aru's gravesite on the 5th of Av, his Yahrzeit. Rabbi Chaim Vital and I resolved our differences before his death and mine, but the Arizal had passed 20 years earlier and has not communicated with us since as we think we really put a kink in his equilibrium. In a way it is a confession that I and many others were spiritually jealous of the high evolution of the Arizal's soul and strived to know how we could attain that. I'm hoping this confession, evidence of my Teshuvah, and congregation with Chaim will help both of us elevate ourselves. You can't imagine the torturous level of discourse on the lower levels of the spiritual plane."

"Are you telling me that you need my help with your Teshuvah? You died a few hundred years ago. Isn't it a little late for that? And the 5th of Av is almost two months from Yom Kippur. We haven't even celebrated Pesach yet this year. It is months until Av."

"Yes, but what I need you to do will be in Jerusalem and Safed in the early days of Av, before the fifth. It will take time to prepare and establish the story we will use so we need time to set this up and establish the credibility of your trip to Israel."

"Trip to Israel? We don't have that kind of money! Serah and I and the six children will be a fortune - then travel, hotels, and food while we are there! OY! It looks like six figures just to do that - we don't have that kind of money lying around! Do you see us in flashy cars, here? Flash clothes, jewellery, new furniture do you see? We are scraping along and the opportunity you had to jump in here, as I suppose it is, created a small marketing event of which I will take full advantage - but it isn't going to give me enough to splash out on a trip to Israel. I'll be lucky if I pull in enough to pay for the funereal party catering. Get real," said Sammy rather derisively, as the mitzvah intrigued him and he was disappointed that the condition made it impossible.

"Sammy, in the spiritual level dybbuks and ibburs inhabit, many things are possible that you cannot imagine. I know what it costs and I can make it happen including vast income amounts to secure your family's time there. The money is the least of the worries. Establishing you as an antiquarian specialist is the larger issue and that needs to be done soon. That is where we will need the help of your friend Simon."

"Simon? Why him?"

"You never talk much to people in your shul, you know..."

"How can I, all they ever ask me is how it feels to be as old as I am... except Simon, you're right. We do talk about my books, but I do not pry into others' lives, you know."

"You should - it shows you are interested in them. It gives them a chance to talk about themselves. Anyway, one of Simon's duties is head of the antiquarian section at his university. We will need a letter of introduction from him to the Curator of Rare Books at the National Library of Israel so that you can get access to at least one volume they have."

"I know from wiener schnitzel about rare books. You are asking me to present myself as an expert in antiquarian matters from which I am so ignorant our dog knows more?"

"Your dog?"

"That's how little I know because the mythical dog that does not exist knows more than I do."

"Not to worry as I can guide these things a bit - you should have no problem if you want to help. You were always able to play the authority when you were consulting, didn't you? How is this so different?"

"Because then I actually had a bit of a handle on what I was convincing people to do. This, I don't. And that was 50 years ago. Though watching what is going on, I'd be stumped in playing a game of 'find the differences'. It is as though the world was put on hold 50, 60 years ago and we're all on a merry-go-round."

"Now that is one of your more perceptive statements, Sammy, but the hold happened over 150 years ago because the fight to control the world hasn't stopped and nobody is willing to smash the villains. However, that is another discussion about which I can do nothing. Now that you are agreeable, I can begin getting things ready for your trip and you have to talk to Simon next week. The reason you will need his letter of introduction is that you will be comparing one of the volumes his collection possesses with the real original housed in the National Library of Israel."

"How am I to do that? I already told you I know nothing..."

"But I do and I will lead you through what has to be done and what you have to say."

"So, I'm just sort of a puppet in all this, eh?"

"Yes... and no; because I could not do this with anyone - there are reasons why you were chosen and they relate to dimensions you cannot understand as yet. So, yes, you have to act as I direct you, but the ability and essence to do that is something peculiar to you and no one else... or at least not to many."

"And all this is to help elevate you?"

"Yes, and Rabbi Chaim Vital, we must resolve a concern that may still trouble the Arizal, and by so doing elevate yourself as well. You'll see, but it may be some time before that is apparent. The time scale in the physical world is inhibiting, purposefully so, but inhibiting nonetheless."

Sammy was more than a little gobsmacked.

"So, wait; are you an ibbur or a dybbuk?", asked Sammy as he knew a little of the differences.

"Sort of both, to you. I am a dybbuk because I am trying to settle a spiritual slight, but aspects of an ibbur because it will elevate you at the same time; but there is nothing demonic about this synergistic relationship. The complexity is why this mitzvah takes you to accomplish it; few others can do it for very few others have your lack of fear. It would be best if you did not mention this to your rabbis I suspect, as they are bound by rather dogmatic and orthodox thinking. This is not a matter of normal orthodoxy, you might say. But if at any time you think I am harming you, please tell me and then tell your rabbis. OK?"

Sammy wondered two things. First, if his thoughts were solely his own and not always shared with his new companion and, two, if he thought the spirit was harmful,

could the spirit overwhelm his desire to seek outside help?
Hmmm... He resolved to think about it.

Chapter 13 - Preparations and Surprises

The lightness of Sammy Silver was that he saw this as a new project, a new challenge, something he had never done before, ignoring the dark and foreboding elements possible in dealing with forces far beyond his capability. This was one of those dimensions why Serah loved him, his ability to deal forward; to strive onward, seemingly oblivious to consequences that he refused to recognise. While this characteristic seemed to put many others in deep hazards, Sammy seemed to sail right through - a blessing that one never fully recognises, perhaps.

He called Simon to set a meeting for next week after he returned from his road shows. Simon was always happy to see Sammy and didn't even ask the reason - for which Sammy breathed a silent sigh of relief because he didn't know the answer, yet.

And, as expected, three local television and three radio shows all looking for "the man that rose from the dead". Sammy formulated the quip: "At my age, you would think it would be difficult to tell the difference, eh?" usually got at least a giggle from live audiences - the dead ones didn't utter a sound.

The one nice thing is that sales of Sammy's books began hustling like mad. They had never sold this well. "Heck, I should die more often," he thought in passing. The line was so good he incorporated it into the responses to the brain dead interviewers. It was as though they had some online script base from which they all pulled their inane questions and commentaries. They all sounded almost exactly the same... until on the final local TV interview, Sammy asked, "tell me, please. I've had three weeks of show tours to local radio and television stations around the eastern half of the US and Canada, and except for a real human in Cuyahoga Falls, Ohio, you and your media colleagues ask almost exactly the same questions. It is virtually the same ones, every interview, radio or TV. Is there a reason for this?"

And the 'talent' froze for a moment. That wasn't in the script. The producer was yelling something at him in his ear but he wasn't paying attention and finally discretely pulled the earplug out and slowly responded to Sammy, "Well, you've observed the secret to networked media and called us on it I'm afraid. We are all given the same script for intervicwccs making the rounds, no matter the station and apparent loyalties, they or we are all networked and controlled like one large, lumbering, mindless android, ensuring that the viewing or listening audiences all get exactly the same pap and dribble, ensuring nothing is extraordinary, honest, frank, or original. It began over 70 years ago and has never changed because what you might think of as the public has never demanded anything different. This way we can indoctrinate the lot of them, program them all at minimal cost and not leave any loose intellectual ends lying about. Is that clear?"

"And, as that statement will be edited out of the video if this interview is distributed, its play will only be to those folks currently tuned in to this broadcast. I hope they appreciate the reality that was just laid out before them IF they hadn't realised it before. Of course, millions recognised this decades ago when it first began, but there was no hue and cry and it just has continued as though it is the way it is supposed to be. Talking heads like myself do not have to exercise even the tiniest soupcon of intellect to conform to the network personality. In fact, any individualistic effort like that would ensure relegation to night shift advertising tag announcing in local television stations. So, I may have just ended my video carer with that admission. However, yours was a fair question for an audience that should have been begging for its answer. Thank you."

"Thank you," acknowledged Sammy gratefully, "honesty is frightening, but far less rebarbative than extended prevarication."

The 'talent' in that interview was later promoted to program manager for the station, virtually ensuring that he will never be given the chance to broadcast such heresy on air for the rest of his career in broadcasting. The Borg, sorry, Network, does not abide anyone going off script. He was fortunate.

Because all this week's show tours were in Florida, Sammy had to endure the indignity of US air travel Gestapo services twice, once out of Canada a few days ago and once returning after the Radio and TV interviews. Sammy created his resolve to drive within certain distances years ago because of the dehumanisation of US air travel back in the early 21st century and while he had driven from Canada to southern Florida in 24 hours before... it was when Sammy was about half this age and he wasn't going to try it now. So, even travelling First Class made no difference anymore and Sammy grudgingly turned off his brain and followed instructions...such as "Ja, ich habe meine papiere, Herr Kommandant." He was not happy that he couldn't so easily goose-step any longer, but the concentration camp guard simulacra they use in airport security don't have senses of humour, anyway, so one must be careful, stepping lightly, so to speak.

There are few things that make one feel appreciated like the welcoming one receives from their family when they return from a few days' trip. It just reinforces all the human dimensions of your life and warms those parts of you no other experience reaches. So it was with Sammy, particularly as he arrived in time for dinner and everyone was waiting for him and wanted to hear, as always, about the interviews and if he had met any interesting people.

The next day Sammy showered, dressed and headed downstairs to his office to prepare for his meeting with Simon later that morning. This time he had to begin the conversation with Moshe, as he had no idea what he was to do with Simon. Now that felt strange.

"Moshe? Are you there," whispering as though the ibbur was hiding behind something.

"Most of the time, but not all - we have not the physical limitations of the mortal world. Why are you calling me?"

"Moshe, I've this appointment with Simon this morning and I have no idea what it is about or what I'm supposed to say to him. Remember, I'm no antiquarian. Can you help, please?"

"Simple, Sammy. You need to tell him you have been studying with the American Antiquarian Society and specifically with John Fitzgerald Schitt, one of the premier antiquarians in North America today - surely Simon knows him. So that sets your credibility. Then, you tell him you know he has come into possession of this reputed Rabbi Isaac Luria bound book from Safed. The only known verified copy is in the National Library in Israel. Since you are going there this summer would he like you to report on validating the copy that is in his possession? Something like that. But I'll be there to coach you. It will go well."

Sammy wished he were as optimistic as Moshe. We'll see, he thought.

Simon's office looked like a nice wooden desk hidden under reams of paper, bound and loose on the one side with three bookcases on the opposite wall similarly filled and with two visible chairs in the midst of all that... and rumours of a third under more volumes in the corner. The shelves mounted on the wall over the desk held a few framed photos and degrees surrounded by yet more paper. Simon was wont to say that if the Greenies ever saw his office, they'd put him up as the man that destroyed the rain forest.

"So, Sammy, welcome to my humble hidey-hole, can I get you some coffee, tea, or something stronger?"

"Simon, thank you, but you know my klutzy touch - I'd hate to spill on the accumulated works of three or four classes," smiled Sammy.

"Sammy. I know what everything is and where everything is... really," grimaced Simon, "some of these students really are bright... some of them, anyway, and I want to encourage them all to literary achievement like yours."

"Oh, now comes the rolling bovine excrement, eh?" grinned Sammy, "I'm just a mediocre story teller, Simon, so far from Dickens that we aren't even in the same city, much less the same ball park." At least Simon understood these older aphorisms and sayings, a cultural heritage totally lost on the current crop of techie-enslaved children.

"That is not what I hear," countered Simon, "I was told your books have risen to the top of the best seller lists, based, they said, on your sudden rising as opposed to their literary merit," chuckled Simon gleefully. "I was there. I remember thinking 'gee, I hope I can pull that off when the time comes', but wondering too, how it would be to look forward to a long rest near Him only to be jerked back to this mundane existence. How disappointing that would be."

"But call me a tool, Simon, I'm doing only as He wants me to do, only without the prophetic and upright spirit of Moses, sadly. Which brings me partly to this occasion. One of the things my studies enable, strangely, is antiquarian texts. I've been collaborating with John Fitzgerald Schitt and am off to Israel this next summer to look critically at some of the rarities in the National Library of Israel while my family sight-sees..."

"Are you?" Simon interrupted excitedly. "Excuse me, but if you're going to be there could you do me a gigantic favour that I just haven't the time to properly attend? I can't get there as my summer is already booked with speaking engagements I can't afford to refuse, so it would be a huge mitzvah if you could do this for me, please?"

Sammy was truly and thankfully surprised, "Sure," he said trying to minimise the grin, "I'd be happy to help you if I can. What is it?" he asked innocently.

"We are in the process of acquiring a manuscript for the school that its purported owner claims to be the work of Rabbi Isaac Luria and printed by Eliezer bar Yitzhak. Since Eliezer printed only 10 major works in the 10 years his printing business survived, that part is easier to determine, but the question of whether it is truly the work of the Ari must be verified by someone that is at least familiar with the issues found in antiquarian investigations. And if you are agreeable, I would forever appreciate it if that were you that helped. We will provide you with a suitable carrying case for the manuscript along with a letter of introduction noting your expertise and our charge to you in making the analytical comparison to support our decision to acquire or not. It would be a great help to me and the entire department, Sammy. If it works well, we might be able to twist some academic arms and get you an honorary phid, sorry, Ph.D. in honour of your invaluable assistance to the department. What do you say to that?"

Sammy's head was virtually reeling on twin tracks: one wondering how Moshe was able to put this together and, two, guilt over misrepresenting himself and the unearned accolades that may come of it. There was the third track, too, the inner torture that he could never tell anyone about this and how it was managed. But Simon has stopped speaking, so Sammy swallowed it for now and assured Simon, "the honourific would be wonderful, but

I'm happy to help just for the sake of the mitzvah, Simon," as Sammy sidestepped all he'd been thinking. "The trip will commence before Av, but when I have the exact flight dates, I'll let you know. How does that sound?"

"Make sure I have the arrangements as soon as possible after Pesach, please; as I'll be gone through most of the summer and you'll have to pick up the case from our administrative assistant or the Chair of the Department just before you leave as we don't want it straying too far from our control for too long. If the university buys this it will be a first and the start of a tremendous collection, we hope."

"I can tell you if Eliezer bar Yitzhak printed the book as it is clear from the binding."

Sammy ignored Moshe as that sounded like the end of the meeting to Sammy.

Sammy got up, "Simon that is a great idea and if I ever remember why I asked for this meeting, I'll get back to you - but I like the idea and I'm ever so happy to help, honourific or not."

Simon stood up. "Sammy, you have taken a great weight off my mind, my commitments, and my calendar. I can't tell you how relieved I am that you'll take this on for me. The next time I see John Fitzgerald, I'll be sure to thank him for helping you, too."

And with that Sammy left, allowing Simon's last passing comment to drive him more than slightly anxious.

While Sammy was driving home, Moshe sprang up to mention that *John Fitzgerald was not an issue as he would remember Sammy well, having read all of his books.*

'Really?' Sammy thought. *'Yes' reassured Moshe,* thus preventing who knows how many accidents due to an erratic old man driving on the freeway. So, by the time Sammy got home he was feeling far more at ease and relaxed. Then Sid called.

"Sammy, I gotta thank you for your Lazarus act a few weeks ago. It was either that or something you said on those interview shows that have put sales of your books into reprint mode. Places have actually sold out and some are asking for signing tours. Believe that? Signing parties for a 120-year-old author. I can't tell you how grateful my son's college fund is for your recent popularity. Can we do a few signing parties? I'll try to schedule them like I did the interview rounds, out on Sunday, back late Wednesday or Thursday, no west coast and I'll try to skip Florida this time because I know how fond you are of flying in the US prison system, err, flight system. How's that sound?"

Sammy really wanted to sit at home, enjoy his children and Serah, work on a couple of stories, and rest. This morning's appointment with Simon had tired him out more than he thought. However, if he was going to do this favour for Simon and Moshe, he needed a lot of money for flights, hotels, and tourist expenses. Sighing, he said, "sure, Sid. Set it up and e-mail me the details, please."

Then it occurred to Sammy to check his publisher account.

Sammy had never seen so much money in an account of his before. It was far more than enough to pay for the flights and errata in Israel, first class, even, with plenty left over. Wow. Then Sammy remembered that Moshe had promised the ability and means to help him.

"Moshe, is all that your effect?" Sammy asked.

"Some, most of it due to curiosity of a rising dead man, I think. Your inebriated and semi-cataleptic recovery act caught the imagination of a lot of people and people read often what piques their imagination. That is how John Fitzgerald came to read you, you know. Besides that, you are easy to read and do not challenge people except for those who seek to alter the traditional culture, so you're easy. Your lack of sales for so many years was just that people gravitate to things that attract their interest - and

you never did before. You refused to put sexually enticing or imaginative covers on your books so what do you expect?"

"It isn't enough to be a 120-year-old author?"

"No, not today. Remember, you're an outlier but not the oldest. And the others aren't comatose in a home, either. So, that is an aspect, but not a strong marketing angle; so get out there and do those book signings gratefully and gracefully."

Chapter 14 - Preparation, Expectation, and Israel

Sid did well. The tour was engineered so that Sammy was able to drive. In the first week the longest leg was the initial jaunt to Boston, and they were always morning signings so that he could travel in the afternoon to the next city. Next week it was Philadelphia to start and the week after that, Pittsburgh, then Chicago, Milwaukee, and Cleveland were the big starting cities, sometimes having two signing parties in the one city on successive days - then an afternoon session could be sandwiched in, as well. It was a six week stint, home for the weekends and Shabbat, and out for book signings. And Sammy was more than gracious, as he figured that all these people meant not just money but recognition, life, and acknowledgement of some level of mitzvah he was doing for them. To his thinking, an author that imparts pleasure or education and growth is much like a teacher, a mentor, one that stimulates people to think outside the prosaic shell the State wants to be the entirety of individual relationships.

And Pesach was almost upon them by the time the tour finished. Moshe reminded Sammy to make reservations in Israel now and that took a week. The three week apart plane reservations with El Al were easy, but after he surprised Serah with the news that they were all, ALL going to Israel, she demanded to see how they were going to afford it.

Sammy showed her the money accumulating to be awarded, and after she got over her surprise, she wanted to tour the country from top to bottom. She was only momentarily curious when Sammy noted that he needed to be in Jerusalem initially for meetings and in Safed for other meetings on other days, but that was all easy to schedule.

The book tours were over, Pesach cleaning was completed as pleasantly painful as it was, Pesach was upon them and finished before it was noticed, then Shavuos and the summer was almost upon them. Sammy made Pesach all the more special by announcing to the children that they were all going to Israel in the summer. Then in the ensuing weeks, Serah and Sammy had to deal with some plan alterations to see and do things the children wanted; the excitement was contagious. Sammy had also given his dates to Simon who got back to him noting that the container with the manuscript would be with the Department Chair and Sammy was expected to pick it up along with his letter of introduction and authorisation as well as the bonding authority three days before the expected departure.

In the intervening space, Sammy tried to work on more stories, but his own tale was preoccupying his mind excessively. And there was the occasional reminder from Moshe about clearing the relic document examination time with the archivist and Manuscript Department of the Library. So Sammy took a look online and exclaimed..."hey, it's all in Hebrew and my Hebrew is not all that good."

Moshe figuratively rubbed his spiritual fingers pensively across his disincarnate forehead, noting quietly that a face-palm is far too unsophisticated for one as steeped in Kabbalah as he - though he had seen the Arizal confront such frustration centuries ago on a level far above his. "Just e-mail the archivist about what you have and what you need to do, please. He speaks English and I will be with you to do the comparison and acquire what we need to acquire from the books. Oh, and also note that you'll need to have access to any of Rabbi Chaim Vital's books on the Arizal's teaching that they have - that is a MUST, particularly if they were published by Eliezer. Do you understand?"

"Okay. I'll do as you wish. This is your mitzvah..."

"No, it is not just me, but Chaim Vital, as well, as he acted according to my Halachic rulings at the time. You are acting for two, here."

"If you say so. I just still find it very strange being possessed, so to speak - and I can't talk or write about it to anyone. I can't share it, my fears, or my frustrations with anyone."

"Not for now - wait until it is over and you can then decide if you want to share your experiences. But let us finish what we can do first, please."

And Sammy wrote the e-mail to the curator and let it rest.

Three days before they left, Sammy visited the Chair of Simon's department at the University to secure the manuscript in its case, the letter, and complete the bond paperwork. In the case, the bound document was secured between two thick insulating layers that would not allow it to bounce around the inside of the case. There were also a couple pairs of latex gloves for handling in case none were available outside. Sammy was cautioned that under no circumstances should he or anyone else pick up the document with their bare hands as the acid remnants would permanently ruin the manuscript.

He took the case home and opened it in his library. Donning the gloves, he took out the manuscript very carefully to allow Moshe to see it.

"I don't want to see the inside contents, yet. Stand the book on its fore-edge so that the spine is facing up.

Sammy complied.

"There, see all those protruding ribs running across the spine at odd intervals, particularly the ones on either side of the title inscription? And see the two circular shields embossed at the top and bottom of the spine?"

"Yes"

Sammy held each end of the book with a thumb and his fingers, trying to get a bit of leverage for pushing with his index fingers on the shields. He was delicate at first, then pressed harder and they simultaneously retracted into the spine of the book! At the same time, parts of the spine cover opened up in uneven sections, swivelling on the joint on the wide margins of the spine. What was revealed was mostly what one sees if the spine comes off a properly bound book, but there were a few pages in the centre of the document that were not single sheets, but looked like envelopes, virtually hollow pages inside which other smaller pages could be secreted. In fact, using very thin papers, almost glassine, entire volumes might be thus hidden. Sammy was more than slightly surprised.

<span segment removed>*government or secret agency to another via Eliezer's excellently constructed books and cooperative academics, priests, and rabbis. This one seems to contain about six envelopes. Is there anything in any of them?"*

Sammy turned the book so that the light was more illuminating, let's say. He fingered the envelopes and noted that two of them seemed to have contents.

"Well, pull them out and let's see what they are."

Sammy pulled out one that was three larger sheets, folded in half, but on such glassine paper that to read them they had to be placed on a paper background. The other one was four half, essentially A5, sheets, but similarly transparent. Sammy first spread out the four sheets on his desk on top of paper he pulled from the printer stack. It was obviously biblical Hebrew and Sammy couldn't read any of them. "So what is it?" he queried.

"Amazing," whispered Moshe almost breathlessly (which is pretty interesting for an ibbur, you have to admit), "Secrets that no one today would understand. Secrets that I yearned to know from the lips of the Ari himself. No wonder he did not want these to be published. No wonder, then, that Chaim wanted me to retrieve them. But what are they doing in this volume, here in Canada? Spread out the others, Sammy, please."

Sammy carefully gathered the four A5 sheets and placed them in an A4 manila envelope. He spread out the A3 size sheets carefully, being careful not to split them where they were folded, three of them, on the white paper. Again, more biblical Hebrew that Sammy did not understand.

"More secret lessons of the Arizal! These are getting very close to things I do not even understand or have the wisdom to understand. Oh, dear. No wonder Chaim has worried himself for centuries about these. Put them away carefully, Sammy. Not back in the book, but separately, please. They go with us as they are actually

more precious than the book itself. The question then, is what are they doing in this book and what, if anything, is in the book in Jerusalem? Please close the spine carefully and let us look at the book, itself, please?"

Sammy put the folded A3 sheets in another manila envelope and without sealing them he put both envelopes aside. Sammy pushed the book back together and swivelled the spine sections back in place and when he had pushed the final spine rib and its section back into place, the shields popped back up and the book was as before. 17th century technology, wow. Rubik's cube with a practical use.

Sammy put the book on the desk and opened the cover.

"Ahh, no wonder, this is Chaim's approved volume on the teachings of the Ari. It is a very significant book and far beyond most of the students and Kabbalists of today, sadly. The Rebbe understood and his antecedents did, as well; but Kabbalah is a level of wisdom over and above even the most erudite of rabbis in most cases. It is like moving from Newtonian physics to Quantum mechanics and those imbued with the former are often unable to grasp the latter."

Sammy paged through the volume, more amazed at the inability to tell the pages that were envelopes, such was the craftsmanship of the 17th century.

"Yes, this is Chaim's approved work on the Arizal. I remember it well. I studied it assiduously and painfully and yet yearned for more that the Ari would never let me have."

"Okay, finish turning the pages and close the book. Return it to its case with its wrapping and insulation... and the gloves as you'll need them in Jerusalem. Put the envelopes with the separate pages in the folder division section of your thin briefcase. Do not label either envelope. Leave them plain and do not seal them. If those

*papers survived a few hundred years in that book, they'll
survive a couple of weeks in your briefcase."*

Sammy finally spoke. "So tell me. Is this volume
real, is it the work of Rabbi Chaim Vital?"

*"Well, without carbon dating or whatever fancy
technology you have, it looks just like the book I studied
back in Safed hundreds of years ago. The Hebrew is right,
the ink seems correct, the paper feels right or acts right, the
book or document case is certainly correct, and what we
extracted from the book is absolutely certain to be the
things Chaim asked me to procure. That they are here as
opposed to Jerusalem will just make things very interesting
when we get there. It will be interesting what we discover,
if anything, in the book kept in the National Library of
Israel."*

Sammy put everything away, sealed the document
case, locked his briefcase, and got caught up in the
preparations for travel because the children were driving
Serah spare.

The excitement of children who've not taken a long
distance flight before is difficult to contain. Sammy and
Serah made sure there was enough in their carry-ons to
keep them occupied because it was a long flight and they
thought even the online and inflight entertainment systems
would not be enough. With the large increase in his book
sales, Sammy could have bought up the first class cabin but
decided to scale back to business where the other
passengers would be just as sniffy, but at least it didn't cost
as much. He and Serah's worries about the children's
behaviour were wasted as even the flight personnel
complimented them on how well the children were
behaved.

Getting off the plane in Tel Aviv, the first thing that
struck them was the heat. The second thing was the wave

of comfort, the feeling of being where you belong, an hospitality in the very air that bespoke of home, a spiritual and physical restfulness that was unknown anywhere they had lived before. It was a warm smile of so many lovely dimensions. It was so obvious that even the children, tired as they were, erupted into joy despite those monotonous hours and hours on the plane.

Sammy's appointment in Jerusalem wasn't for a week. So they decided to tour the south of Israel for a week, historic cities, kibbutzim, Torah tours, and end the week in Jerusalem. At the hotel in Tel Aviv, Sammy procured a couple of stout boxes, a wooden one for the document case and dispatched both of them to the curator at the National Library of Israel, after checking to be sure they would secure the packages on arrival. Once they were told of the contents, they told Sammy they would secure them in their vault awaiting his arrival. There was nothing in the briefcase that he would need while touring southern Israel. And they had reservations to be back in Jerusalem on the first of Av, celebrating Rosh Chodesh[13] in Jerusalem... that just twirled Sammy's propeller so...

---

[13] Rosh Chodesh is the Hebrew celebration of the new month, remembering that the Jewish Calendar is monthly, but precision corrected to keep Pesach, a spring holiday, near the beginning of Spring rather than meandering through the solar year like other monthly calendar cultures.

Chapter 15 - The National Library of Israel

Ever since the official annexation of all of what used to be Judea and Samaria into official, as far as Israel was concerned, Israel, the Empire that used to own them was remarkably hostile, covertly provoking all sorts of hostilities from locals who were sadly not bright enough to know they were just being used as tools. This was the difficult part of the tour of the south where places like Hebron and the Cave of Machpelah were still surrounded by antipathetic pawns of people that hate Jews - or are paid to hate Jews, the difference is never quite clear. But aside from having to interact for a small portion with professional hate-mongers, the south was brilliant, clearing Sammy's sinuses and, except for the occasional scorpion, just a big sand box of lovely, hot weather, camel rides, and skin clearing sun.

Because it was Rosh Chodesh they spent a good portion of the first day in Jerusalem near the wall with thousands of other Jews. Sammy was now glad that he brought his tallis. They were asked to a number of homes for lunch and, then, dinner after maariv, Sammy being North American enough to buy multiple bottles of wine for his hosts even though they said it was not needed. The overwhelming welcome hospitality was so abundant that Serah and the children kept asking if it was real - and the locals noted that this is just a mitzvah, normal life for Jews in Jerusalem, "is it not the same where you live?"

The next day Serah and the children had tours of Jerusalem booked, lunches out, and more tours in the afternoon. Sammy headed to the Library. When he got there he asked about the packages and was directed to security in the lower levels. After showing a few pieces of identification over a metal covered counter, through a small window in a steel mesh gated opening, he commented that Library security was more than he expected. The Shift Commander explained to him that a couple of days before, two men, one of them claiming to be Sammy, showed up to claim the packages and the security team stopped them. "After all, the one claiming to be you didn't even look 60, much less 120. You look more like you," he explained. Sammy wasn't quite sure how to take that, but since it worked...

"What was that about?" Sammy wondered, almost aloud.

"I was worried about this," Moshe said quietly. "Just as there were malevolent influences wanting to use the Arizal's holiness for unnatural purposes 500 years ago, they are still trying to find some of the secrets he knew today. You will have to be careful. I don't know how they knew we would be here, but the line must extend back to Simon's school."

"C'mon," thought Sammy, "that is only conjecture even on your part. Maybe they have someone on the inside at the Library who alerts them when someone is coming in to view the manuscripts like us. That makes more sense."

"Sir," as Sammy addressed the Shift Commander, "may I uncrate my cases here as I need to open them upstairs when I see the curator?"

"Sure. Have at it."

"Thank you." Sammy took out the document case and his thin briefcase, leaving the packing materials on the counter. "I appreciate the security and thank you for bearing with the mess"

"You're welcome. We wondered if we'd see the famous Sammy Silver on this shift."

"Famous? You must be kidding."

"No, sir. Your Lazarus act of a few months ago really caught the imagination over here. Remember, we are the home of the walking dead, if you'll forgive poking fun at one of our apostate sects. And we've had more messiahs than we deserve, so it is as though it is almost time for another... why not Sammy Silver?" he jocularly posited, smiling broadly in his jest.

"You can't imagine how many in the US wanted to go that route. Nearly every interview had some of that aspect to it. I was about to throw up my hands and admit it just for fun until it became apparent what I thought was fun would be deadly serious for far too many out there. There are some strange bunches of people out there... and don't we know it?"

And with another "thank you", Sammy took his cases and toddled off to the Rare Manuscript section with his shadow spirit, Moshe.

Having removed the introductory letter on the way to the offices, he showed it briefly to the receptionist. Sammy was then shown into the Curator's office, who got up and came around his desk to shake hands.

"If it isn't the famous Sammy Silver come to visit our modest almost incunabula," he beamed...the Curator loved the chance to use that word.

"Please, please... is that what everyone thinks over here? OY!"

The Curator giggled. "Sorry, but you are a bit unique sir with your age, your family, and the kittel dance climbing out of the coffin, continuing to write, and now an aspect we did not know in your antiquarian expertise. If you were not aware, your funeral performance went viral over here because there were a few that video'd it and posted it. Surely it was not as funny as it looked. Forgive us, please, but popular excitement is not one of the general benefits of the librarian's life on the job unless we have some sort of celebrity here for a fund raiser."

"Okay, down to business. May I have your introductory and authorisation letter, please?"

"Here it is," quipped Sammy as he handed him the letter still in the envelope.

"I presume the large case contains the volume you are to check against our original? Can you open it for me, please." And as Sammy was opening the case, putting on gloves, removing the volume, and the insulation, the Curator was donning gloves because he wanted to look at it before having the library's volume brought up out of the vault. Sammy set it on the desk and the Curator came around and opened it very carefully. The insides of these 5-600 year old books is not as minutely fragile as the papyrus scrolls also in the Library's collection, but respect demands care and gentle treatment nonetheless.

"Without doing the comparison you intend to do, this looks every bit the same as the volume we have, but that is just a cursory view. You surely do not expect to recover minute fragments of our volume and do any comparative chemical assay tests, do you? If so, we can already give you the report of chemical analyses we had done a few years ago when we acquired our Luria volume."

"Actually a copy of that report would be helpful in framing my report back to the university, if you wouldn't mind. Did you do any X-ray or chromatographic analysis?"

"Just a perfunctory X-Ray and no chromatographic work at all. We thought the chemical signatures sufficient to document the authenticity as we have a few other volumes from Eliezar's press and compared them. Here is an inert plastic marker we would appreciate if you would place in your volume to clearly distinguish it from ours, please. Yes, just a fancy, sure to not degrade, bookmark, so to speak."

"Okay, perhaps enough of this frivolity," smiled Sammy wrapping up his book with the marker and placing it back in the case. "Do you have any other volumes of

Chaim Vital's writing on the Arizal's lessons, please? If so, might I look at them as well, please?"

"Well, yes we do. We have two other works of Chaim Vital's if you'd like to examine them at the same time. I think we can do that."

"Thank you. Then would you show me to an examination room and have your volumes brought up to me, please?"

The Curator took Sammy out of the office and down the elevator to the next floor down. They went through two sets of security doors which required the Curator's hand print and into a long corridor of glass-walled rooms, each with a glass table and chairs. All of the rooms were thoroughly visible to anyone in the hallway or next to them - and outside for that matter, because the back wall of the rooms were glass and offered a live, scenic view of Old Jerusalem. It is difficult to be secretive if your every motion is visible to anyone passing by in the hallway.

The Curator stopped at number five, opened the door with an electronic key, and gestured Sammy to enter. Sammy put the cases on the table.

"I'll call security to deliver the volumes up here if you'll wait for a few minutes. When the guard brings it he will leave them with you but will remain in the corridor as long as you are here. He'll set himself near the entrance to the hallway. If you have to visit the bathroom, open the door and motion him to come here and guard the room while you are gone - obviously he will be sure you take nothing with you to the loo - and will let you back in the room when you return. When you are done, again call him to the room and he'll return our books to the vault. All our manuscript and relic volumes have specific frequency UV coding on all of them so that we can easily distinguish our volumes from those anyone might bring in. Part of the guard's responsibility is to validate the volume with those codes going in and coming out of the examination rooms, which is why there is a UV source that only highlights that frequency in the doorframe of each room. I'll be here all day so when you finish if you would not mind coming back up and informing me of your immediate findings, it would be a nice gesture, please. You cannot imagine the number of times the Luria volumes have attracted very sophisticated thieves - which is strange because we have far older and more rare and valuable tomes that collectors fight to acquire. I hope you determine what you need to know."

And with that, the Curator turned and left.

"It seems they have established a fair security apparatus here. Glad our mission is different."

"Now what am I looking for?"

"First we see if the volume has envelopes like yours and if anything is inside them. If so, it means they have not inspected them as well as they think, but to be fair, these secrets were lost through the ages. Secondly, we will look through the volume to be sure it is real. Your friend Simon and his department are making this check because there are a lot of fakes out there. And I know his volume is real because I remember reading it, though it may have been another copy. I wonder if this is a real copy as their experts have not the way to verify that I do."

The guard arrived, opened the door, checked the code, came in, and laid the volumes on the glass table. He said nothing and left, closing the door behind him.

Strange, thought Sammy, everyone else is very convivial, friendly, and even chirpy. What's with him?

Sammy opened the cases and propped the tops open on the door side of the table so that they at least afforded some shield from passing eyes when they opened the spines. Donning his gloves, he stood the first Library's book on its fore-edge and pressed the shields at the top and bottom of the spine. It took a bit more effort with this volume but just like the University's copy, the spine began separating at the ribs, taking parts of the spine to swivel on the joint, opening up the back of the book so that its binding was visible. And, like the University's copy, there were half-a-dozen or so envelope pages in the centre of the bound pages. But there was nothing in them, no glassine thin sheets. So, Sammy closed the spine on that volume, set it aside, and went to the next. The second book opened like the others and had about six envelope pages in the centre of the bound pages. Again, most of them were empty but two. Sammy carefully extracted the glassine sheets in each of them and placed them in his open briefcase, placing an empty manila envelope above and beneath them as they were resting on his portable computer. He checked to be sure the other envelopes were empty and closed the spine. Both sets of papers were A5 size this time; four sheets each, again in biblical Hebrew from what he could tell. He placed the glassine sheets in the envelopes and without sealing put them in another division of the 'organiser' attached to the top of his briefcase. He took last week's envelopes and moved them back one division in the organiser and put the new envelopes in the front compartment. Sammy set the second volume on the table and tried to open the third. Funny, it looked like the same binding, but the shields were not at all moveable. Sammy looked closer and compared the last spine to this one and the third volume and the ever so slight space around the second volume spine shields was not at all visible on the third book.

"Not all of Eliezer's books were made for concealment, just chosen ones."

So, Sammy set the third book on the table for review, but wanted to start with the second as it was the one concealing the sheets. He reached for the Library's book and opened it so that Moshe could see what it said.

The first thing Sammy heard was, *"It's not the same. It is still Luria's lessons, that I remember, but this is not the same volume I read and studied. I don't know where this book is going for even the phraseology does not sound the same. This is very strange. It is authentic. It is generally what Luria taught, but it is not the same as the University's book. Keep turning the pages. Fast reading this stuff is not easy but let me see where it goes."*

And Sammy kept turning at Moshe's prompts, which was fine because it was totally unintelligible to Sammy.

"Okay, I see. This is a very basic Kabbalah, spiritualism for dummies, not the advanced lessons in the University's book. I was not aware Chaim had done this for the Rabbi - maybe it was a sort of ruse to get the spiritually inept off Luria's back. It is Kabbalah, but not anything that Chaim or I would recognise as serious. Let's look at the others."

Sammy reached over for the first volume, placing the second on the side of the table. He opened it, began turning pages, and Moshe said, *"Ah, general Kabbalah lessons, philosophy, and background. This would be a very introductory volume to set the frame of mind for Kabbalah studies. Turn through the book, let me see what is on the pages and then we'll go to the closed book."*

Sammy finished the first book, placed it aside, and pulled over the third volume. He opened it up for Moshe.

"Aha, a review text, mostly Torah and philosophy, good to broaden a student's grasp of the world, but nothing to do with Luria's teachings. Okay, let me look at those sheets, please."

So Sammy put this volume aside too, and took the new envelopes from his case and removed the sheets in one and placed one of them on the envelope on the table so that it could be read.

Moshe was highly irritated, upset, agitated, when he said *"put on the next one, quick... and the next..."* And Sammy kept putting down one after picking up the other.

And Sammy replaced the first set of sheets in their envelope, opened the next one and put it out to read.

"And the next one.... and the next," demanded Moshe in a very distraught kind of voice.

"This is not good. Put them away. In fact, maybe better we put them back in the book than even let them out into the real world."

"What is it, Moshe? queried Sammy, feeling totally puzzled because he couldn't understand a bit of it.

"Those are literally instructions for meditation that will destroy the person that does them. The strength of those instructions are such that they could warp reality in the virtual implosion they could create with a strong enough mind. The ones in the university's book are spiritual and elevating, but these practices are thoroughly destructive and can cause great damage to the person and everything around them. They need to be destroyed or put away so no one will ever see them because in the hands of someone that does not understand Kabbalah, following those instructions will surely lead to their death and their soul's complete destruction and perhaps that of all around them. I think the entire book where we found them was constructed as a trap by Chaim in order to destroy Luria's visible enemies... and Rabbi Isaac did have some very visible enemies who would not shrink from any means to try to control him. It was our very private opinion that Rabbi Luria was assassinated and how that could have happened with his level of current and future awareness was beyond us. But both within Israel, even Safed, and other countries there were men fighting to preserve an Empire... The Sixteenth Century was a time of cruel survival manipulation and world wars for the time..."

And Moshe stopped unexpectedly. Sammy still had the glassine sheets in his hands with the others set back in an envelope. The reason Moshe stopped is that two men, two very swarthy men dressed in black, were coming through what Sammy had thought was his locked door. They said something unintelligible in Hebrew and held what looked like silenced pistols in their hands.

"They want you to be quiet and put up your hands," Moshe informed Sammy.

"Okay, if you say so. You have the advantage of me and this is a strange place for an armed robbery, don't you think?" People at 120 years seem to get strangely wiseguy sometimes, but Sammy raised his gloved hands to waist height anyway, forgetting that in one hand was an envelope and in the other two of the four glassine sheets Moshe was reading. "So, what now?"

Again in Hebrew, "Give us the sheets, quickly." Moshe translated in Sammy's head and he handed them the sheets in his hand.

"And the ones on the table." Moshe translated, Sammy complied.

"And the envelope on the table." Moshe translated, Sammy complied.

"And the envelope in your hand." Moshe translated, Sammy complied.

The thieves stuffed the sheets carelessly in the envelope, backed out the door, holstered their guns, and walked very quickly down the hall and apparently let themselves out.

"I told you there were people who still wanted to get Luria's work."

"Fine with that, but what about the guard, is he all right?" queried Sammy.

Sammy opened the door and the hallway was empty. No thugs, no guard, no nothing but open space as there were obviously no more examinations being done today, at least in this corridor or at this time.

Sammy took off his gloves, closed the cases, left the Library's books on the table, used the larger case to prop open the examination room door, and walked down the hallway to look for an emergency button. Bright red, as they usually are, Sammy found it near to where the security guard was supposed to sit, so he pressed it, walked back to the examination room, and sat down to wait.

There was no noise Sammy could hear, so even Moshe asked, *"I was there - I thought you pushed it - where are they?"*

And five seconds later they heard the corridor doors slam open and security looking uniformed personnel came running into the hallway from both ends. They stopped outside Sammy's door with the Shift Commander coming in to ask, breathlessly, "what on earth is going on... do you know you mobilised the entire crew and we had to climb three flights of stirs to get here this fast?"

"Sorry, but do you know where the guard is that brought up these books from the vault and who was assigned to watch us?"

The Commander looked around, leaned into the hallway to ask a couple of his staff, then sent four of them to building exits and called someone to lock down the parking lot until they were told to reopen it. He next called to lock down the entire building until a search could be completed and instructed four other guards to begin the search at the bottom.

"So what happened?" he finally asked.

"You might check your security cameras to see if they match the guys from the other day, but two thuggish looking armed men walked in here without any trouble and wanted to steal your books that I was using as a template for comparison to one we brought from Canada."

"But they are still here."

"Right. My book is still wrapped in the case in which I brought it, see," and Sammy showed him his book in the case. "But when they were going to steal your books, 'cause they ignored the case for some reason, we explained that it was electronically tagged and if it was attempted to be removed from its vault / elevator / examination room current residence, it would trigger an automatic lock down of everything in the building including all exits and the parking lots. They had not anticipated that, I guess, and then left with the guard that was not a lot of help to them."

"But that is codswallop," explained the Commander. We aren't that sophisticated and these volumes are not that valuable to deserve that level of security."

"But they didn't know that," noted Sammy.

"And they bought it?" queried the Commander, cocking his head to the side.

"Years ago I used to make a fair living convincing people I knew the ins and outs and every detail of their businesses when, quite often, I knew just enough to use the right words and phrases. I'd later come to that knowledge if we had a work project. It is a matter of presentation of self and phrasing, ya' know?" said Sammy brazenly, cocking his head and proving again why he used to be good at what he did.

"Okay, let me take those volumes back to the vault and escort you to the Curator."

So, Sammy picked up his cases and followed the Commander back to the Curator.

Chapter 16 - Confession...sort of...partially

Sammy was shown into the Curator's office, he put down his cases, the Commander left, and the Curator gave Sammy the copy of the chemical analysis he had promised earlier and Sammy dutifully placed it in his briefcase.

"I heard you had an interesting time with those books. I'm sorry our security was a bit lax on that one but sometimes you just hire the wrong people. Given the people involved, I'd be worried about the man pretending to be our guard."

"Oh, I've had guns pointed at me before. At my age such things are not as threatening as the thugs want them to be."

"No, please understand. As the Curator I have access both visual and audio to virtually every square centimetre of this place through a battalion of cameras and microphones that can isolate almost anything, anywhere in the Library and immediately in its environs. Further, we're not as unaware as your university in Canada. We know what we have and know that Luria volume is not what we pretend it is. It was a trick, a ruse of Rabbi Chaim Vital to give people what they thought was Luria when actually the Ari did not want so much of his teachings distributed, thinking that would bring heavenly condemnation on him and others who knew of them. So, Chaim wrote and published that book as though it was the real thing."

"Yes," agreed Sammy, "that is what I understand - but I was not aware of that before I came here."

"Yes," the Curator went on, "and you really were not aware of the sheets hidden in the book or what they mean, were you?"

For three seconds Sammy played with the idea of trying to bluff the Curator, then he remembered that he had probably seen everything.

"Umm, no. And I am more than slightly worried about the consequences of those sheets being used as meditative directions when I suspect the ramifications could be fatal."

"They will be. But the powers that worked so hard to steal them, not knowing where to find them, will neither know nor care of any negative contrecoup to their acquisition."

"Sammy," droned the Curator, "I am a great believer in things being what they should be, events happening as they are supposed to happen, people being where they are supposed to be, and no matter what we think of those events and the consequences thereof, they are what they are supposed to be in line with a plan that I have no more chance of understanding than I have the ability to time travel. However, it is what it is and those sheets are going where they are supposed to be for reasons we will never understand. I'm just very glad you showed the good sense to not get all Yankee and John Wayne on us. They are going where they are supposed to be."

"Now that we understand each other... and we do, don't we?"

"I see it the same way, Curator; which is why I was not loathe to do as they requested. I am slightly aware of the import of the instructions in those notes and I would not be the one following them for anything."

"Good," beamed the Curator, sitting back in his chair, "now, can we have you here in five days for a book-signing? You see, we are on such a tight budget from the government that we have to raise money however we can and we sell books to do so but usually only books of authors with whom we can host a book-signing event. Can you do it? I confess that finding the famous Sammy Silver coming to Israel and to the library is such a spectacular occasion that we have to take advantage of your visit to help your sales in Israel and our budget squeeze at the same time, please?"

"We're going to be in Safed about that time, but I see no reason why I can't drive up here for that. Of course, Curator."

Thank you, Sammy. I'll start with the promotional activities tomorrow - and hope I can scrounge up enough of your books to make it worthwhile."

"Let me call my publicist and get him to help. His name is Sid and I'll have him call you direct, OK?"

The Curator was happy, Sammy was happy, but Moshe was troubled and let Sammy know on the way back to the hotel.

"I'm sure Chaim would have wanted those sheets left as we'll do with the ones we still have. Why did you let them go so easily?"

"Hold on. You heard the Curator - they are where they are supposed to be. Besides that, I didn't hear you yelling, 'let me handle this' in the back of my head. You were as quiet as a mouse because not only could you do nothing physically, but I'm in no kind of martial arts shape to deal with two guys with drawn guns - unless being shot is a workable outcome... and it isn't, not to my mind. So let it rest, stop being controlling, and believe that they are where they are supposed to be."

Sammy could feel Moshe kvetching under his mind-control-breath, but no more talk.

The Silvers spent another day in Jerusalem, an amazing feat of endurance because the day before totally exhausted the children, to say nothing of poor Serah. Sammy found a secure package service where he had the book in its case bound in a wood frame and sent to Simon's office at the university in Canada. At least that was out of his hair. They then drove up to Safed and ensconced themselves in a hotel where they could observe Shabbat. They made enquiries about services at the Sephardic Synagogue above the old cemetery, but were advised that there was not likely space with the crowds in town and expected for the Ari's Yahrzeit next week. They allowed themselves to be directed to a larger Chabad shul.

Long before dawn on the 5th of Av, Sammy was awakened and knew the culprit. It was time to finish his work for Moshe. He dressed, retrieved the envelopes from his briefcase, and walked to the old Safed Cemetery. It was not difficult to find the Ari's grave. It was not only painted deep blue, but it had a platform built around it, and even before sunrise there were people lined up around it davening, people hanging plastic bags on the tree that grew out of his son's grave next to his, and the real problem was finding a rock on the ground to put on top of the glassine sheets so that they would not blow away. Moshe solved it.

"Here, see that rock on the ground in front of you? Use that."

"But it is not very big or very heavy, I expect."

"Use it. There is no wind and it won't have to hold the papers there for long. Trust me."

So, Sammy picked up a rock the size of his fist. He put it in his pocket while he extracted the glassine sheets from the envelopes, first one, then the other. He took the rock from his pocket. Then, he had to kneel down and stretch to put them on the grave cover and then place the rock on them.

Having done that, he stood up with the empty envelopes still in his hand. He watched the almost transparent sheets, not knowing what was going to happen. While he was watching, each of the sheets slowly vanished from his sight. They didn't melt, or vapourise, or anything but fade into nothingness, each of them, slowly, but completely, until there were no glassine sheets under the rock at all. Wow.

Then he heard a contented, relaxed, satisfyingly long sigh.... and he heard Moshe say, *"Thank you, Sammy. Mitzvah complete. May I know you when you join us someday. Baruch Hashem."*

And Sammy could literally feel Moshe leave, a separation of part of him unlike anything he'd ever felt before, almost like something being sucked physically out of him. And of course, a more apposite place for Moshe to separate could not be found since he, too, was buried here.

Chapter 17 - Denouement

Sammy walked back to the hotel, discarded the envelopes, undressed, and climbed back into bed as it wasn't even dawn yet. He cuddled up with Serah and they slept closely for a couple hours.

After getting the family up, dressed, and fed, they headed out to explore Safed all morning and afternoon. They even made it up to the cave. However, by that time the children were just pooped. Sammy suggested that they find a place for dinner and rest tonight and that Serah and the children rest, swim in the hotel's pool and generally chill as the signs of historic exhaustion overload were beginning to appear in all of them.

The next day Sammy drove down early to the National Library for the book signing session he had promised. In the morning, the Curator kept him company while Sammy signed and talked to the people who'd come to meet him, have him sign their books, buy new ones, and those who just wanted to meet the Famous Sammy Silver. Sid had come through in fine form, overnight shipping copies of all his books as ordered by the Curator. It was just a fine time but after all his activities of the last few days, tired Sammy a bit. The Curator took him to lunch.

When they were seated and ordered drinks, the Curator inquired, "Sammy, you and your family are Jewish, orthodox Jews, why don't you make Aliyah? I know you rely on your book sales for income and the commission rates from the rest of the world translate very well into Shekels. But that has to be a constant pressure and I suspect it gets old on occasion. I inquired of the Directors casually about creating an ongoing educational program built around the art of the story. It would have some attraction for other authors for guest lectures and all that, but you would be the mainstay, the anchor of the program, and I think we could get it accredited as well through the university of Jerusalem. What do you think? And you do not have to give me your answer now, but please talk with your wife and children, as it is their decision, too. Here is my personal card. Call or write when you have questions or have made a decision, please."

And the rest of the delightful lunch made Sammy feel even better. He'd not had a job offer in decades and it felt really nice.

Sammy pondered the offer all the drive back to Safed and was not overwhelmingly positive broaching it to Serah. What bothered Sammy was not leaving all the people they knew, leaving a country they knew, uprooting the children from their friends, having to learn at least rudimentary Hebrew because that is what most people spoke, or even the finances of it all, but the idea of a thrice weekly trip into Jerusalem and structuring a curriculum around teaching people how to write stories. Sammy realised he was scared to death of the routine that he would no longer control... and a 'regular' job which was something he had not experienced in many decades.

He called the Curator and told him of his difficulties. The Curator asked him to wait until he had returned to Canada, had some time to rest and then call him again. The program would wait as it will be built around Sammy.

However, having expressed his reluctance, Sammy called a real estate friend at home and asked for a top of the head number in easily selling their house. He translated that number into shekels and he and Serah made discreet enquiries about houses in Safed. If they were going to do aliyah, it would be to Safed and that area.

That is pretty much the story. Sammy and Serah decided to move. Sammy reported to Simon that not only

was that volume real, it was advanced Luria-taught
Kabbalah knowledge written by Rabbi Chaim Vital and
should be kept in a vault or under high security protected
unbreakable glass because it was hugely valuable, better
than the Israel volume, and far above and beyond the level
of most of today's students. Simon's department awarded
Sammy an honorary Ph.D. that autumn.

Rabbis Blum, Goldbaum, Helfenberg, and
Rosenberg were all relieved to see Sammy acting normally
and not possessed.

The Silvers sold the house and moved to Safed.
Sammy took up teaching the Curator's course in story
writing and progression, which led to the development of
many new, and brilliant writers over the next few years.
Rachel, Sarah, and Margaux became skilled artists with the
training available in Safed's art community and the boys
generally drifted into techie fields, working near Jerusalem
or north of Tel Aviv. Altogether, it was a happily-ever-
after ending to a story that began as a funeral, an event that
Sammy and Serah have yet to experience for real.

Nobody in the everyday world really paid much
attention to the highly controversial story that was lost to
Sammy and Serah during all the hustle and bustle of their
move to Israel. The famed and fortified 5th century BCE
Aragonese Castle, connected to the island of Ischia, owned
and inhabited by an unbelievably rich and one of the old
Venetian fondi who were refurbishing and rebuilding it,
blew up one night, throwing some debris as far as the
island, over 700 feet away. The castle was not so much

reduced to rubble as it was literally vapourised along with the entire volcanic island almost to the waterline on which it was originally built as a fortress to protect the main island from pirates and Venetian privateers. No bodies of the family or the construction crews that were doing the work were ever recovered, no trace of the construction equipment or tons of granite and marble of the castle were found anywhere in the ocean nearby, and no cause was determined for what must have been an immense blast, though no one on Ischia reported hearing anything unusual that night. Similarly, there was no seismic activity registered by the Italian government earthquake monitoring office. Neither the Italian Federal Police nor UN Officials nor Interpol conducting the investigations could find even a single clue as to what happened.

Time flies like an arrow...

It is just a short tale of heroic evolutionary ideals thwarted by intellectual incompetence in the face of the demands of biological reality.

Finally Sheila had gotten away from what felt like thousands of relatives and children and she and some of her brood were heading to the swimming pool for a rest. She could see it in the distance, that white inverted cone above the pool. More than that, she and her children could smell the alluring odour that drew them nearer and nearer. They literally followed their noses to the pool's entrance.

The closer they got, the more delicious it smelled, so difficult to resist and the youngest were trying to race to get there. When they did, they had to figure how to get in because the entrance wasn't marked. "Neat places are like that aren't they?" they thought. "Enticing you to come in then playing all loose and cagey about satisfying, the engaging anticipation driven mad by the attraction."

And like youngsters, their first thought is "that isn't fair". But Sheila tried to instill a little patience in them.

"Move back, move up a bit, get a view all around to find the entrance," she encouraged them. But, no, they mostly just stood around, walked around the entire perimeter. A few walked toward the top edge of the cone and while it was a great view all around, none...err... few looked down. Then a few tried walking down into the cone and as the odour that was driving them mad became stronger, they tried to call out to the others outside, but they didn't hear them.

So, Larry and his buddies that had already begun walking into the cone, took off and headed straight in, whooping, hollering, and yelling at the top of their spiracles. And all their peers already hanging out above the pool and on the walls just jeered at them, "Ya' don't know what you're doing.... wise up, save your energy."

So they pulled up after clearing the end and landed on the side of the cone and began walking... walking around and around. Larry stopped and just stood still. When they came around from the other direction, he remarked to his friends that they looked an awful lot like guys he knew that just took off, 'that 'a way'... so they walked faster to try to catch up to the other guys. Funny, they never caught them, but Larry kept telling them how they just passed him just a little bit ago, time after time...after time...after time.

Larry became tired of this game and flew over to talk a guy clinging to the side of the jar - a pretty good achievement since it is a lot more slippery than the cone. He asked what the guy was doing and he said, "hanging here for my life because if I let go, I'll fall into the pool and it isn't what you think. It is a monster that eats us, not a Pool. I know it smells great, but so do those Venus plants that the blue bottles like and you know what happens there, don't you?"

"No," said Larry, curious now, "what?"

"The Venus eats them. They suck them in, trap them, and eat them. It is horrible, the deception and prevarication. You'd think they were members of the Great Bug Parliament, you would."

Larry began realising how little of the world he knew and it frightened him.

"Just hang out here, young fellah, and you'll be fine until you can figure a way to get out. I thought it was easy, entranced by the white light and the great smell, but finding your way back through the light is not so easy. There has to be a way, but it is disguised."

Now Larry was getting frightened. His mother had brought them all to the Pool thinking the odour was delicious - which it was - but she didn't know what came with it. Larry began to think, not such an easy task for a few assorted nerve ganglia. If The Pool is a place of death, how do we stay alive now that we are here? Worse, what about girlfriends? There is no place to romance discretely here. Larry was having the classic conflict in himself: being vs. breeding, as once in the Pool, maintaining life superseded family and raising bunches of broods. Larry was amazed at how certain pressures tended to focus his attention. He asked the old-timer how he approached it.

"Sheila and I didn't have that problem, Larry. We were spoiled for choice in the fruit bowl. Heck, we just kept breeding as it seemed like the right thing to do, 'ya know?"

"You're my father!?" exclaimed Larry. "What are you doing here?"

"Same thing as you, sucked in by the attraction before I realised the trap. Heck, we're the bright ones. You can't imagine how many come in and literally dive into the Pool, never to be seen again. I've watched them. No breeding time for them! Not even enough time to give them Darwin Awards. So, you've got a future to fulfil and need to get out of this trap. I'm getting too weak from hanging on so long to wing it, but you can still get yourself out if you try."

"But how?"

"Put those ganglia together because you have at least 100,000 neurons that can help figure this out. What is your strongest sense? Use it."

"Hmmm," thought Larry, "strongest sense? Strongest sense. Hmm. AHA! Smell! We smell things long before we see them! AHA! Umm... umm...so what?"

"Sometimes, Larry, I worry that you got your mother's eyes. Think, boy, think!"

"All right...think...smell got us in here. Yup. I followed the smell right in here, sure did, yup. So how do I follow the smell out? How? Hmmm.... well, if I can tell when the smell gets stronger, then I can tell when it is weaker, too, no? And if I can tell when it gets weaker, then I can follow the decreasing concentrations of olfactory redolence out of here."

"Now that is using your noggin, Larry. Well done!" congratulated his father.

"What did I just say? I'm confused." Larry was running over his neuronal capabilities for a Darwinian moment.

His father couldn't do a face palm because he thought he'd fall in, but he responded, "Larry, you said that if you followed the scent getting stronger on the way in, finding the path where it gets weaker will get you out, dummy."

"Oh, yeah... did I say that?"

"LARRY! WAKE UP, BOY!"

"Ok, I get it. I just don't want to leave you, Dad."

"Don't worry about me. I'll be here. I'm not going anywhere. I think I'm glued into place or at least I can't feel my most distal tarsal claws any longer."

"I'll be back, Dad"

"Yes, son, you just take care.... find a nice girl with different coloured eyes and make lots of broods... don't worry about me. I've had plenty of fun already."

"I'll be back, Dad... just hang in there."

And with that Larry detached himself and began flying around above the Pool, sniffing, trying to find lesser concentrations, almost finding himself in the Pool a couple times when he went the wrong way.

"More...no... less...yes - and went that way; then more, no...less, yes and went that way. It was painstaking sensations, time after time, after time. He passed his friends still walking around the cone end and tried to get them to follow him out.

"We will as soon as we catch up to those other guys," they said. Larry wrote them off.

"More...no... less...yes - and went that way; then more, no...less, yes and went that way. And this resulted in Larry going up the cone, getting yelled at by his cousins going the other direction.

"You're going the wrong way," they yelled.

"You're going into a trap," Larry screamed. Only one turned around and followed him, Clyde.

"What do you mean?" asked Clyde, joining him on the way out of the cone.

"It is a death trap down there and I'm going to warn the rest of the family," boasted Larry.

"They won't listen. They only follow their noses. They're as thick as flies. I'm only following you because I have sinus problems and I was just following them 'cause I can't smell anything. It would be nice to find a more uplifting discussion outside of eating and breeding, don't you think?"

"You have different coloured eyes, don't you? asked Larry.

"Yeah, they used to tease me about that."

"Well, where's your mother and sisters?" queried Larry salaciously, certain thoughts already beginning to supersede images of leading a developmental Darwinian revolution.

"Over here," as Clyde led Larry to the fruit bowl and a mix of peaches, nectarines, various pears, and there Larry found Desdemona on an Anjou Pear. Her eyes were a different colour than his.

"Oooooo, you're one of Sheila's boys, aren't you?" she drooled.

"Yes, how can you tell?"

"Oh, it's in your eyes.... and you're bigger... and you don't have sinus problems."

"How can you tell that?"

"Nothing is dripping from your proboscis, silly. Look at Clyde. Gross me out with a foreleg sex comb that does. And you just got back from the Pool direction which is a surprise because most of you clear smelling folks end up in it."

"Well, I was in the Pool with my father, but I escaped and came back here to.... to.... to....," and Larry had forgotten what he was coming back to do, forgotten completely while gazing enraptured into Desdemona's multi-faceted eyes. There is a limit to the memory capacity of a hundred thousand neurons, you know. Moreover, like a trait that seems to carry-on as one progresses all the way up the phylogenetic scale, he can think of only one thing at a time.

So Larry settled down with Desdemona on that Anjou Pear, breeding, eating, and discussing the qualitative advantages of Anjou verses Bartlett Pears, a discussion Clyde always wanted to lead.... 'cause they all smell the same to him... except bananas. Clyde likes a banana.

Isaac Meets NeoGeorgian

Note: This is one of the more recent stories, strangely attracting input ideas from too many places. It is not the usual offering in this genre, I believe. However, the main antagonist is only a metaphor for what the author sees as a long-term hegemonic political battle that will not cease until the beast has fallen and taken its minions with it. As a genre, this theme has a very niche following, no?

It is best read, perhaps as the protagonist suggests in one of the penultimate paragraphs, "Later that afternoon, after putting on his copy of Mike Oldfield's first album..."

And, to add a bit of current flavour to the story,

"*ROME — An Italian exorcist has denounced a steady rise in demonic activity as more and more young people abandon traditional spirituality and dabble in the occult.*

"Satanism is getting much more aggressive and also diffused," Dominican Father Francois Dermine told *Crux, an online Catholic news outlet.*

"Secularization leaves a void," said the priest, who has worked as an exorcist for the Archdiocese of Ancona-Osimo since 1994. "Young people do not have anything to satisfy their spiritual and profound needs. They are thirsting for something, and the Church is not attractive anymore."

Since the Church is no longer perceived as a valid option for many young people looking for answers, he said, 'they try to find something elsewhere. This something is, many times, the demonic world.' "

Sourced on 23 December 2019 from: https://www.breitbart.com/faith/2019/12/23/italian-exorcist-decries-rise-aggressive-satanism/

It was a lovely autumn day, temperate with a slight breeze, plenty of sun, a few diaphanous clouds, and just the barest whiff of decaying flora in the air - you could almost imagine the smell of burning piles of leaves, but the cultural barbarians in charge of governments don't allow that any longer in the cities. Sigh....

Isaac turned the car into the driveway in front of the impressive neo-Georgian style house with a wide semi-circular drive in front and an extension off one side to a three-car garage offset in the back-yard. The yard lights lining both sides the drive and front walk were lit during the day to give the full impression of the upscale level of this house. The owners wanted out. Now. Isaac wasn't sure why, yet, but he suspected he would, soon. He met Marie as she drove up behind him and he asked again about the price on the house.

"Oooo, it is priced to sell, immediately," she gushed with a smile and a dimple. "It has seven bedrooms including a master suite, ensuite bathrooms are in the master and shared between adjoining bedrooms and in the guest room with WC's in the hallways upstairs and down, and off the library. The kitchen....."

"Yes, Marie," said Isaac, trying not to sound annoyed, "I know all that, read it over three times. Can we just go in, please?"

"Of course, Mr. Notwen, but I should tell you that the current owners wanted to stay here for this viewing."

"Oh?" Isaac's eyebrow shot up, "that is unusual."

"Well, they said it was necessary and we can only advise of usual and customary -- it is their house, after all."

"Okay, we shall see what this means; lay on McDuff."

"Umm, it is McAlester, not McDuff, Mr. Notwen."

"Sorry, let's go then, please?" This was becoming tiresome. Isaac was only here because Marie virtually begged him to do the showing. Frankly, it looked far too upscale for him and his small family, generally preferring more rustic ambiance than OTT fancy. However, the price was more attractive than he could resist so he thought, 'what the hey, let's at least look'.

They walked to the front doors and Marie pushed the doorbell while he used the large brass door knocker incredibly prominent and duplicated on both doors.

"Hey, it's hot," he exclaimed in surprise, "that is very peculiar. Who's got a heated door knocker?"

Marie was doing an excellent "deer in the headlights" look when the Davis's opened the doors.

If you've ever been to visit mourning relatives after 24 hours or so, this couple had that drawn, haggard, morose, and exhausted look even though they propped up the sides of their mouths with wan smiles. Dressed very well, they were not the most cheery of hosts when they invited Marie and Isaac in.

"Thank you for coming to look at the house. Can we get you some coffee, tea, or water, soft drinks," they offered.

"Maybe when I've seen the house. How about you, Marie?"

"Yes, later, please. Let's take a look around. Can we begin in the living room?"

"Of course. I know this is usually your work, Marie, but if you don't mind, I'll conduct the tour. By the way," turning to Isaac," I'm Doris and this is Dominic," gesturing toward her husband.

"Okay, I'll be the tourist," chirped Marie as they moved though the large, marble entrance foyer with floor-to-ceiling columns at the base of each of the semi-circular staircases winding their way to the second floor from each side of the foyer. Between the columns there was a Colonial framed opening to a hall that extended back to the kitchen with a coatroom, loo, and a door to the basement along it. On the right was a set of entrance doors to a large

study / library / office and on the immediate left, an ornate
frame to the living room/parlour with matching column
style pedestals on each side, topped with vases of dried
flowers and flora.

Very nice, thought Isaac, but far too much for us.
But let's not be rude. So Doris Davis walked everyone
through the parlour, the adjoining formal dining room, and
the kitchen with the family room off it on one side. Then,
in the midst of the virtual glass wall comprising the back of
the house were two sets of French doors leading to a large
deck across the back of the house, a deck with a two-level
staircase to a large manicured lawn with stone paths
meandering around various stone garden pieces, fountains,
and a guest house at the bottom of the garden. Wow,
thought Isaac. The nice thing is that there were already
twin stoves, cooking surfaces, refrigerators, and
dishwashers, a huge island preparation area with a sink and
faucet, and still plenty of room for a casual kitchen dining
table and chairs for eight.

Next to the kitchen, pantry, laundry room, and
another door facing the garage was a large guest suite with
ensuite that was touted as a potential servants quarters or
granny flat. They went through the central hallway to the
library, then up the stairs to look at the bedrooms. Marie
had forgotten to mention the Sauna in the Master Bedroom
ensuite. Nice touch, along with walk-in closets that could
hold a couple of third world families each and have room
left over for their goatherds. The other four bedrooms, two
on each side of the main hallway, shared an ensuite bath
between each of them and the guest bedroom at the end of
the hallway had its own ensuite as well as a covered deck
that looked out over the back yard - and a few others at the
same time, curiously. Wow, a lot of house for a small
family on a less than seven figure annual income, thought
Isaac. We don't even have the money to furnish it. And the
property taxes? Isaac just shook his head in his

imagination. Why did Marie bring me here? Oh, yeah, the giveaway price... but still...

All this time Doris' husband had said nothing. He let Doris do the talking and he just toddled on behind them. Isaac wondered what that was about, but he didn't ask these things so that people wouldn't be embarrassed.

As they were walking down the incredibly stately curved staircases back to the entrance foyer, Doris turned her head to Isaac and said, "Well, that's the house. What do you think of it Mr. Notwen?"

"You have an incredible house Mrs. Davis. It is actually far too much for me and my small family at this time; but one thing, please. We did not see the basement. I can see it has a basement and there is a door to it on the left after the coatroom. Is it finished, unfinished, used for storage, surely the forced air heating and hot water tank is down there? Is it oil or gas? Can I see it please?"

Isaac had seen granite floors that were softer than the look that came over Doris' face when he said that. Dominic finally spoke up. "No."

Doris turned to Marie, "didn't you tell him we can't show that part, Marie?"

Marie turned red, "No, I did not get around to it because you insisted on doing the show."

Isaac just looked back and forth from Dom, to Doris, to Marie, wondering what was going on. They were all in the entrance foyer, now. So, Isaac said, "Okay, I'll just look for myself. I've got to see the equipment and the state it is in at least." And with that he turned and headed for the basement door.

"NO!" yelled Dominic, "you can't. Please." And with that Dominic began moving over to block the door.

But Isaac was faster and already had his hand on the doorknob. Again, he thought, it is warm, why is that?

As Dominic was still a step or two away from the door, Isaac opened it and an overwhelming redolent stench of sulphur sent him reeling back on his heels.

"Okay, now you know, we have a plumbing problem down there," said Dominic tersely as he tried to cover for the strange odour, moving over in front of the doorway. Doris was beginning to cry softly, turning to Marie's shoulder for comfort. Isaac was confused, saying, "Just let me turn on the light and go down there and take a look at the problem. If we have to bring in a plumber, we have to get a contracting plumber, but I have to see it to try to describe the problem. Just let me take a look," he said as he tried to gently slide Dominic out of the way.

Dom, though, was not willing to move. So Isaac leaned forward and flicked on the light switch he had seen at the top of the stairs on the wall just inside the door on the left... sort of where you'd expect it to be. The stairs lit up as you would expect and Isaac could see what looked like a normal finished basement at the bottom of the stairs: painted walls, floored, carpeted - Isaac was a head taller than Dom, you see.

Dom looked over his shoulder, looking everything like a man fearful of his imminent death at any moment. Isaac asked, "What is wrong Dominic? Why the problem? I don't see anything that would bother me - it looks like the basement is fine. Let me just take a look, please."

Dom was unmoved. "You don't want to go down there. Believe me. There is something about which we cannot do anything, but losing you will not help it."

"Losing me? What on earth do you mean? It is just a bleedin' basement, Dom."

"No it isn't. Trust me. It has already cost us Richard and a copper.   We don't want it to get you, too."

"Richard? A copper? What do you mean?" asked Isaac as he backed off slightly and gave Dom more room.

Dom began to tear-up as he looked at Isaac. "Our son, Richard, went down there a couple of weeks ago... just went down the stairs... and he never came back up. We looked all over the house and finally went down there and discovered his cap down there, but not him; we couldn't find him and that is when we heard the voice down there. It said that it had him now and wouldn't give him back. We saw nothing but a swirling mist in the corner, but the voice was very menacing and as it came closer we ran back up the stairs and it laughed at us, laughed at our fright. While we were trying to figure what to do, the school sent a truancy officer the next day that looked at least like a real copper. We explained to him what we knew and he laughed at us, too. Then we showed him the basement, he went down the stairs, and we heard nothing more from him. The school did not even call to ask about him or Richard. That was when we called Marie to get rid of this cursed house as it just meant only heartbreak to us."

The light was still on in the basement and perhaps it was a trick of angles but there appeared to be this slight but dark mist on the stairs.

Isaac shook his head and looked at Dom. "This is just silly. No, not your Richard or the truancy officer, but letting a disembodied voice intimidate you...really. You seem to see fear and I see just superstition, no offense. I'm going at least part way down there, now. I've had enough of this folderol." And Isaac pushed past Dom and began walking down the steps. He stopped after four or five and sat down on the steps. He did see a dark mist scudding across the floor and sort of in a corner. And then there came a disembodied, but deep and resonant voice:

"Good afternoon. Have you come to play?"

"I somehow do not think that your definition of many words is the same as mine. Identify yourself and show yourself, here, please."

"My, my, my, aren't we pushy, now. Okay little man. You can call me "Bob" and in what form do you want to enjoy my visage?"

"John Wayne would be nice. I'd rather not see Julius Caesar or Napoleon; they are far too short. Clark Gable or Humphrey Bogart would be all right, too. And I'll bet you cannot do Martin of Tours."

"You're correct on the last one but almost any Pope is easy. Wayne isn't as easy as Douglas Fairbanks, Jr. How about Captain Blood?"

"If English, then Terry Thomas, please or, better, and I'm sure he is easy for you, Neville Chamberlain."

And, {{poof}}, at the bottom of the stairs appeared Neville Chamberlain, tweeds, pipe, and all.

"How's that, little man?"

"Not bad, Bob."

"So, before we enslave your soul for eternity, pray tell us what you are doing here."

"Bob, first, you need to back off and calm down. You may have convinced many or most of the world that you are the 'bee's knees', but you are not in charge here or anywhere else. You have these poor mortals kerflummoxed, but that is only because they are superstitious, probably Catholic, and indoctrinated.... like so many others these days. I mean, the entire social platform scene today is a virtual playground for you, isn't it?"

That set off Neville, laughing hysterically, holding his sides.

"For a little man you have some interesting perceptions - but you are correct. We forces of malediction are virtually free to roam and take control of whatever we like because a few of you dim humans think they are in charge and think we are virtually doing their bidding. They do not understand that they are our tools, silly children. They think they control their physical universe

but never understand that it is all a delusion, an illusion, not as real as the spiritual dimension which lasts for the eternity."

"So how come you came to visit yourself in Doris and Dom's basement? What did they do to attract the enmity of such an important spiritual entity as yourself?"

"It is not them, per se, though picking up a couple of souls carelessly contributed was not so bad, but it is just a convenient place as I'm spawning minions so fast in your national capitol that I cannot afford to be too far away."

"Excuse me, would you mind explaining that to a naive little man as I, please?"

"Ah. As the base malevolency for this sector of the universe in order to create demonic minions of sufficient power to more easily overwhelm the sybaritic and symbiotic mentality of those who would create their own demons, this base near the centres of political power is perfect. This is a far nicer basement than others that I've known... remembering that we live below the surface of things, eh? Isn't that subtle enough?"

"Ah, so it isn't them, it is that they have this house sitting on a convenient set of ley line intersections, eh?"

"For a little man, you do know more than most of these dullards. Usually even Catholic priests ignore that aspect and do not know that we are working from a position of strength while they are trying to impose their spiritual laws in our back yard, so to speak. They usually have not the strength to succeed, but they try."

"But why are you not afraid like all the others? You're just a material mortal like them."

"Yeah, true, but I'm Jewish and we know who runs things, see?"

"So what does the magnificent base malevolency do, exactly; if you don't mind the question, and how do we deserve the honour of your presence?" trying to inflate the demon so that he wouldn't remember what was said.

The Neville character had moved up a few steps while talking and was now only a few steps below Isaac. Pungent as he was, Isaac noticed the demon was becoming more relaxed, of all things... or edging closer to seize him, perhaps. Isaac was not really used to dealing with direct emanations of evil

Speaking in the manner of a Subject Matter Expert, Bob continued, *"The greater malefic portion of the universe is anticipating the complete conquering of the few western Earth lands that have resisted it for so many centuries. Since those who listen to us convinced the philosophical and educational worlds that He does not exist back in your 18th and 19th centuries, it has been a success run of unmatched levels. The more who refute Him, the more you flimsy mentalities accept us as the default, as we easily convince these ego-centred dolts that they are the centre of the universe and they revel in the false ego our support gives them. We own them. They have no idea what they are doing to themselves."*

"Your silly excuse for science and academia thinks there is no free will and thinks everything is more or less determined by the unimaginative conditioning that the sheep simply follow and all the media and information services support this false reality. What a bunch of maroons you silly humans are. So I'm here to complete the job, take the credit for all the souls we have captured, and ensure that the entire planet is ours, overseeing the end of humanity, including those snivelling little snots that call themselves Jews. Some of them are the easiest to seduce. They only need to be told that they are right in following a secular government, and they fall into line like little tin soldiers, throwing His Torah and over 5,000 years of history out the door as we ply them like all the others with materialist rewards. They have no idea what they are losing. Our servants have done an excellent job dumbing-down the entire West because all the other versions of

*organised religions are the same - so materialistic that they
are led like cows with rings in their noses, all of them.
Promise them money and power and they'll do anything for
you, even sell you their own mother and their children.
You silly beings were so happy to get what makes your
miserable and meaningless lives easier, you paid no
attention to the price to be exacted in exchange for material
toys and vain pleasures."*

"It sounds so easy, Bob. But it has taken centuries
to get to this point. Why do you think the end of humanity
is near now? What if those stiff-necked Jews refuse to
cooperate? What if the few saintly Catholics arouse and
inflame the not complete wash-outs? What if the
Evangelicals find a few real believers? What if the Sufi's,
the Hindus, the Buddhists, and the Sikh's that believe in
what they know fail to line up? What then?"

*"They are nothing - at most a drop in the bucket of
lost souls - we own the governments at every level."*

"But there is still the military, the police, and I've
seen some pretty independent US Sheriffs in so many areas
that take their responsibility seriously."

*"Piffle they are. Nothing. Our servants have
organised literal armies of brain-dead minions to serve us
and fight those who think they are defending principles.
We may not outnumber the military, but the people we
already own will rise up with us and overrun the forces of
normalcy. You'll see,"* inflated Bob incredibly over-
confidently. *"We own all the communication means and we
can condition the masses to do as we want, no matter what
anyone else wants. So that is that,"* resolved Bob, speaking
with a level of cock-sure confidence that usually comes
from believing that one knows everything.

"So what had Richard to do with all this? He's just
a little boy."

*"He was a disturbance. He would be in the way.
He would be a distraction if he came down stairs whenever*

he wanted to where I am working. He is just another useless human. He needed to be a lesson to his parents not to disturb me," with such an overabundant arrogance that Isaac could not see all of that existing even in Neville Chamberlain; which was correct because with that declaration, Neville stood up and began transmogrifying. First he turned all maroon and red, lost the pipe and the tweeds, then sprouted a long set of horns and his body became more and more satyr-like, entirely losing the masquerade of clothing, then sprouted the tail and the feet became cloven hoofs.

"Ah," remarked Isaac, "there is the demonic form we more easily recognise. Sorry the basement is so short you cannot reach the height you could under less constrained circumstances," derided Isaac, as Bob climbed back down the stairs to the basement floor.

"Well, I've pretty much had enough of this conversation, little man. It is time to take care of you..."

"No, apparition; it is time you returned Richard as he was," and Isaac stood up on the stairs.

And stretching out his right and left arms and pointing his hands at the demon with the side fingers together and thumb separate, he commanded, "RETURN RICHARD NOW AS HE WAS OR FURNISH US WITH THE PROOF OF PERMISSION YOU HAD TO DO SOMETHING TO HIM. YOU MUST HAVE PERMISSION FROM HIM TO DO EVERYTHING YOU DO, EVERYTHING. SO YOU EITHER FURNISH US WITH PROOF OR RETURN RICHARD AS HE WAS, NOW!"

"WHAT ARE YOU TALKING LITTLE MAN? YOU CANNOT ORDER ME TO DO ANYTHING!" And with that Bob literally stretched himself, leaned all the way up the stairway, and stuck his very red, sneering, horned face in Isaac's.

"Correct. However, no matter how wonderful you think yourself, sulphur breath, you cannot do anything without HIS approval. Think back very carefully as we all know that and we've known it ever since your chief did a hatchet job on Job."

Bob was fuming silently, thinking, looking for a way out, silently summoning all the demons attached to this usurper... and none responded, none showed up, none revealed themselves. That's impossible he thought, nobody is that clean. Nobody.

"Now return Richard as he was, no changes, no perversions, no devilish alterations, just an innocent 8 year old boy as he was when you took him. NOW!" commanded Isaac, as he dropped his arms.

And with barely a puff of sulphurous smoke in the corner, Isaac heard the small and tentative steps of a small boy on the stairs, steps that increased in speed as they got closer to the top, sped past him and into the arms of his waiting mother. Isaac only heard because he was in a virtual staring contest with Bob, neither of them willing to break off the focused glare.

"Now the truancy officer, Bob. You had no approval for him, either."

And Bob got this wiseguy look on his red, horned face, a smirk of ages, and whined, *"and how do you know that, little man?"*

"I confess Bob, I've had help behind me here but it was not always apparent. If you do not know them, let me introduce Gabriel, Raphael, Michael and Rodney." The archangels appeared standing behind Isaac, including Rodney, all dressed in current casual array *sans* wings because that could get more than a little bulky in a basement stairway.

"Okay, here he comes," resignedly noted a crestfallen demon.

And the plodding feet of an older man could be heard across the floor and onto the stairs, Isaac still in his gaze lock with Bob, climbing the stairs and exiting past Isaac and between the angels to whom he paid no attention.

"Okay, you've done your good deed for the day, now, boy scout. Bugger off and let me get back to corrupting the rest of the western world."

"Gee, sorry, Bob, but there is a reason the archangels brought Rodney along, if you did not notice. I'm told he is a new archangel, sort of, just getting used to his wings and he specialises in a huge power: he turns black holes into glistening white galaxies, literally turns giant gravity sucking nebulae inside out and distributes their contents toward populating new galaxies. The key property of the talent is the dispersion of formerly coherent and far too tightly packed fabricated matter in such a way that it never coalesces negative again."

"So what, "sneered Bob, "I do not belong to or am governed by your dimensions."

"Correct, again. But while He allowed you to play 'j'accuse' at will and gather in souls who will need a mountain of cleaning if they are to progress further in the future, He has found that your influence and seduction of so many vulnerable people has led to conditions not wholly unlike the Noahide times. But since He promised to never decimate the entire planet ever again, it seems that He has decided to purge the planet of its serious detritus in order that the even mediocre and young souls might have a chance to live and grow toward Him in peace."

"What does that have to do with me?"

"Perhaps you have forgotten that He did not give you permission to degrade the planet's entire population. As you confessed to me earlier, that is your objective and has been for centuries and you have scads of willing minions willing to commit heinous crimes to realise your goal of controlling the entire planet and its innocent population. Right?"

"But He always wanted me to test everyone to push them toward denying Him so that they can eventually seek Teshuvah, redemption, and return to Him," Bob was almost whining.

"Perhaps, but you did not just test, you organised virtual armies around congruence with your plan of total control to create the end of humanity...'the end of humanity' were your words, Bob. You are supposed to be working for the Father of humanity and why do you think it would be in His interest to see their end?"

Gathering the archangels closer around him, Isaac motioned Bob forward. "You went too far, I'm afraid, and have tried to conquer this planet and created organisations to reflect that nihilistic objective. It is time to stop and He asked Rodney to help us."

"Come closer Bob." And Bob stretched his head closer to Isaac, looking now not so filled with bravado but like a child anticipating a spanking. "It will be like this. Rodney, please, help me here." And Isaac stretched out his right index finger and touched the tip of Bob's left horn, then immediately reached out with his left index finger and touched the tip of Bob's right horn.

It began slowly at the tips of the horns, the disintegration, hardly noticeable, but continued and accelerated, then creating sparks and flashing lights like Fourth of July sparklers as it continued.

"Wait!" Bob stepped back, *"What is going on here? I'm the head of millions or billions. You can't do anything to me! My minions will take over everything. We have a Plan B and the consequences will not help your humanity. It will be a bloody massacre in the streets. No one will survive! We are in control here, not you."*

Isaac and the angels watched as Bob ranted, raved, and raged and continued to disintegrate ever more quickly, quantum bits of it flying off through the walls and off to places around the universe, never to coalesce again. It was not burning, just coming apart at all the seams, along with the seams, themselves.

Michael finally asked when Bob was almost nothingness again, "Isaac, why He needed Rodney is very clear, but what about Raphael, Gabriel, and I, why were we here?"

Isaac thought for a moment. "I think Gabriel was here to help get Richard freed, Raphael for the truancy officer, and you to give me the courage to face this demon... and to give me the flattery ideas that made it a soft target in the end, I think."

"Thank you for your help and support. I am so grateful to Him and all of you. Now we shall see how effective the contamination effects of Rodney's power might be."

"I'd best comfort the people upstairs, I think. They might think I've been done in."

There was no one in the foyer when he came out of the basement. He turned off the light, closed the door, and began looking, heading back toward the kitchen. He found four adults and a very smiling child at the kitchen table having coffee, cake, and soft drinks.

"Isaac," beamed Doris, "thank you for giving us back our life. If you will forgive us, Dom and I have decided not to sell and stay here since the danger has been resolved and Richard is back. We need to make a larger family for Richard and this house."

Dom got up, extended his hand and went on with the expected "if there is anything, anything at all I can do for you..." speech. Dom was completely sincere but Isaac wondered what an award winning, world famous electric pole and grid designer could do for him. Marie looked up at him and winked, but she was too busy romancing the truancy officer to pay much attention to Isaac. And

Richard was a picture of contentment, back with his parents and cake, lots of cake. He saw that he could play this for a good long time. Isaac silently wagged his finger at him semi-seriously to caution him not to take up his former captor's behaviour. Richard blushed.

Isaac excused himself and drove home, amazed that it had only been an hour at the house because it had felt like six. Later that afternoon, after putting on his copy of Mike Oldfield's first album, he logged on to the web and the instant news was bursting with very curious headlines...

- 80% of Congress collapses in unexplained epidemic...
- A former president and his wife collapsed and died onstage where they were speaking to a group of...
- Another former president and his 'wife' collapsed and were in ICU, not expected to live...
- All the still alive former US presidents collapsed and one died along with his spouse...
- Many Federal judges across the country were rendered unconscious by a mysterious cause...
- The leaders of the EU, Britain, France, Germany, Sweden, Norway, Israel, Turkey, Spain, Saudi, Lebanon, Iran, Iraq, Ukraine, Yemen, Egypt, Libya, Tunisia, Pakistan, Denmark, and over half the countries in Africa all collapsed in office, some died, just like the strange epidemic that hit the US Congress. South America, China, India, Australia, New Zealand, and Canada... all their leaders and ministers mysteriously

collapsed, as well. Again, some dying on the spot.

- Scores of movie and video personalities in the US and Europe also collapsed, as did hundreds of music artists, some in the midst of concerts, performances, or recording sessions.
- Most broadcast news outlets were staffed by stand-ins as most of the talking heads collapsed, some on air and some off.
- Newspaper offices were full of collapsing writers and editors, but few died there.
- It was an epidemic in every level of government at federal, state, county, and city or local levels in the US and abroad. Fewer collapsed in the local areas, but state house politicians across the US and provincial and local officials in Canada and elsewhere were being carried out by the busload, so to speak.
- Many Churches, Cathedrals, and Synagogues were reporting the same malevolent influence - they called it.
- Hospitals were overloaded with ordinary people who had just collapsed on the street, in schools, universities, in their parents' basements, in every sort of government office across the nation.
- Apparently the Pentagon, FBI, CIA, NSA and other acronym agencies had over 70% of their staff decimated due to attacks of the mysterious epidemic, some suffering highly animated jerks, twitches, versions of St. Vitus' Dance, and more than a few ran from

their offices, screaming, and all the way into the Potomac River for some strange reason.

- And universities across the US, Canada, Europe were struck with professors, instructors, adjunct and junior professors fainting dead away in the middle of lectures or in their offices. Administration figures were similarly struck on most campuses, some leading to fatalities.

- Spokesmen for the FDA, CDC, and WHO had no idea what was happening as no organic cause could be found tying the apparent epidemic illness to anything they could find as common amongst all those that suffered. Some blamed it on the Russians and Chinese, but there was no visible link and no organic trace of disease.

Well, well, thought Isaac, Rodney's contamination reversal is pretty powerful, after all. I wonder...

BRRRRRRRRRIIIIINNNNNGGGGGGGGGGG
SLAM

"IT IS ZERO FIVE THIRTY," THE RADIO ANNOUNCED.

Damn! Oh bugger, that was such a nice dream, why did it have to end?

He and She Pointless

This is pure whimsy. Is it a slice of life? Not just now, and not even likely in the future. We all have thoughts that nestle in the quiet, dark caverns of memories not dredged up very often and when they do, are they significant? Not usually, but they can be the base for thoughts when we are not preoccupied by other requirements, maybe. But sometimes those errant thoughts stimulate concepts we'd not broach otherwise. Then we just forget them, eh?

While the writer's style is often best described as "stream of inspiration", this is reminiscent of the old stream of consciousness style, moving, like thoughts, from one fluttering idea to another occasionally with clear connections from one to the next, but sometimes we traverse very thin and rickety bridges from one mental place to another, no?

Years, no, decades of time and millions of miles, millions of dollars, billions of memories, uncounted places and ideas, scores of people, generations of families, and innumerable active and benumbed feelings later, he remembered her. It was not a "wish she were here" kind of thought, nor a "where would I be had she been here" kind of wish, because she might have not well tolerated the hurdy-gurdy kind of life road down which his path had led. It was more a wondering, maybe a longing to have explored the life that would have been had they been together as his memories tell him they should. It was one of those frayed loose ends of memories, self-tattering in the relentless winds of emotional churning, the chaos that is the uncertain and never fully explored.

It was never a thought that tortured him because memories of her were only occasioned by thoughts of places they knew together or times they had shared; often fleeting, bringing a brief smile, a lightness of mood, a reminiscence, a memory, and often followed by a brief pang of guilt or remorse - but more for not knowing than a surety of what was missing. After all, at the time, when they were together, he had no certainty of her intentions except... except by dint of her behaviour on occasion.

Why Philadelphia, he kept thinking? He had never figured that one out except as maybe just a lark in her mind, as it was in his at the time. And he could barely remember visiting her family that one time, sadly. But he was like that often, ignoring details because some other worry was pre-occupying his mind. She was not the only one whom he had slighted for that reason. That was the advancing and initial stages of his disassociation, the main thrust of his relationship mentality for the next 40 years. He had worked hard to eliminate or bring under control much of his anxiety, substituting it with performance in his chosen work for he who excelled could be less anxious, he believed. And that became the sole focus of his work as

only through excelling could he free himself of the chains
of fear and loathing. Was it that focus that separated him
from her? Was it the self or the drive to find something of
which he was consciously unaware that did it?

He was driving himself to something in all those
years and it had various names along the way, names that
gave way to new names when they were presented as
something new, bright, and shiny. Yet none of the new
names were sufficient to hold his attention for very long. It
was not that they were insufficient, just perceived to be less
than the new vision before him, a vision that may be more
in his imagination than reality. Years later when he wrote
out a list of his positions over his career life, perhaps that is
part of what drove the fact that the single spaced list ran
over into a second A4 sheet of paper.

No, he kept coming back to the idea that his
separation from her, though not an official act, just a failure
to keep the relationship, was no failure of hers, but
thoroughly his and one that he was not sure still to this day
that he regrets or merely muses about the path of life had
he... had he... had he... stayed with her as he sometimes
thinks he should have done.

But then he remembers that they never talked about
such things as a future, he thinks, telling him that she was
not heavily invested in their future, either. But he also
remembers a level of downright comfort, peace, and right
feeling with her that he had not had before, nor since, with
others. And it wasn't just calm, but peace with ebullience,
a lightness, a carefree that he does not remember
elsewhere. That, THAT is what drives him back to think
he erred - for with no one else has he ever been that relaxed
and airy. It was as though two people who had not known
each other ever, before, met, got along and enjoyed each
other as though they had known each other all their lives.
He did not know how to handle it. He did not know what
he had. He walked away from a mate with whom he had

been close before, in another life, perhaps. He is not sure if they are feelings of regret or pangs of unmet curiosity as one wonders if she would have tolerated the life he has led - then again, would he have made the same decisions with her counsel added into the mix? Would THEY have made the same decisions?

Sitting in another place, decades on from prior realities, the ability to intuit is no better now than then, but the incapacity was not as much due to a lack of perception as it was to a drive whose source he still did not know. Occasionally one questions whether that ill focus is a realistic or a vain attempt to avoid the guilt for screwing up an entire life for the sake of objectives of which he was not fully aware. Sigh... he can't tell. A decision is not necessary. It would not advance his thinking or perception at this time, so it is of no use, either way.

What if he had done the right thing? The definition of that "right" being getting together with her for a marriage or at least a trial period, as they came to be for many.

He would have continued to do what he was doing at the time most likely, never branching out into the frenetic search for "more" that led to his repose here, far away, and scores of positions later. She would have continued at the bank until it was bought as happened years after he left. She would have likely been promoted and perhaps included in a higher achievement group in the larger corporation. He would have eventually or sooner become programming manager, maybe eventually even Station Manager. That would have given them enough money for a family, house, and all the things that tie people to a place, style, method, and process. Maybe it would have led to higher positions in the corporation that owned the station, who knows? But it would also have been the intellectual trap that he still is not sure he can handle.

But is that what she would have wanted? Remembering the little he knew of her family, such an eventuality would not be out of line with her upbringing. But would she, too, feel trapped in that scenario? Would it matter that both of them might feel like that?

Aha! There is the question that has launched a bazillion divorces and unhappy lives ever after for decades. Usually, the story with the "feeling" is single sourced, not taking into account the other side of the story, never ever imagining that the thinker could be a source of mindlessly boring and brain dead routines as seen from the other side of those eyes. No. It is always the "other' side that is such and strives to maintain credible stability despite the clear wishes to be free expressed by the one with the "feelings". What codswallop that is. Self-centred egoistic prattle it is. And that pair of descriptions fits no matter which half of the supposedly adult pair has them and finds themselves "trapped".

Would they have progressed to that?

Maybe not. While he has always tended to get catatonically enwrapped in what he does, she was always more outwardly looking, open, effusive, and lively. It was that hysterical dimension of her personality that interacted so well with what was often his passive-aggressive core. If he thought about it, there was that dimension to his parents, as well, strangely. He'd not considered it before. It was more apparent before his mother went through therapy, but his father... his father... his father never did but he changed in some dimensions with his wife's improvements.

No wonder one of the more consistent sets of dimensions that brings people together is hysteria and passive aggressive and keeps them together IF, and it is a big IF, their conditions are not too, too pathological and severe. If their mental condition, i.e., a paucity of emotional maturity, is severe, they stop enjoying each other as they age because the emotional energy needed to keep one's self together when the pathology requires more and more to maintain the self and leaves less and less for the relationships to keep the two of you together. Thus, the ties do not sever naturally as much as they softly, silently, invisibly vapourise as the people only have enough emotional energy to maintain their own mental health instability; but mutuality, a partnership, a marriage has needs in excess of that which they can generate; so they silently withdraw their energy from the relationship in ordcr to maintain their own self, driven by the 'feed me' emotional energy demands of the neuroses. Before long, the couple notices that they are no longer a couple but two distinct individuals only supporting themselves and what happens? Most often, they split because the egocentric energy is still there that says they are right and the other is no longer with them. In many cases, such a feeling is perfectly mutual. And they are both correct. They just have run out of the emotional energy that bound them together. This also springs a trap that they can never escape because unless they find solutions to the mental self-support energy problems, they will never be able to create another viable coupling. Life will remain a challenge of living within the energy bounds required to maintain a cogent level of self in a world that is not likely to become one creating easier to relate situations.

Would he and she have gone through that? Would he and she have been the victims of their own energy dwindling and egoistic self-centredness? How many angels can dance on the head of a pin, anyway? He will never know.

A few years ago, he took a brief but unenergetic look for her as few have her Christian name. It seems that some many years before it might have been she that married a fellow in central northern Ohio. He thought that was good and hoped it was a joyous and fruitful marriage.

That did not stop him from wondering, but gave him a bit of peace in that she found her love.

He sometimes thinks of her these days when he's running through a bout of self-pity, maybe, but that is probably a defence mechanism. If lives are enriched by mistakes, he thinks he must make Croesus jealous. However, in one's mind one always imagines or fantasises about meeting certain people who were critical at certain points in their past, today. You wonder what has happened in their lives. Maybe what you wonder most is whether the lack of your presence made any difference in their lives at all. Most times and for most people it is not difficult to understand that the answer is not only no, but perhaps an emphatic NO! But for some it is a kind yes. And for most it would be a contest of political sensitivity because, as extolled above, how do we know? Even those relationships that feel correct may be only so because of the circumstances, the timing, the place, the sum of extraneous factors that, together, created an inclination that would not have existed otherwise. Perhaps it is those temporal relationships that blossom, bloom, grow, wither, and die within a palpable time period, as noted like the ones specified above. But those are not the people about whom one imagines "what life would have been like with..." are they? No. Once such almost purposefully temporal relationships are abandoned, they are usually never revisited. Thoughts of other women he had known do not share this state of enquiry, ever.

So, where does this leave him? Pretty much where he began this introspective soliloquy, no? Yes. Though he has long theorised about the role of emotional energy in maintaining relationships, it is better to get it on paper. It provides no new insights as healthy people with healthy levels of energy NOT distracted by the million mundane mental mishaps called neuroses, have enough energy to surround themselves and their loved ones with care, not needing to withdraw energy to bolster one's own fading ego strength as they age. However, that is not to say that there are not incidents where one is challenged by events, situations, dangers, threats, and other aspects of life fraught with fear that draw a lot of energy into handling them. But also in those events, the people close to them can perceive a problem and offer as much support as possible to defray the need to divert so much energy to the resolution. That is what spouses are for, as well as all healthy people close to the target. That is how emotional support is exemplified.

Such is life.

So, he asks, what about her, anyway?

OY! What do you think this is, a Sophie Tucker reprise?

He never engaged in the "what if" scenarios he'd heard that others do and that are staple themes in romance novels. Oh, he often regretted his poor decisions and mistakes, but mostly for the impacts they had on others. When things began piling up badly he'd often say to himself and whomever was around to listen, "okay, what's next?" He saw all these challenges as tests, many of which he was sure he was not passing. Life is like that. One day you do the right thing and next day you don't. It all depends... but whatever it is, life goes on.

It is an old approach to philosophy and life, but he believed that he was where he was supposed to be, often, but not always, but often doing what he was supposed to do... and from that learning something he needed to know. He did not believe in determinism, knowing that it was his will to follow these opportunities. HE may control the universe and everything within it, but it was always his decision to go one direction or another -- the two realities were on completely different dimensions that, for humans, meant that His knowledge of what he was to do did not determine that he did it because living as He does in a dimension without time (as humans know it) the mundane connection between causes and events is irrelevant and does not exist. He also understood that most people fail to see the dimensional and time separation required to allow free will. Being mere humans, there is another dimension that says everything forward is a matter of probabilities and He has the option to "load" the decision tree, but can also choose whether to do it or not. But such is the way when dealing with the everything that is the universe on more levels than mere humans can understand.

Now what has this to do with her?

Ah, yes. She is a thought, then, a reminiscence, not a stimulus at this time, in this place, under these circumstances, for the thought implies neither action nor impetus to act. Okay?

Leave it. Should there ever be the circumstance where he and she meet again, the variables of that event and other things around them will control the outcome, not any fragile and tenuous fantasies constructed outside real dimensions. Just leave it.

OK.

This set of ruminations was pointless, then.

Mostly, yes.

Ladies, Ladies, on the Wall

The author admits to NEVER, NEVER doing any real field research on the subjects and scenarios noted in this story. It is just another of his examinations of the animation of things often thought as inanimate and unthinking. After all, haven't you ever pondered the idea wondering what one thing or another might think or relate to us if they could talk?

No, you haven't?

Oh. Never mind then. Just read the small story, please. Sheesh.

Mabel was just positioned there at the end of the line with the other girls. She checked to be sure she was clean as things just splatter when you aren't watching, don't you know. But not an issue for she was spotless, reflecting the great care she took in her presentation. But it was early yet, not even Eight A.M. and lots can happen between now and Six P.M.

Next to her, on her left, Greta was looking a bit streaky and she tried to fix it, but only made it worse. Greta was unfortunately a bit more than a little O-C-D, but the other girls did not like to mention that as there was little Greta could do about it as things stood. They just learned to live with it and the incessant whining if things weren't perfect for her. Sigh...

Everyone told Greta not to cry as someone would be along to help shortly. But the whining commenced. Shirley, on the other side of Pearl, was getting cross, but being a bit thicker skinned she did not let her words or demeanour reflect her irritation... but you could see that she was getting cloudy.

While all this was going on, Pearl, always the centre of attention and the group, just spaced out and glowed iridescently, as usual. She always felt it was her responsibility as the centre of the entire group to establish a high level of personal discipline and reflect the shining character and view of them as the fixtures of deliberation and ruminative appearance.

Twinkle, on the other end from Mabel, just hummed along as usual as though she was in a different world - and part of that was probably because she had the best view of the foyer and lounge area. Sometimes... well, sometimes she just couldn't even say what went on in the lounge and on the divans. Such carryings-on, she was not so polished that she could witness these things dispassionately, you know. So while she could not close her eyes to the happenings, she just whistled and tried to find distractions elsewhere in front of her.

The routine was boringly the same almost every day as the early birds came in to inspect themselves which began the litany of women mostly doing the same, though some actually used the facilities, having just arrived off public transportation. Some washed up, splattering Mabel, which upset her to no end. Someone used a paper towel to wipe the vague smear off Greta, for which she was brilliantly happy... and so was everyone else as the whining stopped. Those who brought their entire make-up kit into the room gravitated toward Pearl as she was perceived to be the brightest of the bunch - and the lights centred there.

All of them had small ledges and don't you know the kits took up all the space, sometimes spilling over with occasional unidentifiable bits rolling away. However, the girls were properly trained and never offered any opinion on what they saw, nor did they offer any suggestions when they knew and when they could see that alternative techniques would have worked better. They had an operating philosophy that related to the freedom of all their customers to choose what they thought best for themselves. After all, they weren't paid cosmeticians, now, were they? No, they just reflected the choices of their customers.

And as it progressed from 8 AM toward 9, it was the cacophony of so many voices talking at once, some standing doing their faces, some sitting on the divans or reclining, some using the facilities.... seeming as though all were talking at once. Greta always was put on edge from the incessant noise, voices which could not be discretely followed. Pearl and Twinkle were oblivious, Shirley began muttering words customers should not hear and Mabel just sighed and blocked it all.

It was no use letting the babble upset you as these were conversations that went in one side and out the other, never stopping in between... except and unless it was about the CEO's PA or a new member of the crew because both of those topics had some traction to them and could be revisited later.

And after the early morning rush, that nice cleaning woman came in and made sure all of us were clean and sparkling. Greta, poor Greta, always tried to tell her what to do and how to do it, but she paid Greta no mind and did her work quickly and efficiently, anyway. Which was a good thing because we got attention from the women on our floor throughout the morning. Some just came in to use the facilities and wash afterward...some didn't, ugh.   There was always a mid-morning rush when Twinkle would tell the rest of us what was going on as most of the activity was in the foyer and lounge area. Then everyone would clear out, our cleaning woman would come in for a look to make sure everything was fine and then we would be pretty much alone to talk amongst ourselves until the human lunch time, when there was another rush for our facilities and checks of cosmetic presentation levels before some went out to lunch. There was intermittent use of our facilities through the hour as people finished their lunch and came in to relax away from their desks for a while, perhaps to hide as well. Then there was a rush as people came back from outside.

Amazingly, a few actually brought some instruments used to clean out their oral cavities, much the same but smaller than the brushes our cleaning woman used on the facilities. We always wondered what on earth similarity there could be between the two as comparability was unimaginable until one day when Pearl remarked that we should listen to what they say. There is a reason Pearl is our leader.

Afternoons pretty much were the same as mornings except on rare occasions when one of the women came in convulsed with grief and tears. That usually brought in a couple more to support or help her, but because they were in the lounge area, only Twinkle could see what was going on. She'd tell us what she could but most of it was incomprehensible except that "fired" usually meant that we never saw that woman again. Oh, sometimes she'd come back to show off new jewellery or a ring, but most often we'd not see her again, either.

Occasionally, Twinkle would see that one of the women had come back from outside and even before hanging up her outer clothing, she'd throw it on the chairs out in the lounge and lie weeping on the divan. That would bring in others or those who came in would stay to comfort her. Sometimes they would have told her colleagues or master of the problem and communicate back to her as she could not face anything but whatever tragedy set off this emotional outburst. After a while, the outburst would diminish and her friends would help her back to her place in the office after she tried to put on a better face in front of Pearl. The poor cleaning lady used to work like mad to get some of the mascara stains out of the divan upholstery.

Then, later in the afternoon, Twinkle would alert us when she saw many coming in to prepare themselves for going elsewhere. For some it was "home", for others it was "out", for some it was shopping, for some it was to a health club, for some it was to a salon or saloon, for some it was out to dinner, and for others it was someone else's place for a gathering or "date". And there they would go again, a babble none of us could understand or distinguish as they all talked at once. But they'd then check their watches and begin to drift out until we had an empty facility and they only thing to wait for is the later cleaning person who would inevitably leave streaks on Greta just to upset her, she thought. We all began to think that such was part of their training as it was so consistent.

And it was virtually if not exactly the same day after day after day after day after day after day and so on for years. It was almost predictable but, reflecting the best taste of the firm, none of these monitors would ever repeat

any of the prattle of their customers. The primary reason
being that it was just not the thing that was done in a world
of human respect. Secondarily, the level of truth of what
was said was an entirely different dimension and varied
more, one suspected, with the source than in reality as
viewed by dispassionate eyes. Third, there was the
dimensional communication barrier after all, of which none
of them spoke, so to speak. Well, I mean.... one just
doesn't, does one?

Then there was the day that the ladies lost Greta. It
was a horrible accident where absolutely none of the
women or fellow shining examples were responsible, but
an event that left so many involved traumatised for weeks
thereafter, even though such things have been happening
more and more frequently in many states.

It was a normal weekday and the room was filled as
usual with many cued up to inspect or repair their faces in
front of the wall, when two swarthy, unshaven MALE!
terrorists slammed the door open and marched in to the
facilities room, in front of the sinks, pushing the ladies out
of the way, brandishing automatic weapons and indicating
that the women in there were to get back into the lounge
area. They were yelling and displaying a lot of bravado so
that they didn't notice Belinda and Carla holding onto their
purses and whispering to the women in front of them where
they had stopped in the doorway to the facilities section.
The terrorists stood in front of the sinks and yelled as to
how they were taking over and were going to use the
women as hostages and punctuated their comments with a
couple of shots into the ceiling. Well, that let fly the dust
and bits of granular ceiling tile. And as Belinda and Carla
nodded to each other in the midst of the flying muck, they
simultaneously screamed "DOWN" and while all the
women in front of them hit the ground, they pulled their

.357 short revolvers from their purses and drilled the
terrorists a new hole in each of their heads.

It was the fact that Carla was not using hollow-
points that allowed her shell to go not just through the
relatively empty, spongy space of the terrorist's head and
blow out a large section in the back, but then into and
breaking Greta behind him, as well. This preference for a
greater distance penetration sent uncountable shards of
Greta all over the floor, the sinks, and the now dead
terrorists who, by this time, were lying inert on the floor of
the ladies room, leaking a horribly bloody mess of things.

Following the very loud report of the guns, it was,
strangely, deathly silent in the ladies room. It took almost
ten of the longest seconds the surviving ladies had ever
experienced before anyone even screamed, at which point,
Belinda noted dismissively, "it's a little late for that, isn't
it?" while she and Carla replaced their pistols back in their
purses. Most of the women just gasped, grabbed their
purses, and streamed out the door, headed for the facilities
on another floor where they might sit and decompress for a
while. Carla called 9-1-1 just in case no one had done so
yet. Belinda sat down on the divan, shaking like a leaf ...
soon thereafter followed by Carla.

Pamela, the CEO's PA, came in, surveyed the scene,
retrieved a cloth from the cleaning closet to cover the
bodies, and called her boss to tell him what had happened,
unaware that a similar scene had been acted-out in the
lobby of the building with three more wounded or dead
would-be terrorists down.

The driver of the van that brought them all to the
building heard the shots, decided that this was not the day
to be in that business, and sped away. He ditched the van
and the outer outfit he was wearing and had the presence of
mind to try to wipe down every surface in the van he could
remember touching before sauntering casually over a few
streets to a bus stop. On the walk to his pad, he picked up a

newspaper for the want ads. He perused them, found one
very close to him, made sure he looked presentable and
applied for the job. It wasn't more than a minimum wage
job but he kept it for a few years and got promoted. He
kept at it and had worked his way up to General Manager in
ten years. Along the way to that achievement, he picked up
a loving wife; they had three children, two boys and a girl;
they eventually got a house in a decent neighbourhood; he
pushed the children to study and they got scholarships to
university, all of them. The children went on to get
graduate degrees and all placed themselves successfully in
business careers or academia. The driver never forgot what
inspired him to follow this course and volunteered to lead
classes helping children from less financially fortunate
areas to help them avoid thinking they should be a driver
for urban terrorists someday.

But back to the ladies....

They were aghast at what had happened to Greta.
Mabel and Shirley clouded over while Pearl lost her sheen
and Twinkle almost jiggled out of her casement with
hysteria. There was nothing they could do - there was poor
Greta all over the place, in a million shiny pieces. It was
too much to ask them to be all shiny and bright seeing that.
It later took the cleaning specialist over 30 minutes to clean
them partially back to shiny.... but with a giant hole on one
side, empty. The ladies never shone as they used to for
weeks after that. Even when they put Gladys with her
bright and chipper attitude in the vacant space, it took a
while before the ladies could explain the full story to her.
Belinda and Carla thought they were in for real
trouble. The emergency services guys had come by and
carted away the black bags after the forensics crew had
taken lots and lots of photos. However, the police
questioned them for 10 minutes, asked for the weapons to

run tests, actually gave them receipts, and were far more sympathetic than they expected. They gave them the name of a counselling service to which they could go if the shock was too traumatic. Their bosses came by and told them to go home after the police were done - which was pretty good as neither of them had finished shaking yet.

There is so much of it in the media that people are fairly inured to scenes of shootings and death... until you do it yourself. Police are more aware of this than anyone. It is not an action anyone can undertake lightly. Sure, you practice on a range, get your skills right, your aim correct, and know what you are going to hit when you fire. But none of that prepares you for seeing the dead body in front of you knowing you have done it. Some shrug it off, disassociate from the reaction... but it always comes back and usually far more intense if you don't deal with it up front.

Belinda and Carla came back to work the next day but were not "right" for some months. They used the counselling option and that helped. It took over six months for activity and normalcy to return to the ladies room on the executive floor. The ladies on the wall took that much time to get used to Gladys as she was more like Twinkle but a cynical version, not like the ever so often prissy Greta. The women that came in still every day didn't notice so much but the ladies knew that none of them were ever as much a shining example as they used to be before.

Bodacious Bob's Boutique Blessings

This story began as a light-hearted treatment of a guy in a small southern US town who makes his living blessing people out of the side of his house... yeah, drive through blessings... for a modest tip. It was not intended to deride the real folks who live by expanding the reach of their real religion, but surely to deride those who exploit it for personal gain exclusive of human respect.... the commercialisation indicative of Las Vegas and TV evangelists may come to mind.

It ended up not as light as the author originally intended it, but such may be the way with things that actually do affect lives. No, no new Messiah lines here, but interesting as to how one discovers his business model, eh?

And you never know where things may lead.

Introduction

BLESSINGS BY BOBBY.... TIP $1

...read the large sign cantilevered on the ground near the circular drive that Ol' Steve used to use for drive-in customers for his bootlegging business dealt out of the side of his house there on Vine Street. At first few folks ventured down that drive as they had no idea what that meant. But once Bubba Hornswagon began spreading his story, Bobby had regular and sometimes long lines of waiting customers for a blessing.

Blessings from the Lord were nothing really new in a highly Baptist Padyurwallet, Georgia, where every Preacher finished Sunday's services with a general blessing of the congregation. But unlike some religions, most Baptists only met and recognised Him on Sundays, so active blessings during the week were hard to come by. It seems that a few people thought they needed some spiritual support through the week and reading the good book and prayer committee meetings were just not "it" for them. So, they and soon more and more drove by Bobby for a blessing almost any time of the day.... or night, much to Bobby's sleep's discomfort. And you didn't have to pay Bobby as what he asked for was merely a $1 tip that you would throw in the bucket hanging on the hook to the side of the window on the side of the house.

It was a large picture window sized space on the side of the house, half-framed, its bottom about even with the middle of most car doors, with piano hinges to open inwards like a window. Ol' Steve used to dispense quantities of moonshine and commercial alcohol and beer out of it - one of the first drive-through liquor stores anywhere... except that the city was dry and so he was technically a bootlegger even though the county was wet.

Most of the southern US states had created similar entrepreneur opportunities for enterprising people decades ago through the judicious use of alcohol blue laws to designate certain towns or counties either "wet" or "dry" dependent on the local preferences and practices... and who stood a good chance to make money off the designations thereof, including the necessity to buy protection from the local law. And Yankees had the nerve to think free-enterprise was a non-starter in the South. It just proves that they know so very little up there.

For a long while Steve had a good business going and nobody really bothered him. He was said to have the best "shine" for miles around and even gave free samples to the state and county cops that occasionally came by for a rest in the middle of their shifts. Steve actually loved them parking their squad cars out front 'cause it gave him a break and provided his perpetual rationale for why he had to charge more for bottles that were cheaper about 10 miles away in the county.

But after about 20 years, Steve became a bit sloppy, began seriously sampling his own wares, and either forgot or refused to pay off the county Sheriff and state cops one year. It had been a mutually profitable relationship but something happened and Steve got all bent out of shape and stopped paying for his insurance. One day the county Sheriff and county prosecutor stopped by and you could hear the Claude Raines impression, "I'm shocked, shocked that there is alcohol being sold here!" exclaimed the Sheriff before putting his usual quart Mason Jar in the squad car boot. So, Steve was arrested, the shop closed, and for pure stupidity, he got 20 years for selling booze without an insurance policy, whoops... for selling alcohol in a jurisdiction that prohibited it and without a license, either.

So, to pay for the attorney that, unbeknownst to Steve, the Sheriff had already paid off to lose the case, Steve sold the house to Robert Buck at a real steal... mostly because it needed a lot of work as bootleggers are not known to be overly house-proud.

While it took a while to get the house and yard fixed up, it also took months for Robert to discover that he wanted to be in the Blessings business after he bought the house.

Chapter 1 - What you don't know can't influence you

Padyurwallet, Georgia was a quiet village west of Atlanta. It used to be fairly bustling with agriculture in the decades before Atlanta became the behemoth it is. But these days there are two sides to Padyurwallet, the old town and the new suburbia and they do not mix very well or at all. Where the old town is typified by neat family homes, white picket fences, sidewalks, large and tall trees overhanging the quiet streets, small shops, modest churches, parks, and an elementary and a high school, it is organised around the old square with a confederate War Between the States memorial statue in the middle of it and the suburban area is built up all around it... surrounding it, you might say. In the old town, segregation was never enforced, but it just sort of happened that black families lived generally in the southern side of the town - though nobody made them do it or restricted sales elsewhere in the town. It just grew up that way; and it happened without a train line running through to have different sides of the tracks. That was not unlike the big cities where the Italians, Poles, Germans, Jews, Ukrainians, etc., tended to live in the same area, that's all it was.

But outside the old town, the Atlanta bedroom community with its feeder roads to the freeways grew up much like a hostile force enclosing the old village. The entire surround was dotted with shopping malls, a few bike trails, a few parks, elementary and high schools, and more than one mega church competing for the spiritual dollars of the locals. It was just as ugly, depersonalised, vain, and soulless as any urban landscape, only out in the midst of the few remaining farms holding out against the voracious developers. The county had had to negotiate to get bus lines coordinated with MARTA to serve the entire community as the old bus lines that plied a few routes in the old town refused to capitalise and serve the new area with regular service in and out of Atlanta.

The industry of the old town was mainly small ventures providing building, repairs, plumbing, automobile mechanical, petrol, surveying, real estate, retail, pharmacy, grocery, butcher, bakeries, barber shops, beauty salons, shoes, ladies' clothes, a cobbler, a couple diners, with some law and medical offices as the closest hospital was on the outskirts of Atlanta, 30 minutes away. While the shopping malls built into the expanding sections outside the old town proper brought in all the modern convenience shops and services, that only made the contrast with the old town more stark. The mentality of the two areas was so poles apart that there was virtually no crossover in shopping or church attendance between the two areas. That was actually one of the saving graces that allowed the old town to survive amidst what could have been the crushing competition of the mass-market [meaning predatory] retailers in the suburban section.

The town council remained generally the province of the old town, as the bedroom community residents were far too busy in their chosen life styles to participate and everything just ran tickety-boo, anyway. This is another grace for the predatory retailers had exerted considerable lobbying and pressure on the town council to change the zoning laws to allow them into the old town area, but the council would not allow it, refusing monetary and other enticements and threats. They figured that since Padyurwallet had survived Sherman, it could more than survive a Wal-Mart's onslaught and hold off the modern carpet-baggers, particularly since Arkansas was viewed as one of those places where genteel people did not go... excepting Hot Springs, of course.

Now in Padyurwallet lived one Robert Buck. Robert's family had come to the town back before WWI and his great grandparents had been attorneys that mostly worked in Atlanta. Just before the first war they had changed the family name from Bockstein to Buck as the former sounded far too German and they could see the writing on the Wilsonian wall that the English would suck the US into the war just because Wilson was such a lily-livered coward and suck-up to the Brits no matter what. Besides that, the lawyers could see how the Dreyfus Affair, polarising religious sentiments in Europe, would migrate across the Atlantic and more of an Anglo-American sounding name would be not such a bad idea. Anyway, in expectation of the w-a-r, most of the German Muellers were changing to Miller, anyway, so if the Guelphs in England could do it, why not them?

The investments of his great grandparents had been such - and had avoided the crash, curiously - that the returns thereon still paid for Robert's education at the University of Georgia, then allowed him to buy Steve's modest house in the old town section, and gave him a modest lifestyle as he was one of those well educated folks that, at this point, still did not know what they wanted to do in life. Robert trolled the Internet in search of his life's calling daily and was highly blessed in having the luxury of looking for fulfilment, rather than having to substitute earning a living for seeking satisfaction. But he was beginning to look for something to do locally just to defray the mind-stultifying sameness and boredom, not knowing that those are exactly the detested fruits of most employment situations in this wage-slave world. And in the midst of deliberating as to whether to apply for one pointless position or another, his mother rang him up.

"Bobby?"

"Yes, Mum."

"You won't believe what I've found. Actually, I never told you about it at all so you would have no expectation of knowing what it is. So, please come over and get it as it has always been for you, but I never got around to giving it to you."

"Okay, Mum. I'll be there in a few minutes." Bobby was not surprised at his Mum's approach as she often talked as though you already knew what she was going to say.

Given the tranquil and temperate weather of Padyurwallet, the only reason to drive is because you expect to carry something that will be easier in a vehicle; so Bobby drove, not knowing what it was his Mum had for him.

When he got there they went through the usual "No, I don't need anything to eat, Mum. I'm fine" routine; as well as the rather sentimental greetings, always more intense since his father died. He told her of looking for some meaningless work to keep him busy and tried to head off a detailed discussion, as he didn't know what he was going to do, yet.

"Okay," she finally said, indicating a change of topic, "I was going through the attic and found this box that your grandfather had left for you decades ago before he passed on. But before I give it to you, I owe you an explanation, I think."

Bobby could not imagine anything his often verbose mother would not have told him a number of times, but let's see, he thought.

"Surely you remember the reasons your great grandfathers changed their name from Bockstein to Buck, don't you? I know we told you that. But I don't think I ever fully explained to you that you are Jewish, did I?" she began, watching Bobby react the way people might when they realise a tidal wave is coming upon them soon. You see, in a small southern US town in Georgia, rarer than the

Che Guevara Fan Clubs are generally Jews. Not so much in Atlanta, mind you, but highly rare in Padyurwallet. It wasn't a matter of discrimination issues as much as it was that in the South, Jews always lived in the big cities to avoid creating those kinds of issues. In fact, Bobby searched his mind quickly to try to remember any Jews he knew in the village - and there were none. His mother continued.

"Both, well, all of your great grandfathers were Jewish lawyers that moved down here to live but worked in Atlanta - not an easy thing back before WWI. Seeing the building discrimination and hate issues elsewhere, they just kept their religion very private and kept it amongst themselves. It was the same thing with your grandfather. By the time your father and I went under the chupah - that is a wedding canopy under which all Jewish weddings take place - it was more a formality than an observant practice. You see, there is not a synagogue within 30 minutes of here and not enough observant Jews to make a minyan here in town. Oh, there are a few but they, like your father and I kept everything very private. By the way, a minyan is ten male adult Jews and is a necessary quorum for some prayer services. We never had you or your brothers take Bar Mitzvah and I doubt you ever saw us actively daven - that means pray if you're Hebrew. You often saw me light a candle on Friday night and mumble things, but you never asked and your father and I never explained what that was all about. Do you want that drink yet?"

Bobby was more than a bit perplexed, confused, and almost astonished as he nodded yes to the drink, now. A little Bourbon would soothe his fevered thinking. He wondered where his mind had been for all those years when he remembered seeing his Mum do that every Friday. He used to wonder why they never went to the little Baptist Church down the street like their neighbours, but always let himself get distracted from those thoughts with things to do

with his brothers. He remembered early in high school
asking his father why he didn't look quite the same as his
peers, something he noticed in the locker room. His father
has explained that for reasons of personal hygiene all males
after WWI were often circumcised, a practice that many of
the more rural obstetricians did not follow, but his family
had required and it was done when he was just eight days
old at a special place in Atlanta. Bobby wondered how he
had survived just allowing his parents' easy explanations to
assuage his inquiries all those years. How had he been so
preoccupied that nothing ever clicked? Parental love and
trust is an amazing thing.

Before his Mum sat down, he asked for a refill,
drinking all of it down in an instant. He took a bit more
time with the second one. It wasn't being Jewish, per se,
that was shocking but the idea that there was part of his
family and his history of which he was thoroughly unaware
- and he had been kept unaware for 25 years! It was similar
to discovering that you had brothers and sisters you had
never known. Gob-smacked is perhaps one of the more apt
descriptions of Bobby's mental condition as his mother sat
down and began, again.

"When your brothers and sister moved away after
their schooling your father often went to visit them and
help set them up in the cities where they were working. He
explained to them what I'm telling you now so that they
could choose to explore and join in local congregations.
Your brothers were fine and said they had always suspected
it was so as they were the only circumcised children in their
local schools. I had to visit your sister to calm her down
and get her the books she needed to learn if she was going
to become observant. Even though we could provide all of
them with the proper paperwork to get them accepted, they
still needed to learn what was expected of them as Jews.
Just going into a prayer service in a local shul can be
thoroughly confusing and embarrassing if you are not ready

for it. By and large, they all took it well. Even your sister calmed down after a couple of days and constant explanations and going to stores and getting her books, dishes, candle holders, and everything she needed. I think your father was hugely disappointed that he could not talk to you before he passed on, but you were still in school and only here for the assigned holidays. Besides, nobody expects to be run down by a crash of Rhino's in the middle of Atlanta these days - so surprising was your father's untimely demise. The Chevra Kadisha had an awful time trying to put some of him in his kittel for burial, so it was no surprise that the simple pine casket was nailed shut. It was an awful surprise for all of us it was."

Bobby, spoke up, "did they ever figure out where the Rhinos came from or went?"

"No. That is the strangest thing, like something from the Twilight Zone or Ionesco. Nobody ever figured it out even though it had plenty of witnesses. But now that you've heard most of it, do you have any questions?"

"How many other Jews are there in town?"

"Oh, half a dozen or so still here, mostly older as their children have moved away, too."

"Is that why Dad was buried over in a corner of the graveyard along a few others?"

"Exactly. Your great grandfathers and a few others bought that section of the graveyard for use by Jews decades ago; they had it consecrated, and it is dedicated to them and owned by a self-financing trust to take care of the landscaping and care. Because Padyurwallet is such a small town and there were so few of us, it made no sense to have the separate graveyard that is normally required."

Bobby just sat there in stunned silence, letting all this roll about in his mind, not knowing whether to be stunned, anxious, fearful, awed, angry, upset, or just plain old gob-smacked. He chose the latter and asked his Mum if he could ruminate on this for a few minutes. She said fine and went off to fix them lunch.

"Does this mean I have to find a nice Jewish girl to marry?" he yelled at his mother who was in the kitchen by now.

"That would be what your great grandfathers, your grandfathers, your father and I would prefer, you know," she replied unhesitatingly.

"Oh."

"Why, did you have someone in mind already?"

"No, just wondering because if there are only old Jewish families left here in Padyurwallet, I'll have to begin looking elsewhere, that's all."

"Oh, I can find a *shadchan* if you need one."

"What is that?"

"A Jewish matchmaker. They are still around for the more strictly orthodox families."

"No thanks... I'm not desperate, yet."

"I don't think it is desperate so much as letting someone else sift through the available mates to find the ones with the best potential..."

"Thanks, Mum.... I'll try on my own as I have."

"And that has gotten you where?" she asked.

Bobby just let it hang in the air like a slowly deflating helium balloon, bobbing slightly with the ambient wind and heat currents in the room.

During lunch Bobby quizzed his mother about what traditional Jewish practices were. But she actually knew very little as her family was never what orthodox people call "observant" and her husband's family the same, having kept minimal traditions in light of being invisible Jews in a small southern Georgia town where there wasn't so much antipathy or hate as just ignorance and they did their best to be totally non-visible as Jews. Even though the village was relatively tolerant, there was plenty of anti-Semitism in the surrounding states to make up for it and recommend an invisibility that kept them from being an object of malevolent attention. By the end of the lunch, Bobby had decided to find out more and drive into Atlanta in search of what he had been missing. But first, the box left for him by his grandfather.

It was one of those cut-down sized steamer trunks, about the same footprint but one-third the height with handles on four of the six sides and huge clasp locks on the front and steel reinforcing on all the corners. Fortunately the clasps were not locked because his Mum noted she had no idea where anything like a key could be found. They opened it and inside were stacks of papers, books, a few kippahs, a string tied bag with Tefillin, a large Kittel, white cotton tunics with knotted strings hanging off the corners, and a large Tallis or two.

On top of the papers were documents in Hebrew with a couple of certifying stamps that had his grandfather's name. Under that was a copy of his mother's birth certificate, the ketuba (mother's marriage contract with his father), a copy of his birth certificate, and a letter written by his grandfather signifying the family lineage and stamped with certification by a Beis Din in Atlanta. Basically, to his inexperienced eyes, it looked like all he needed to prove that he was a Jew of proper family and parentage. Wow.

There were three siddurs (prayer books). One entirely in Hebrew, one transliterated and translated into English with the Hebrew on the opposing page, and one with Hebrew on one page and English on the facing page. There was also a Chumash, his mother explained, the Torah in book form with notes and explanations, but everything outside the Torah and explanatory notes was commentaries by Sages. There were a few ordinary looking books on what it meant to be a Jew, Jewish practices and procedures, everyday and food Blessings, a few more on various aspects of living like a Jew, and a compendium of Jewish Humour in English and Yiddish. It seems that his grandfather knew well the vacuum from which he would be presented with all this. Amazing, it was. Instant life change...maybe. Bobby was not convinced that was the direction he wanted his life to go, nor was he opposed to it. He was just confused, baffled, and, frankly, stunned. He thought about calling his brothers later.

"Your grandfather," his mother explained, "felt horribly guilty for creating the isolated environment in which the significance of our spiritual and familial heritage was erased. He regularly mentioned how he might have done it differently if he had known the emptiness of life outside Judaism. I couldn't relate to that as I'd never been elsewhere, but I think practices and traditions were followed in his father's house that he did not migrate to ours when we were growing up out here. Of course, back then and by then they were also fighting a depression and many local resentments that people allow to metastasise when economic conditions are tough just to think they are relieving the pressure of misery when they are only creating another whip for their back."

"Okay," ventured Bobby, "so what do I do with all this? I've already decided to try to find a synagogue... is it synagogue or shul?"

"Both. More orthodox communities often term their synagogue a shul - it is an old Ashkenazy reference. Umm... Ashkenazy are (mostly eastern) European Jews and Sephardic are those from North Africa and Israel. Most over here are Ashkenazy in origin."

"Right. I'll make some calls and find one with a Rabbi willing to walk me through all this. Surely, there will be one, somewhere, don't you think?"

"As much as Jews distance themselves from others in order to maintain their traditions and beliefs, they are truly welcoming for returning non-observant Jews and even converts. They just do not easily accept converts because they question: 'who would willingly join a sect that has been systematically hated, excluded, ostracised, tortured, murdered, vilified, subject to genocide, and thrown out of countries for no more reason than just being Jewish for thousands of years'? Well?"

"But on the other hand," Bobby retorted, "how incredibly valuable and fulfilling Judaism must be that people would endure all that hardship just to retain their beliefs. It must be incredible that people would sacrifice themselves to maintain a cherished culture that has defined and defied a level of suffering unknown to any other group for so long and yet, survived. It is just amazing."

"You need to find out for yourself," his mother advised parentally.

"Thank you, Mum. I may or may not go orthodox but I certainly appreciate the fact that I'm actually part of something much bigger than I. Cool." And with that, Bobby closed the trunk, hoisted it onto his shoulder, and thanked his Mum for opening the door for him.

She watched as he loaded it in the car and mused to herself, "I wonder if my father had any idea what he might be loosing on this village with this knowledge," because Bobby had that look of zeal in his eyes that could make things very interesting for more than just him.

Chapter 2 - Discovery and Determination

Indeed, Bobby found an orthodox shul and Rabbi that was more than interested in bringing in a non-observant Jew. It was not the first shul he contacted, nor the second, not even the third or the fourth because all of them were either not very interested, having their own resourcing difficulties, or just far more interested in their problems than Bobby's. Some of this was apparent when he talked to them; the attitude of the others was deducted by the length of time it took for them to get back to him. Bobby drove in to meet with Rabbi Blum and because they seemed to connect, agreed to weekly meetings or classes to bring Bobby back into the traditions of his fathers. This meant that Bobby had to get up especially early some mornings and drive to the early service, learn how to wear the Tefillin he had inherited, and learn how to say the later services on his own with the Siddurs he was given. Bobby was learning how to be a practicing Jew... except Bobby was not ready to tackle learning Hebrew just yet, even though he knew it had to be done eventually.

Bobby also borrowed a few books from the shul to help him learn Torah background to which he had never been exposed. He was especially taken with Abraham's devotion and commitment, a deep duty far beyond that of which he thought he was capable. It was the serving and humble deference to all those that passed by his humble abode that struck him - and began him thinking about how he could do something like that in Padyurwallet. It couldn't be to make converts, as had been Abraham's intention, but simply to serve and help because going for converts in a small southern Georgia town is about as close to social suicide as one can get without putting a giant statue of Abraham Lincoln on your front lawn and playing "Battle Hymn of the Republic" through speakers in its base. The

Baptist Churches were never and should never be insecure about their position in the community; that was never Bobby's idea.

But while wanting to be a 21st Century Abraham, Bobby also had to look at what he needed to do to earn a living as his funds were not running out but did not allow for a lot of travel, a wife and children, or even many sumptuous feasts for holidays. He had found new direction, but still had not advanced off the mental square he inhabited when he went on that fateful visit to his Mum's. His desire to uplift humanity was not so different from so many others' desire to do the same these days and not so differently bereft of practical mechanisms to make it happen.

Bubba Hornswagon had known Bobby since they were in school together and they didn't see each other too often these days because Bubba was driving a wood rig for Georgia Pacific, hauling tree trunks to the sawmills. It was long hours and mostly unrewarding, but Bubba didn't mind as it did not interfere with his pursuit of Astronomy and visual searches for asteroids within the solar system... at least that is what he told the girls to whom he showed his telescopes and visual sight records. All in all, Bubba was quite a subject matter expert on what one could see through his fairly sophisticated telescopes and showed many a girl some things they had not seen before on those warm summer nights in Georgia.

Bobby was in the local grocery one evening when Bubba came in and they spent 20 minutes exchanging life stories, thereby Bubba learned of Bobby's lifestyle change and Bobby learned what Bubba was doing, driving and all. In fact, Bubba shared the fact that driving the big rigs through steep and narrow dirt roads on hills and down was often not the safest, particularly after or during rains when the Georgia clay roads were slicker than ice. Often the reason Bubba's first after work stop was a saloon was to quiet the nerves jumping out of his skin after a particularly dangerous day. Bobby could actually feel the genuine fear as Bubba related his work stories.

Without thinking when Bubba had stopped for a moment, Bobby put out his right hand, facing his palm toward Bubba, separating his fingers into two and two and separating his thumb, and began the blessing he did every morning during Shacharis, the early morning prayer, *"May the Lord bless you and safeguard you. May the Lord illuminate his countenance for you and be gracious to you. May the Lord turn His countenance to you and establish peace for you."* And while Bubba looked at him kinda funny, he seemed to calm down as well. Bubba did not know how to react to that. Bobby apologised and said it just occurred to him to do that as Bubba looked as though he needed some words of higher strength and that was all that Bobby could think of. They wrapped up their conversation, finished their shopping, and went on their ways.

The next day, Bobby began thinking of how, rather than food and drink in the desert as Abraham had provided, perhaps a daily blessing would uplift the lives of ordinary people, reflecting on the actual effect he thought he had on Bubba the previous night. He kept thinking of that and went outside; he was looking carefully at the semi-circular drive through the wooded lot that still existed on the west side of the house as it faced Vine Street. It was still reasonably paved and the folks that mowed his lawn kept up that part of the yard as well. He looked over at the window on the side of the house and how it could be opened. The pressure sensor line across the drive was still there, the one that rang a bell in the house to let Steve know he had customers; it was just unplugged.

Hugo at the hardware store used to make wood signs. Bobby called down there to see if he still did and could make one that would lean up, about four foot tall and three foot wide. "Sure," said Hugo, "usually they are 3/4 inch plywood and if it will be out all the time I can have it varnished to keep it from warping in the rain. What did you have in mind?"

"Blessings by Bobby, three lines, cursive, slanted going up left to right, and TIP $1 below that. But because I'm not sure, would you might drawing me a small picture of that and I'll come by this afternoon to go over it with you?"

"Sure, not a problem Bobby. That is one of the more interesting business ideas I've ever heard - think the Preachers will mind the competition?" joked Hugo.

"Maybe...but just to be sure I don't upset them, maybe I'll close on the weekends," he ventured, half seriously, conscious of his commitment not to work on Saturdays, already. "I'll see you this afternoon," and Bobby rang off.

It took a couple of days for the sign to be made. Meanwhile, Bobby had to decide what to say. The general blessings would be the mainstay, but there was also the blessing for having come through a dangerous trip or situation, the blessing for new children, blessing for those in the armed services, a general blessing of families, for leaders of schools and congregations, and he modified the standard blessings of the government and state of Israel to conform to local concerns... and hoped his Rabbi would not hear of it.

Then he opened the window, set a background like those space dividers you find in IT offices behind enough space where he could stand in front of it, found a large hook he could screw into the outside window frame and a bucket to hang from it. Oh, and he turned on the pressure sensor and tried it to see that it still worked. It did. He got out one of the tallis' and figured out how to drape it over his head and shoulders so that raising his arm wouldn't cause it to fall off. Then there was the kippah. The ones left by his grandfather had been pretty small and were intended to be kept in place by a bobby pin. In a Hebrew clothing and bookstore in Atlanta, there had been lots of larger, knit kippahs that sat securely on his head without bobby pins. He had bought a few. But with the Tallis over his head, nobody would see the kippah, but he thought he should wear one anyway and began wearing a cap outside no matter where he went to wear but not display the kippah and to keep it on his head. It is one thing adopting a new lifestyle and culture, it is another exposing people who've never seen certain things in their day-to-day environment to challenges they may not understand... and Bobby did not want to find out just yet. And Bobby was ready to begin his business, waiting for the sign.

After the sign arrived, Bobby leaned it up near the entrance to the drive, pulled a chair into the alcove between the window and the background... and waited. After a couple of hours and Bobby nodding off to a nap, the bell rang, waking up bobby like a start in time for him to see an older F-150 pull slowly up to his window with an even older man driving it.

"Say young feller, is Steve back?" he inquired.

""No. He's still doing his time. I'm Bobby and I confer blessings. What were you looking for?"

"Oh, a pint of Jim Beam, but that's ok. Thanks anyway. Hope the blessings work." And he drove out of the drive and off down Vine Street.

Bobby had a couple more like that before noon. Jim Beam was real popular around here.

He was beginning to think that he missed the bet by not advertising before he opened up when a small grey sedan pulled up to his window.

It was a rather withered man, looking like he was in his 80's, who said in a tremulous voice, "Father, can you bless me 'cause I'm sore afraid."

"What is it, sir?"

"I've got to go to the hospital. They say I have to have a surgery and I'm horribly afraid. I've never stayed in a hospital in my life and I don't know what to expect."

Rather than try to minimise the old man's worry, Bobby stood up, looked the old man straight in the eyes, assumed the hand position, and read out part of the morning blessing about the Lord blessing and safeguarding, then adding lines form the Thanksgiving blessing for after a dangerous situation so as to make it a blessing on the outcome before the situation.

He could see the old man almost tearing. He said, "listen I don't have any money right now but let me come back after I get out, ok?"

"Sir, you will be fine and I'm happy to wait to see you well and fit again."

And the sedan slowly pulled out of the drive and up Vine Street. Bobby did not recognise his second grade teacher after all these years as he was fairly old and close to retirement even back then, but as he drove off the old man thought Bobby had turned out okay after being such a pain as a child, as mule-headed stubborn as he was.

There! Bobby had delivered his first blessing! He was rather pleased with himself and truly hoped the old man would come out fine and fit.

Remember Bubba?

On the day after Bobby blessed Bubba, it had poured down rain in the forest where they were logging. That didn't stop the work, but it sure made hauling the logs out of there real chancey. After three loads, Bubba was there with his last, just heading out of the forest and down that slippery as can be red clay road. Getting traction up the even minor hills was difficult and only possible because the loads were so heavy and they dug in so deep in the mud. One of the tricks was to drive just barely onto the embankment side as the sides were more solid and gave more traction than the roadbeds. But you had to be especially careful lest you drive your load up the embankment too far and it begins to tip either because it is angled too far or the load is too top heavy. Either way, if it begins to tip and you don't have enough speed and forward momentum to bring it down again into the roadbed, it will flip the trailer, the logs, and take you and the tractor with it, turning over and over again as many times as it takes to roll down the hill, spilling the logs everywhere. The company recovers the logs with a bit of effort, but always writes off those trucks and the drivers thereof. So few had walked or been carried away from those accidents that it was always assumed they were fatal.

Well, Bubba went just that ever so little much too high on the embankment with the trailer and he wasn't moving fast enough to recover so when his trailer turned, it just went... over and over, and over, and over, twisting the tractor with it. It and the logs all came to rest about 30 feet below the muddy road in a formerly dry creek bed. In the forest with the chain saws going nobody hears those events. But toward the end of the day when most are off and put away for the night, that kind of crash makes more noise than a steam railroad piling through the centre of town without rails! The super piled into his truck and drove down the creek bed as it was easier to traverse than the mud road. When he came around a turn in the creek and saw Bubba's truck, one giant mass of twisted metal, logs splintered and splayed all over, and still rotating tyres, looking like a dead beast with its legs in the air, he was afraid and sure he'd have to make another one of those awful calls to relatives... then he saw Bubba kicking the piss out of the rear tyres on the tractor. Bubba had just figured out that it would have been better to deflate some of the tyres on the inside of the road and leave the outside tyres full air. The super just grabbed Bubba and gave him such a hug. He began talking a blue streak and didn't stop expressing his amazement that Bubba survived an almost sure death wreck. Bubba was just numb, in shock from it all. So the company gave him a paid two weeks off for medical and set him up with a few doctors to see before he could return to work.

But that isn't the end of it. While recovering, Bubba remembered that Bobby had blessed him the night before the accident and Bubba convinced himself that it was Bobby's blessing that had saved his life. Maybe it had been, maybe not, but Bubba talked it up first at the bars where he used to hang out, then to whomever he met that talked about the accident and his miraculous recovery, then to half the Anaconda Aireheart Baptist Church as a true miracle. Then, when Bubba heard that Bobby had begun a small business offering blessings, he talked that up and every morning, early, before going off to work, Bubba came by for a blessing as Bobby had done before and dropped a dollar in the bucket.

Following Bubba were a lot of other people going off to semi-hazardous jobs who thought, "Well, ya' know, I don't know if it works or not... but for a dollar, what the hey..."

And so they began arriving before five A.M. to get their morning blessings. It was a good 50 to 100 every morning. Padyurwallet's local police began to wonder if they needed to put in traffic lights on Vine Street for that time, or maybe widen the street and put in a left turn lane mostly because they were in line, too. But people were orderly, polite, and happy to interleave their turns - mostly because they all knew or knew of each other. Remember, Padyurwallet was a small town. Bobby's service did not so much attract the attention of the folks in the outlying suburbia as they were far too sophisticated for something they deemed that backward and old fashioned.

Bobby's bucket kept filling and he kept emptying it. Dollars may not add up quickly, but the occasional fiver always helped.

Bubba's story became what passed for an urban legend in Padyurwallet. So did the story of two high flyers that came up to Bobby's window early one morning, ignored what he said, grabbed his bucket and dumped the contents in their car, threw the bucket out, and made to speed away. But when they went to turn right onto Vine, they did not look to the left and an 18-wheeler, one of the few ever seen on Vine Street, took off the entire front of their car. The entire engine compartment was dragged 50 feet down the street and they were fortunately left sitting in the middle of the road with people running from Bobby's drive-up to be sure they were all right. Bobby came out and performed the Thanksgiving Blessing for them. The driver was fine and his cab had only scratches despite demolishing the engine section of that car... and Bobby blessed him too 'cause he was shaking as to what could have been. The boys lost their driving privileges for a year, but used that time to do a bit of a turn-around and eventually joined the county sheriffs' force. Thus, another village legend was born.

A month or so later, after the morning rush, an old grey sedan pulled up and that old man threw a fiver in Bobby's bucket. He told him how the operations had been so successful that he was a new man, had a new girl friend, got a new job, went dancing three nights a week and could never thank him enough for the blessing. This time, Bobby was getting tearful. This was the purpose for all this, after all.

Chapter 3 - Life Goes On

Around lunchtime one day, Bobby's Mum came over to visit. She had not heard anything and he never called, so....

He apologised profusely, made her some tea and sat down to explain what he had been doing.

"You know, I hear about your business all the time. Sol Gold came through here one day and had not heard the morning blessing in so long he began to say one or two prayers a day. A miracle he calls it. I think it is something we mistakenly cut out of our lives in fear, but that is the way times were back then."

"It is going really well, even financially. I do somewhere near one to two thousand a week, one dollar at a time with the occasional fiver."

"Wow, Bobby, who woulda' thought?"

"Then I recorded the standard blessing for the radio station in Douglasville. They play it first thing every morning and pay me $50 every time it airs. Amazing. But I didn't even know or recognise Sol Gold, I wish he'd have stopped and talked."

"He said he would have but you had a drive full of people waiting. He said he'd come by some day to talk. I think he wants to see if you would meet his daughter when she comes home to visit, but don't tell him I told you so."

"That would be ok, I suppose. I've been hesitant to meet women because what do I tell them I do, bless people?"

"But you do - and you do well at it. People tell me they feel uplifted after they visit you. They indeed feel blessed. Isn't that what you want?"

"Yes, but..." And all of a sudden Bobby was having that ancient conflict of materialism try to stretch out to smother him. He'd almost forgotten his objective to be an

Avraham as well as he could - and he'd succeeded, but what next, was it enough for him... and what about someone else? Then, behind the someone else thought, was this hidden fear called family.

"Mum, I think there is something next. Yes, this is exactly what I wanted to do and it is unbelievable that I've been able to do it. But now that I have, is there something more I should tackle? I get a feeling that there is but I can't identify it."

"Slow down speed demon. Just like finding this avocation, it takes time and events and, if I recall correctly, it is said that we always are where we are supposed to be and do what we are supposed to be doing."

The bell rang and Bobby went to bless some new parents. He came back.

"Okay. I'll be patient. If you see Sol, ask him to stop by after the morning crush some time for a coffee, maybe. Would you like some lunch?"

"No, I have to get home to prepare for the bridge ladies. At least some things don't change."

It was kisses and hugs as they parted with Bobby asking his Mum to be more forward as he is sort of trapped by his business... and seems to be davening late all the time.

A few weeks later after the morning crush, Bobby was sitting in his space behind the window. He had moved a comfy chair in there as he seemed to have developed the habit of taking small naps after a round of blessings - they were actually tiring. So he was semi-sprawled out, his tallis covering part of his face when the bell that went off was his doorbell, not the sensor. So after looking outside, he straightened the tallis, closed the window, and went to the door, opened it, and there stood a man he recognised from blessing him in his car and a young woman so lovely he could not take his eyes off her.

"Bobby," the man said, sticking his hand out, "I'm Sol Gold. I came by your window a few weeks ago and I want to thank you for your blessing and tell you how it changed my life."

"Bobby?" queried Sol, seeing him staring at his daughter, "hello... I'm here...Bobby?"

"Sol, Sol," stammered Bobby, recovering, taking his hand, "I'm sorry I was a bit taken aback. Please excuse me, for a moment I thought I was blessed there..."

She blushed, Bobby blushed, Sol looked a bit pleased.

"Please come in, please," entreated Bobby, backing up and opening the way for them. "Please have a seat," as he showed them to the parlour. "May I get you anything to drink? A coffee? A tea? Soft Drink? Something stronger? Maybe a few biscuits with that?" And as Sol and his daughter indicated that a coffee and tea would be nice, Bobby went off to get them ready, saying, "please excuse me a minute while I arrange things. I'm so glad you stopped by."

Bobby first turned on the urn for hot water, then set up the coffee to brew, then distributed all sorts of biscuits / cookies on a plate and took the plate out while the waters were heating. Meanwhile, he was thoroughly infatuated with Sol's daughter...at least that was his assumption. He was now hoping that she was his daughter and not the young bride of an older guy.

Having retrieved the coffeepot, teapot, cups, saucers, milk, sugar, lemon, he returned to virtually decorate the coffee table, volunteering to be "mother"[14]. After all was settled, everything poured, cookies offered all around, Bobby sat down in expectation of an introduction for there had been none as yet. Okay, blessings over the

---

[14] "mother" in English Tea serving circles respectfully means the one that serves the others.

beverages were each person's responsibility, but after that Bobby looked expectantly at Sol. Sol stared back for a moment, twinkles in his eyes before he smiled and said, "Bobby, this is my daughter Rachel," gesturing toward his daughter, "she came by to visit me for a few days while she had a break between projects. I spoke to your mother and she thought it would be nice if you two met. Bobby, Rachel; Rachel, Bobby. Okay, can I leave now? Sol joked.

Rachel blushed, Bobby felt himself blushing as well... mostly because he was thinking, "yes, Sol, please?" But he wouldn't say it.

"No, Sol. My mum noted that you have celebrated a bit of a return to practices since you asked for a blessing. That is wonderful to hear for you but surely it is due more to your commitment than my mere words."

"Yes... and no. It was a tipping point I needed, as I'd not heard our morning blessings for years. We do not have a minion here so the few of us have davened individually and when you do that for so long, you begin to fall off as I had done. But I brought over my daughter so that maybe you might provide some attraction to get her to visit here more often, "chuckled Sol, smilingly.

"Sol, we haven't any kosher restaurants here, but if your daughter isn't keeping strict kosher, perhaps we can step out and get to know each other."

Upon which minor insult, Rachel spoke up, "Excuse me," frowningly," you could ask me, you know."

"Rachel, please do not take offense. I was trying to find a suitable segue out of your father's broad hint. Let me ask, then, is there a suitable place in town or the suburbia that you would find attractive for a dinner with me, please? I must confess to being far too solitary as the blessings business is one that asks for your attention at almost all times of day or night."

"Well, then, how are you going to leave it? How do you go shopping or do anything away from that window?" gently challenged Rachel.

Bobby shrivelled slightly inside. She was correct. It also occurred to him that he might smell a manoeuvre of his mother to get him to broaden himself, as he had been pretty much a prisoner of the business ever since he started it over three years ago. And within him the argument raged from one side, "but that is the nature of the business, you have to be there when you are needed" to the other, "you can be the occasional support for these people, but if they need more, have them come in for talks, but you need a life outside the business.... AND A FAMILY." And it finally twigged in Bobby that there was an aspect of the service he'd not explored!

"Thank you, Rachel!" he brightened and replied, "you helped me realise that there is a dimension to this business that I'd not really considered, one that will expand it and allow me to better control it. Wow. Thanks. Do you know of any good kosher restaurants in Atlanta, then?"

Rachel brightened considerably, smiling, "of course. In fact, let me make the arrangements. Can you pick me up at Daddy's at around seven this evening?"

"Absolutely," Bobby, brightening to this, perked up and smiled as well.

After Sol and Rachel had left, Bobby closed up shop for a while, went out, and had the car cleaned inside and out, something he'd not done for months. It was not a new car, but an older European one that worked brilliantly due to the conscientious work of Dougie the local mechanic. So, it cleaned up well but Bobby was wondering if he should have a new car... no, this one works fine and if Rachel needs new cars, she doesn't need Bobby. He even wore a sports coat with a bow tie in a pocket just in case.

When Rachel got in the car her first words were, "nice wheels, where did you get it?"

Bobby explained the vagaries of online auctions and how one finds cars as far away as New Jersey if they are looking for specific Marques, the transport, and how it is a toss-up as to what one gets unless it is through a Marque specific car club, usually. As he drove off and headed to the freeway, he asked where they were going.

"Do you know the Beth Agudah Synagogue?" she asked.

"Rabbi Blum's shul?" he replied.

She started, twitched, turned toward him, saying in a subdued but excited voice, "you know Rabbi Blum?" And she had a curious smile on her face.

"Yes, he has helped me turn to being at least sort of orthodox ever since I was given a trunk from my grandfather." And Bobby explained the trunk, its contents, and his journey to Orthodox Judaism, which also led to his blessings business. "So, how do you know him?"

Rachel smiled and related how she found him as she, too, was seeking to revisit and begin practicing as a Jew that her family had never done when she was a child.

And so the conversation progressed between minor directional suggestions from Rachel, but most of it on how they both discovered things that made the process of life deeper and more meaningful... knowing that such was going to be absolutely meaningless to so many others they knew; but that was an aspect of Judaism that was not so usually explored.

They arrived where they were going, went in, were seated, ordered, and talked all through it. The details of the meal, despite how good it was, were almost irrelevant as they explained to each other what they had been doing, what they do, what future it had, Bobby telling Rachel of the potential for a therapeutic practice that worked off the blessings business, Rachel telling Bobby of how she was looking to move back to Padyurwallet since her business was online and required few face-to-face interactions but occasional travel for projects, and both of them looking at each other at that point as what they might both want was coming to a conjoined idea that was amazingly shining in each others' minds. Bobby talked of how he had bought the lot next to him and had thought of enlarging the house to accommodate more bedrooms and an office. It was then when Rachel said that Rabbit Blum had mentioned this person he knew in Padyurwallet that she might like. Bobby asked if she had ever asked Blum about what they do at Beth Aguda about a chuppah and how that works. Her eyes filled with tears, so did his, she took his hand, he said "Please," she said "yes." And there they were, the two of them, tears streaming down their faces, holding hands, and smiling beamingly into each others' eyes... while the service personnel were standing a bit back, waiting for them to pay and leave as they were the only ones left in the restaurant and the bill had been delivered to their table an hour before but was ignored.

The Maitre D' came up to the table and asked, "would you kiss the bride, please? And, pay the bill so that we can go home?"

Now they both blushed, stood up, embraced, kissed, and Bobby finally gave them some plastic to pay, signed, and they took off hand-in-hand, kissing again before he opened the car door for her.

On the drive back to Padyurwallet, they talked about wedding plans - meaning that Rachel's father and Bobby's mother were going to plan everything so they might as well relax and learn to say "yes" as things just work like that.

After Bobby left Rachel at her father's house, promising to see her in a few hours, he returned home to a couple of stalwarts sitting in his drive, waiting. He went in, donned his tallis, opened the window, and asked how he might help. The answer was not what he expected. He invited them to park at the front and come in.

Bobby spent the next two hours decompressing a set of parents who had just lost one of their children to drugs. They needed not blessings but comforting and options on how to pull their heads out of the dismal misery that had come to surround them. Bobby let them talk, interjected a bit of direction here and there, let them cry, but mostly let them vent whatever guilt and self-accusations they sought to explain in a self-interested vanity to understand and try to find a way to exculpate themselves. Bobby tried to walk that thin line between guilt and a lustre-less way forward with soft spots of hope. At the end, they were too fatigued to offer anything reasonable or workable - so Bobby suggested they come back tomorrow after work. They asked how much Bobby charged for his counselling. He said $50 per hour. They promised to bring the money tomorrow. Bobby now had his new business line.

After a couple hours' sleep, Bobby got up to run his morning's rush hours of blessings. He then went back for a couple of hours of sleep, followed by conversations with contractors about estimates and plans for building additions onto his house: bedrooms, two offices, parlours, dining rooms, two levels, maybe a deck and patio? How many bedrooms? Hmmm.

Bobby's mother called a couple of hours later, so excited she was tripping over her words. She's just talked with Sol and they were planning on driving together to see Rabbi Blum and discuss the Chuppah and make arrangements for the wedding. Bobby thought for a moment... it was one of those thoughts one wonders if it is fantasy or prescience... no... Do you think so? Maybe. We'll see.

When Bobby's counselling couple came back, they still looked like wrung out towels that had been left in the spin cycle for days. They re-hashed their earlier conversation, but Bobby stopped them. He asked, "How long has it been since you two have had a vacation somewhere together, alone?"

They looked at each other; they could not be sure of the exact time, but years and years. He asked again, "Do you have the money to get away, just the two of you, to a warm place, a secluded place where you can be alone?" They nodded in assent. Bobby continued, "Doesn't this seem like a good time to be together, just the two of you, nothing else? I'm sure if your employers knew the circumstances they will understand and allow it... and if they are hesitant, I'll go and speak to them about it."

The couple thought for a moment, looked at each other, smiled wanly, got up, paid Bobby, said "Thank you, great idea. We'll see you when we return." And they left.

Bobby thought about the general flow of the blessings business. It was mostly in the mornings, but another, smaller chunk between four and seven, with a few random requests through the day and a small segment between two and three. That meant that he had a lot of space in the mornings and early afternoon for the counselling business. He dropped by the stationery store to find a detailed diary for his appointments, then over to Hugo to order another sign: "Bobby's Blessed Counselling, appointments available..." and his phone number. Then he ventured into the wasteland of the suburban shopping malls to find an electronics store and an answering machine. When he got home he looked at how he could best arrange his parlour for counselling sessions. He also gave some thought as to how he would keep records and what records he would keep. Okay, so he needs a filing cabinet and folders, and to design a patient intake sheet. Then, there was the added space needed for parking... maybe a few spaces near the street in the middle of the blessings window drive semi-circle. Then another sign that the parking is for counselling appointments only. Hmmm.... this is more complicated than he had thought. Then he called Rachel to set a time and place for dinner.

When he finally got to Sol's house, he was so relieved to see her it was as though 50 pounds of ugly detritus evaporated from his mental shoulders. He straightened himself up and if his smile had gotten any broader, it could not have made it through the doorway. They embraced and kissed for the longest time but they did not sense it was long at all.   Sol came over to shake Bobby's hand and say "Mazel Tov!"   He noted that he had been over to Bobby's Mum's house to begin to work on the arrangements. Then it hit Bobby that he had not phoned his brothers or sister as yet. OY! He recalled with chagrin that it must have been Sol that told his Mum, too. He obviously did not know how to bring his priorities into focus - but he had better learn how to do it or the lovely Rachel would surely remind him strongly. He did not want her to have to do that. The saving grace that popped into his mind is that Sol and his Mum had not worked out a date, yet, whew. He can always self-excuse as the addition of a date always begins to put things in motion.

As he opened the car's door for Rachel, he briefly noticed that she was carrying a small backpack tonight rather than the purse of last night. He thought no more about it.

As they drove in to Atlanta, Rachel talked of her father and his delight at working with Bobby's Mum on the wedding. She did not directly say anything to confirm Bobby's earlier bit of prescience, so he did not share it with her. He asked her about her work and moving it to a remote location. She had been doing things that day to progress the idea - all she needed was a workspace.

They began discussing the alterations to Bobby's house, number of bedrooms, offices, baths, how they would array across two floors, the addition of a basement for storage, and more and more details through the perfunctory dinner, once again. Then talking of what they might do to re-arrange things in the interim until the construction was done took up the time until, again, the manager had to ask them to attend to the bill that had been put there a hour earlier. Well, Bobby thought, at least we'll have the same reputation in all these places.

Bobby did not connect the dots on "rearranging things in the interim" until they were in the car driving home and it was a contest of paying attention to the road or Rachel. The next thing of which he was fully aware was that he and Rachel were horizontal in his bed at home, something he had not done with anyone for quite a while.

The next morning, conversation amidst the loving AFTER the morning rush hour turned to the idea as to how Rachel might move in with Bobby, thus scandalising the orthodox community - but in reality, the two of them were the only people close to an orthodox community in Padyurwallet, so......? There was not a surfeit of space in the house, but enough to add some of her clothes, another dresser, a flat workspace and chair, electric and phone access, and still be able to have a nook for counselling sessions that was perceptibly private. Okay, for now, Bobby thought... and later called the contractors to get a timeline on drawings and construction time estimates, while she drove to her father's house to get a few things.

Because Bobby had not yet torn down the house on the property next door, he went over to check the basement and called a structural engineer to test if the foundation was still usable for another or could be expanded. Fortunately, old construction was often more sturdy than the new stuff and the best idea would be to dig out whatever additional footprint was needed for a new addition to his house. That reminded him - it looks as though he has a basement, but Bobby has never seen it. There is no door to a basement stairway. There was no external opening like so many root and tornado shelter basements. How do you get in?

Remembering that Steve was a bootlegger, Bobby began looking at the floors in the house. There was the massive oriental rug that had always covered part of the floor where he stood by the window. Bobby lifted a corner of the rug, then began rolling part of it back and there were lines in the floor and what looked like a large trap door in the floor with a brass handle on one side of a fair sized hinged rectangle. Bobby pulled on the recessed handle and the door raised easily on large hinges, folding back to lean on a chair Bobby had there. Below the door Bobby could see stairs going down into a black pit... but by going down a couple of steps and feeling around the top of the apparent basement ceiling near the door, AHA!, an electric switch. He turned it on and the entire room lit up. Below him were about three rows of standing shelving units with more against the walls, mostly filled with bottles and sealed cases. The names on the boxes were Jim Beam, Jack Daniels, Old Forrester, Maker's Mark, Jamieson's, Johnny Walker, Crown Royal, Gilbey's Gin, and so on. Then, in another section, cases and cases of PBR, Budweiser, Miller's, Schlitz, Old Milwaukee, Lone Star, and so on. It was Steve's inventory before he was busted, never disturbed, kept dark and cool in the basement. No, there was no wine. Nor did Bobby see any filled mason jars - just as well as surely there is a chemical half-life to that stuff. Wow, though, what a discovery. What to do with it? Technically it came with the house, but knowing a bit of bootleggers and that culture, Bobby thought better of disposing of it.

That was a wise move, too. Because 10 years later when Steve got out early on good behaviour, he came back with a truck one day and asked for his inventory. Bobby was more than happy to even help him take it out to the U-Haul Steve had rented, Rachel and the children were watching in awe, none of them ever knowing all that was down there or even that there was anything down there.

Fortunately, the oriental was far too heavy for the children to lift it up and get to the trap door, so the imaginings of a great hiding place were quashed with that heavyweight rug.

So after Bobby had discovered all this, Rachel returned, stuffed the closet in the bedroom and made some decent progress on filling the modest dresser they had for now. Finishing that, she asked Bobby if he had any preferences for dinner and asked if the dishes and everything were tevilah'd. He noted that he had Rabbi Blum come out to kasher his kitchen after he'd had it cleaned and, yes, he'd taken all his pots, pans, dishes, utensils, glasses, etc. in to tevilah[15] every one of them. Bobby deferred to her as to the choice for dinner. He asked if she wanted help preparing it, but she said she'd take care of it for now and went off the store after checking the kitchen as to what she'd need.

Well, it is fairly predictable from here, isn't it? Aside from the typical "happy ever after nature of Bobby and Rachel, yes, Sol and Bobby's Mum also wed making it a foursome under the chuppah. Well, think about it, combining like that also provided some economies in the catering, no?

And while Rachel and Bobby only planned on three children, it seems that other influences helped them have five, proving that all the beds planned in the original addition were barely enough after all.

Bobby's blessing and counselling business went so well that he not only had the morning blessing shot on a Douglasville station, but he picked up one in Atlanta, too. From that he got attention from the governor's office and Bobby was appointed to deliver a blessing over the entire Georgia Legislature when it convened and that ceremony was repeated every year for the next 50 years, by which

---

[15] to purify all cookware and utensils, it is all run through a certified free moving stream or water source near a Mikveh before using it.

time Bobby was performing only celebratory blessings as he was not so young anymore and neither was Rachel.

But years before that time, seeing Bobby's success in that small town, many more Jews moved to the serenity of the old town of Padyurwallet and they opened three new, small shuls over time. One, the orthodox attended, one, the reform or conservatives attended, and one other that nobody attended. Such is the way of old jokes. But the shuls were never much larger or more ostentatious than the modest residences around them as competition to existing institutions they never wanted to be, not in small town Georgia.

And while it did not strike Bobby as mirroring the accomplishments of Avraham as there was no real stream of converts, there were many more that returned to observances when the minyans became available. In the ethereal but more beneficent current Canaan that was Padyurwallet, Bobby accomplished far more than he ever thought he would.

Mazel Tov.

He Knew He was Standing There[16]

This brief story of expert discombobulated in a setting closer to "Through the Looking Glass", excepting that the Red Queen takes on an entirely different personality. There is much to the metaphor that can be made from this story... but just enjoy the whimsy, perhaps.

---

[16] *"He knew he was standing there" was originally self-published as part of a series of novellas and stories in 2019, the other stories all being written prior to 2010 so this is the only recent output in that volume which is the reason for its addition to this "Opus Two: B".*

He knew he was standing there next to a street. He also knew he had to move... but how, when everything else was moving, too. He so hated to be like everything else. Past him hurtled images like a visual hurdy-gurdy, bright, colourful, almost neon they swirled past him, yet he stared and did not react as close as the cartoon, paper-mache, parade images swirled, twirled, and bounced around and around, turning, gyrating, pressing in, for they were just the distraction from the bright scroll that wove its way behind them, ever moving higher and lower flapping like a flag in a strong wind, as though the world were turning around him at the centre of it all.   And on the scroll were calculations, integrals, formulae, asking him for input. "Well, well, well," the scroll demanded, "what is the next input? What do I do next? Where am I going?" The scroll kept demanding as it flapped at him spewing a rainbow of colours here, there, and everywhere as a punctuation to equations without grammar, flapping like a loose shade over a window in high winds.

"Pi," he yelled in desperation because he could not come up with anything that made more sense. The scroll hissed, "Oh well, if we must we must..." And it erupted in a flash of self-generating formulae and danced like a drunken sailor rolling more formulae up, down, generating a reality integrated with which he was not.

Meanwhile, he began walking not aimlessly, but not with a purpose, either; wandering through what might be streets, by-ways, or paths that ran through lop-sided and leaning structures, talking to him, saying "where are you bound now that you've started it?" Also, "why did you have to do THAT?" And "Are you sure this is the way you want to go?"

None of it impacted him as he was elsewhere, distracted, disassociating from it all; immune to the rushing and visuals, the cartoon cars, the clowns in garish paint make-up, male clowns with bright orange hair, female clowns in black leather looking nasty, caricature animals in colours that were not their own walking alongside him. Red elephants and striped cows were not of the world he knew. And yet the scroll flapped on, humming Bach to itself, creating more and more calculations, formulae, while he suddenly ducked into one of the swirling shops to get away from the animals that were getting a little aggressive and shockingly chartreuse.

Funny that. When he stepped into the swirling shop, it stabilised and became an old-fashioned ice cream shop with a long counter and burgundy vinyl covered stools with a mirrored back bar with stacks of various sized glasses and serving bowls. Opposite that, against the facing wall was a row of burgundy seated banquette booths each with a jukebox control on the cream coloured Formica covered tables between the vinyl pillowed bench seats. On the mirrored wall behind the counter were large menus featuring short order snack foods, sodas, sundaes, ice cream cones, and coke floats and a pretty blond with a ponytail behind the counter asking him what she could get for him. He was tempted to ask what the horse was doing with a bobbed tail, but just mutely shook his head, glancing back over his shoulder to see if the animal parade had followed him. But no, it was he and the girl and no one else in the shop.... even the scroll was still outside.

"Well," she said, "if you don't want anything why did you come in here?"

Gesturing toward the street scene behind him he asked, "Don't the chartreuse animals out there seem a bit strange to you?"

"You're new here aren't you," she queried. "It is after 3 o'clock and they always turn chartreuse every day until 5. I don't know why. I think it is something the local Council demanded before I came here."

That stopped him and he stared at her silently, thinking. What am I doing? Why did I stop? What on earth is she talking about? Shouldn't I get back to doing what I was doing or I'll never be done? And with that he turned slightly and nodded to the girl with the pony's tail and left the shop, feeling it beginning to swirl behind him as he did. But as all that was just slightly abnormal, seeing the chartreuse goats and waving stores across a strect that was filled with a herd of tap-dancing pink buffalos singing "Back in the Saddle Again" and sounding a lot like Willie Nelson caused him to wonder what he was doing. Pink?

He began looking for his colleagues, spying them hanging out of every door on an open tram half a block ahead of him, waving and yelling at him to get on as the numbers hadn't finished and his was about up. They did not like his choice of Pi and had a meeting to decide that "Big G", the gravitational constant, would have been much better. He reminded them that they were lucky he hadn't chosen "c", one of the options he had when confronted by the scroll, could they have found their way home if he'd thrust them all into a relative quandary? That shut them up... except for the newly minted MBA who always had to have the last word - but it was not a word the group wanted to hear. So, they beat him senseless with their flashing striped slide rules.

He noticed they were going around the same set of city blocks time after time, wondering if they were on a hiding to nowhere, but if he got off he'd have to confront the scroll once again as it was having a difficult time generating many more formulae and needed a new boost. Clambering off the trolley, as was necessary because it wasn't slowing down for anything, even the corners, he was slapped in the face by the scroll demanding a new variable.

"Big G," he yelled, as the scroll released a double surge of colour snaps and hissed in pastel overtones. But the equations and permutations wrote on as the scroll flapped merrily along, singing a Bach-time tune.

Walking along the block of wavering and slithery buildings, he then came upon a surprise - a tall, willowy, woman with iridescent maroon hair dressed in a long slit-up-the-side shimmering dress standing by what generally looked like a car. And as he drew closer to her, she asked him in a very gentle voice, "Don't you live in the Tower?"

His head snapped up and to attention. Suddenly, he had a reference point he had mislaid.

"YES!", he almost yelled. "The Tower!"

Then he recovered and raised an eyebrow to her [because he wasn't wearing a hat] and asked suspiciously, "Why?"

"Oh," she replied offhandedly. "I've seen you in the lobby and I'm driving back there out of the colour parade and wondered if you were done playing with the scroll and would like a ride, that's all."

Shocked was he, as he was not aware that all he was doing was scroll playing... he thought it was real when if he thought about it, this rainbow stuff was all just imagination, mental illusions, and fancy dress-up animals. Pink buffaloes, indeed! How silly. Time to get back to being a grown up.

"Sure, that is very kind of you"

"Not an issue as all this stuff is pretty silly and one gets fed up with the semi-acid trip delusions pretty quickly if you don't take them seriously. It is the chartreuse horses with the bobbed tails that gives it all away. Hop in."

So he went to the passenger side of what now looked like a Byzantine Blue Shelby Cobra convertible, roll bars, pulsating white racing stripes, and flashing sapphire blue Reccaro bucket seats that were murmuring "sit on me, sit on me, please" in a voice not so different from Julie London on full seduction. Unnerving as it was, the seats stopped speaking, mostly, when he sat down, but began to purr like an imaginary lion, adding a most disconcerting vibration to the seat.

She hopped in the other side, straightened her dress, inserted the key, pressed the starter and what he heard was that fully throated 8-cylinder Cobra roar. It wasn't the alto Japanese motorcycle hysteria of a 12 cylinder Ferrari whose very personal parts have been grabbed by surprise, nor the quiet dignified burble of the V8 Daimler, but more like an SP 250 Dart on hormone treatments with a healthy dollop of baritone on top.

She drove like a demon; accelerating so fast his head was visibly jerked back, reeling around a couple of corners whose wild colours reached out to ensnare them but missed, driving then straight and accelerating. All around them a pastel mist whirled and churned with no other visible traffic or lights or stop signs until they broke out of the colour fog and far more slowly proceeded into a grey smoke, a dimly more bright, but clear, perceptible, 90 degree world where buildings sat as they should and the road was visible as drab concrete. Concurrently, the Cobra became a Morris 1000 with a sewing machine engine, vinyl half-bench seats, a Bakelite steering wheel and fascia, and no more vibration except the uncomfortable bump of a highway of potholes and breaks in the pavement challenging woefully small tyres. Afraid of what else had changed, he glanced over to his driver and found a not-so-different and demure willowy woman but the iridescent maroon hair had given way to long tresses just on the red side of strawberry blonde with no appreciable other change to her appearance. Oh, except that she now drove a Morris like a Morris, not like a Cobra. Those fantasy segments of culture do have their narcissistic dimensions, but when you get back to reality... Sigh...

She sighed, too. "As deceptive as those fantasy dimensions are, they do provide a more pleasant break from reality when you can create what appears to be to be what you want, you know", she pined. "One almost desires to make the unreality the environment in which one lives, but nothing can be done there, just enjoying the delusions. Eventually, one has to face the reality of making a living and the real world as much as one might wish it different..." He was surprisingly jolted to a pleasant view of this newfound intelligence, not being used to rational and realistic ideas being bandied about publicly. For the first time in a while, he wanted to know more of this woman, as there are so many nice enough, but who are not just drab for humility's sake, but actually drab to the bone, a studied ennui, as he had once found Cleveland. Nice place, nice people, but one of their vaccines upon birth had to be an advanced strain of tedium. He looked back for a moment, remembering the girl from Cuyahoga Falls he might have married. Oh, well, would she have put up with his travel and career wanderlust? Never to know, some of these things.

Even at the Morris's slow pace on city streets, he soon saw the Tower approaching in the distance. An impressive structure, rising from deeply buried safety rooms far beneath the ground to a height well above the ordinary level of "smouds", the smog and clouds that generally covered the city for miles. In fact it was a good 50 mile drive out of the city before you broke out of the "smouds" and could see real sunlight, unfiltered by the pollution and particulate smut that passed for unfiltered air in the city. The other option is to live where he did, above the level of the "smouds", where there was often this iridescent shimmer dancing in the breeze across the tops of the "smouds", particularly in the morning where the dew sitting on the "smouds" seemed to give a sparkling sheen to their tops, like sheets of living chemical prisms.   But the best part up where he lived was the unfiltered sunlight, giving life to the plants, him, and the space where he tried to live.

Before he knew what he was doing he was asking this woman what she was doing after they got back to the Tower.

She smiled modestly. That was a good sign, he thought. But he didn't know why she smiled.

"Okay, maybe we could get to know each other better," she conceded through an amused visage. "What if we meet in the Lounge at the top in an hour or so after we get to the Tower?"

As it was late afternoon, this would mean a segue to an evening in conversation, he thought. "Yes, please," and he smiled, too, imagining the change in ambient light from the setting sun, always brilliant from the Lounge, and the gently increasing glow of muted ground lights through the "smouds". Two large potholes brought him back to reality from his reverie as he almost hit the roof of the Morris with his head. She pulled into the parking garage entrance and continued down to her space, one strangely close to his old estate wagon. His was the old car that alternatively spent time parked here or at the airport when he was travelling for work or on the road with him as he refused to fly for clients less than 12 hours drive away - he hated the airport oppression that much. Odd, he thought, perhaps she saw him down here on a chance passing rather than in the lobby as he rarely went through it except to get his mail. No matter he thought as they exited the mini Morris and walked to the elevator where she asked that he push the button for a floor a couple above his. They rode up in respectful silence excepting that as he exited the elevator at his floor he nodded at her, saying that he'd see her in an hour or so up stairs. She just nodded and smiled demurely, again. So, very Mona Lisa he thought.

  He was an old fashioned kind of guy. He disliked the totalitarian electronics that seemed to control so many people's lives with their faces constantly buried in it or attuned to it with ear buds that shut out the real world. His small mobile phone sufficed even though it had none of the walking computer controls of those large lummox electronics people allowed to control their lives. It was a mobile telephone, period. So when he returned to his flat he checked his answering machine, a device many thought Neanderthal - but one that controlled more those who wanted to speak with him rather than control him by their whim. That meant that he was one of the few who still had a fixed line and a real telephone, one step evolved from the old rotary dial machines. As a luxury, he had second lines put in to the kitchen and bedroom so that if he wanted to answer he didn't have to run like a madman for the study.

  Occasionally his visiting younger colleagues would pick up the phone just to hear the dial tone, something utterly foreign to them. Even more rarely, they might ask what one does with a phone that has a tone. Sigh... the utter degradation of cultural awareness propagated by the indoctrination education programs of The State. For shock value at these combined business/social gatherings, he sometimes would put on a CD of three or four old western movies that ran one after the other and let it run on the monitor in the study. The sound track of gunshots and horses galloping, if nothing else, usually attracted people into the study to watch something they'd never seen before. Sigh... never knowing the western holiness of Randolph Scott. Then, he'd flip it over to "Blazing Saddles" to really trigger them! The naiveté of those under 30. If he continued on this habitual rant, he'd never get ready and changed. So, NOW, shower, dress with the uniform, and listen to messages or check e-mails before going upstairs.

He was gazing out the western windows at the sunset, watching the golds and pinks play over the tops of the chemical clouds, glinting greens, azures, and yellows performing a dance with wisps of artificially coloured bits of condensing moisture rising in twisting tendrils, only to fall back into the churning plane. And out of the corner of his eye, he saw her exit the elevator hallway... and so did every other male set of eyes in the Lounge. He observed and thought of offering a cocktail napkin to the few that were visibly drooling but that might be a bit rude. He was not sure what she had done between the parking level elevator and arriving up here, but the willowy strawberry blonde must have either swallowed male magnets or was wearing a long slinky, slit, gown that had them implanted in the seams.

He walked over smiling a bit obviously, took her arm, thanked her for coming up here, and asked where she preferred to sit. Her choice was on the opposite side so that the setting sun would not get in their eyes. As they walked over to find a banquette on the east side of the lounge, the feeling of eyes following them was palpable. He wasn't really used to this as he did not like to be the centre of attention; it was his business to place his clients in the spotlight, not himself. But this was unavoidable. She chose one of those semi-circular, high-backed banquettes facing the eastern side, but still getting the reflection of the sunset through the windows.

As she scooted in from one side, he did the same on the other side and they were almost right next to each other when the hostess came over to take their drinks order. That done, he finally could wait no longer and blurted out, "you know, you were a highly attractive woman this afternoon when you gave me a ride back to The Tower. However, I have to declare or ask or something else similarly tongue-tying as to what on earth you did between then and now as you are now the apparently perfect embodiment of every quality males seek in women. And it isn't just me. You had this mesmerising effect on every male in the lounge when you walked in. I'm sorry, I don't mean to put you on the spot or embarrass you, but you seem to have the beauty, poise, awareness, and magnetism that attracts the attention of every man around here. I'm thoroughly impressed and somewhat flabbergasted as I feel uncomfortably drab even in the same room with you."

She was gazing out the window as he was talking, but now turned toward him and, placing her hand lightly on his arm, said "thank you. I confess that I did do a bit of a special clean up for you but I didn't think it that over the top. I'm really a very plain girl and do not seek that kind of attention, but I appreciate the compliments. I've had to learn over the years how to make myself look a bit more special in order to do my work as it often requires me to be a bit of a stand-out sometimes, but that sometimes gets me more attention than I expect."

"By the way," she continued, looking directly at him, "what do you do?"

"Oh, I manage consulting and intermediation projects for my clients, basically telling them what to do, mostly in IT and strategic business processes." He sighs. "It means I'm almost always on the road and live in airports, hotels, and on client premises. It is so bad that I had to get a service to come in and tend to my plants so that they wouldn't die while I was gone. People say how wonderful it would be to travel for business, but only because they haven't had to do it day after day, year after year for far longer than is fun anymore. The only real positive is that I do not get bored. I can live with that. What about you," he said looking up at her, wondering sincerely what a knock-out like her would do outside of modelling and the vanity theatre?

The sun chose that precise moment to reflect off the glass and into her eyes, showing a bright sparkle, vibrant green eyes, and a moistness that looked like a tear.

"Funny," she said, "my work is not so different as I travel for my clients too, only I'm more in PR, propaganda, and direct politics, getting people to do what my clients need."

"Hold on," he said suddenly, straightening up, "you graciously gave me a ride, we've been talking and I never asked you your name. I'm sorry, you must think me a complete dolt."

She looked at him soothingly, moved almost imperceptibly closer, and purred, "I think it would have come up at sometime or another, don't you," the last query said looking closely and directly into his eyes which were about the size of saucers by this time. "You can call me Lily, I think." As he felt himself melting into a small puddle on the seat.

There was this uneasy pause, like waiting for a conclusion that was not realised, during which they both edged closer to each other.

"So, Lily," he murmured, "tell me more of your work, what works, what frustrates, what infuriates, what you hate, what you like, how you got into it, why you do it, what makes it you..."

And she moved back a bit, so that she could use her hands because she had been awaiting someone to sincerely ask that kind of question for what seemed like a millennium or two or more... the dam burst and she talked...

You see, having her job, it was always she seductively pulling information from the dupes and targets, getting them to trust her, to talk to her, to reveal things they should not tell anyone, giving her insight as to how they thought and reasoned - all information that would be used against them or their colleagues by her bosses or their employers. But now it was her turn for a change that had not been so since she was so, so much, much younger. So she talked.

She talked of countries, ranks, positions, people without names, Regents, petty officials by title, circumstances, history, and geo-politics of which few were aware. She unloaded. He listened. He asked occasional questions, some of which she could answer, some she could not, some of which she would not, so she launched into another set of incidents and stories of wars, crimes, escapades, adventures, and the clear paucity of integrity of every known government on the face of the earth. She spoke of her opinions, how nobody cared about them, and how the world she knew was steeped in corruption so vile that it hurt her just to be near it... she said.

He nodded, empathised, supported, understood slightly because corporate politics were almost the same; but she was working on a global level he did not fully understand, but he listened and was not appalled, shocked, or afraid of what he heard - as some of it was at a level that left him amazed that she was involved with such malevolence and yet looked so materially unaffected by it all. And the more he listened, the more she talked, sometimes softly, sometimes emotionless, sometimes ruefully. Then, interrupting all this, the hostess came by, placing a small tray with the tab on it near him, saying, "it is almost closing time up here. I can get you another round if you like, but it is time to settle and leave, I'm afraid."

He looked at his watch and it was almost midnight - five hours had virtually evaporated and he had not noticed. He looked at her but before he could ask if she wanted any more she gave a small shake of her head. He put some plastic on the tray and she continued where she was, but wrapping it up, saying, "have I really been talking that long? I'm sorry," touching his hand, "I just prattled on and on and you were kind enough to let me."

"But are you hungry?" he blurted, feeling as though he'd forgotten his responsibility, "I know we could find a place for a dinner of sorts...."

"No, no, that's fine - and I'm fine, thank you. I think it is best to retire now, shall we?"

Ignoring the invitation he retrieved the plastic from the tray, edged his way out of the booth, moved the table so it was easier for her, and took her hand as they sauntered to the elevator lobby where he pushed the button for an elevator.

On their way down to her floor she looked at him and offered, "I have to leave tomorrow for a week or so, but I'd like to see you again so why don't you come by for a moment and get a card so that we can coordinate when we are both back here?"

They walked hand-in-hand to her door and after she unlocked it she took his hand and led him in - but he stopped in the foyer as she began to turn on lights and went to get a card. He was a bit overawed as the entire decor was mostly warm reds and gold and mahogany, with different shades on the walls, carpets, and upholstered furniture. This contrasted significantly with his simple wood, plants, forest green, and a bit of chrome decor, but it fit her it did, he sensed.

When she returned she handed him the card and moved close enough where a kiss and embrace and the promise of more were achingly within a mere leaning... but...

"I think we'll wait, if you don't mind, as I can sense that we'd find a kiss thoroughly insufficient once we began it," he said with more self-control than he thought he actually possessed, far more than he thought he possessed to the extent that he thought he was moving like an automaton, not controlling his behaviour. Simultaneously, he thought this unbelievably strange, as he had never before walked away from such a visible, warm, and inviting entre; and had never before been so close to a woman so beautiful and desirable that parts of him virtually ached just watching her.

The disappointment in her eyes was momentarily visible, but she backed off demurely and purred, "yes, perhaps next time we can have dinner - maybe you can let me prepare our dinner when we both have a bit more time?"

The thought of that melted parts of him he had not had melted in a long, long time. And all he could stammeringly say was, "please, that would be lovely and I can't say that I've ever looked forward to anything so much as that. Thank you."

And with that he found the door lever behind him, opening it, and backed out of her doorway, saying, "thank you. I loved listening and I'm looking forward to your dinner more than you can imagine. Have a successful and safe trip, please." And he shut the door quietly, not finding any trouble in remembering the vision of beauty he was leaving behind as he strolled almost drunkenly toward the elevators.

In the elevator, he finally looked at her card. Aside from the phone and e-mail contact details and a euphemistic position title, there was her full name: Lilith haRishon.

Bertrand Meets Venus

There is little to say about this very brief story, perhaps mirroring the short life span of the protagonists. Surely there was a line from Larry's father than inspired it all, if you remember.

However, one thing the author has never forgotten was being asked, decades ago, "how is a fly like a tree?"

Well?

Bertrand was just cruising around the forest in sunny North Carolina, taking in the myriad of scrumptious smells that came to him and excited his imagination when he saw these fabulously beautiful plants covering the ground, they sported a red pillow that he was compelled to explore. But Elmer was right next to him.

"Bertie, don't go there," Elmer quipped, seeing his eyes going in that direction.

"What do you mean?"

"Let's rest for a minute over here and I'll tell you and you can watch," cautioned Elmer.

As they sat in the sun and preened their wings, Elmer directed Bertie, "Just watch them, those red things, for a while, as difficult as that is for us, eh?" Elmer was referring to the basic lack of visual acuity that results from the form of their eyes - but since that was a general issue that bugged everyone like them, it was no worse than being like a giant with later stage diabetes.

It was difficult to keep Bertie from going off because Bertie did not have the attention span of a Drosophila Melanogaster even though they had about the same number of functioning neurons. It was a function of his poor upbringing in a garbage scow of a place. Elmer and his siblings had the advantage of a dead carcass in his pre-transforming youth. As Elmer thought, once again, it proves that it is nurture, not nature, eh? Simultaneously, Elmer wondered what that meant because 100,000 neurons does not get you a lot of computing power.

"HEY! HEY!" yelled Bertie, "I just saw an ant crawl up on one of those red pads."

"Yeah," drawled Elmer, "you jes continue to watch and see what happens, y' heah? Don't move!"

Bertie was grumbling. Every unconditioned reflex in him was pulling him to those red pads. He just mulled over in his minuscule mind, what there was of it, what Elmer had said, "don't move, don't move, don't move, don't move, don't move, don't move, don't move, don't move, don't move, don't move, don't move." And within a minute, though to be fair, Bertie did not have a watch to tell the time. Which is probably best because in his stage of phylogenetic development, being able to tell the time would probably be depressing, besides the fact that he can't count and wouldn't know a number from a discarded bit of pasta... except that he likes the pasta, especially if there is sauce on it. See, absolutely no focus in that pitiful excuse for a brain, reminding one of some people from particular parts of the US, Canada, or Ireland, or Eastern England, Nord Pas De Calais, or European governments, for that matter.

So, Bertie watched and all of a sudden that splotch of red he was watching when the ant crawled on it was gone! He couldn't understand. It just disappeared... which is what you might expect of the thought processes of 100,000 neurons, eh? Bertie got real excited and told Elmer what he had seen and now what he doesn't see.

Elmer just eased on back, preened his antennae for a minute, and said, "didn't I tell you to watch it?"

"Yes," blurted Bertie excitedly, "but what happened?"

"Is there a green area or leaf near where you saw the red pillows?"

"Well, yeah."

"Can we land on them and NOT, I repeat, NOT touch anything red?"

"Of course. There are what look like leaves next to where the red pillows were."

"Okay, you lead and I'll come along and explain what happened."

So, Bertie went down and stood on one of the leaves next to what used to be red pillows and Elmer joined him.

"Bertie, See those two big semi-circular leaves with spikes all around the edge?"

"Yup, sure do."

"Can you see anything between them, behind the spikes?"

"Well, it looks like there is something between them, struggling, fighting..... ARRGGGHH," screamed Bertram, grabbing at his antennae in fright, "it is the ant! It is trapped! It is..." and before Bertie could finish, one of his cousins, Boomer, came down by them but lit upon a set of the red cushions!

"Boomer, get off there, NOW, immediately," yelled Bertie, "you can't stay there, it will...." but Boomer had moved and the hinges on the leaves snapped shut and Boomer was caught between the leaves of that other trap.

"Elmer," pleaded Bertie, "what can we do now? How can we help Boomer"

"Say your last respects, Bertie; for within a little while Boomer will be with us no longer. We have not yet found a way to save anyone trapped by those deadly red leaves."

Not giving up, Bertie climbed up on the leaves that enclosed Boomer and began jumping up and down.

Elmer tried to reason with him, "Bertie, that isn't going to do any good - once the leaves have him they start dissolving him. Even if you got him out it would only be part of him. Remember that scary story your parents told you about the Monkey's Paw?"

"What are you on about, Elmer? We can't read, remember?"

"Oh yeah, ahead of my Darwin again," murmured Elmer in self-reproach. "But after a few days, those leaves open back up and all you see is some detritus that blows off the pillows with the breeze. Everything else is gone, digested, eaten by those deadly plants. At least they don't talk and say 'Feed Me'."

"Whaaaaaa??" whined Bertie.

"Sorry, I spent a few weeks visiting an art house theatre bin some months ago. What those giants think is entertainment is beyond reckoning."

"Well, that's it," declared Bertie, "I'm going back home to warn and educate my cousins about this danger out here."

"Are you sure they will listen and learn? Remember we are not the swiftest of fauna, no matter how fast our reaction times compared to those giants."

"Well, if I don't, who is? It won't be you since you are not even of our tribe and do I see you going back to educate your relatives?"

"No," stated Elmer flatly, "because we already know of this danger - we get that training even before our wings even come out. That is the difference between our species - not enough but enough to survive better... crap, that sounds like more Darwin. I wish I knew what a Darwin was and if it was correct."

"Well, while I have this in my mind, I'm going back to my garbage scow and tell as many as I can about this danger. I wonder if we can embed it in our pre-flight training? What am I saying? We have no pre-flight training... it is all fly for your life and the devil take the hindmost parts! Sheesh!"

And with that Bertram flew back to the garbage scow and began to lecture anyone that would listen to him about the dangers of the red pillow plants. He didn't stop. He found part of an old white board and used a discarded mascara pencil to draw on it so that his peers and the youngsters just finishing their coming out party would recognise the danger. He threw himself into this saviour gig night and day, to the point where the female peers wondered if he'd lost his sense of perspective. After all, the game was to breed like flies, so to speak, to provide the proper level of decomposition in the world, remembering that ecological renewal depended on carrion eaters like he and his relatives. They came and lectured Bertram on how trees are like flies.

This gave Bertie an even more exalted reason for keeping his tribe away from the deadly plants out there. If they were to be a cohort of the trees, well, there should be enough of them to provide the decomposition effects of the lofty tribe of flies. But in following that line of thinking, Bertie got confused and was eventually seduced by the females to help the tribe proliferate. And, like all males subject to that drive, he soon lost whatever else was on his small mind. Some things don't change.

Elmer, on the other hand, already knew to stay away from those plants. He went to the Research Triangle Science Park, planted himself on the window outside a lab, and stuck out his tongue at the fruit flies in the genetics labs. He then went on a long trip down towards Okefenokee Swamp, down Georgia way 'cause he heard the feed chickens just hung out there. And true it was. There were bins of feed chickens just sitting out. Elmer picked a fat one and just flew right in, letting his nose guide him. After a while he found he was being jostled and bounced, but then it settled down after it seemed like the chicken was being crushed. Elmer never knew that he was just an additional bit of protein fed to Allison Alligator by the park caretakers that day. She wasn't aware of it either.

Come Fly with Me...

Now the author was having a terrible time, it seems, and you will see this where I had to step in and ask for a correction as the story progresses. He woke up and made it right. Thank you for your kind tolerance of an author's bad day. You're wondering..."whaa...??", but keep reading, and you'll see. Thank you. Ed.

Out amidst the great galloping wheat fields of
Nebraska and the other plains states there were special,
small, VFR (Visual Flight Rules) landing strips and airports
with large white arrows embedded in the ground before and
after them. These directional arrows continued at specified
distances, pointing the way for the first airmail planes to
traverse the US, delivering post to the west coast and "flyover" country in between in all those years before
politicians were so blatantly arrogant about creating
divisions in this broad land. Many of these arrows and
small landing strips persist. But many were ploughed over
or incorporated as part of towns growing bigger and
needing the land for houses and commerce. But a few of
those strips survived.

Out in Flyover, Nebraska, a very small rural
community in the middle third of the state, there is a 500
foot tall steel aircraft directional antenna with a revolving
red light at the top, a light that can be seen for a good 20
miles or more on a clear night. It is accompanied by an
even brighter revolving white light on foggy nights.
Similar stationary lights, red and white, are posted along
the superstructure of the tower every 100 feet in line with
FAA regulations.

The structure was built as part of the WPA (Works
Progress Administration) in 1936 and in order to defray
political complaints about costs at the time, the primary
supplier of the airstrip's aviation fuel funded a great part of
the cost IN EXCHANGE for a gigantic, lit, company logo
on the east and west sides of the tower. The Standard Oil
Company furnished the 60 foot tall lit logo that was placed
above the split base of the tower. You see, the tower itself
was a virtual duplicate of the Eiffel Tower in its wide
stance base and narrowing superstructure to the aircraft
beacon at the top. This one is almost half the height of the
original Paris, France tower, which is over 900 feet tall.

The fascinating thing about the tower and the strip is that the tower straddled the lone airstrip - and it was a single direction because it wasn't just prevailing winds that only went west to east in Flyover, they were the only winds. You see, the overall geographic topology put the Flyover airstrip in a slight trough between a couple of rolling hills, probably the only ones in Nebraska, funnelling the winds easterly and any odd North or Southerly winds generally went over the top of the hills. This made it interesting for planes taking off as they had to be careful of being thrown south almost immediately after they took off and climbed 100+ feet IF the North winds were running strongly across the top of the hills. For many, that phenomenon made "Flyover" a real experience with high winds. However, to help pilots, the small terminal office had an anemometer set up on the hills North and South of the field to enable them to prepare for needed wind sheer counter-manoeuvres. There had been talk of adding a 00/180 or 30/330 runway at the west end of the current 90/270, but there was never enough interest from the pilots or any air companies for that.

One of the other 1930's features of the airport was the hot-dog bush pilots literally flying through the wide opening in the bottom of the tower. Under the broad base of the tower, there was more than enough space to fit the width of a B-29 actually, but just the thought of it gave the non-pilot locals 'palpitations', or so they used to say. The vertical clearance was enough, generous, but some pilots liked to give their passengers a bit of an underwear-dirtying thrill by coming in high and making a low swoop. Because it was a VFR field at the time, there were more than a few underwear-dirtying incidents with pilots intending to take off while cowboy bush pilots were showing off going eastward. Remember, if you are not familiar with aircraft routines, the general direction for landings and take-offs at that field was westward. The only thing that saved some was that the tower base was square, like the Eiffel Tower, and the centre of it at the base was hollow, cross struts and superstructure supports began at least 50 feet above the cross members tying the support beams from one side to the other. Whew! Needless to say, the local dry cleaner and laundry business had far more trade than expected for the size of the town around it. They found it profitable to specialise in a dry cleaning or laundry while you wait special service.

Some years later, the airfield added radio support in order to eliminate the risks that were driving insurance rates over the local ceiling.

Flyover, as a viable town, developed as the airstrip was built, roads improved leading to it, and support services like the fuel businesses, lodging, and food and beverage services began expanding with cross-country mail and passenger services. By the time of the late 30's, cross country passenger services no longer had to stop at this field for a break and fuel services... but the signage and tourist nature of the tower drew people, and not just local pilots. Because it was a place of natural calm and peacefulness, as it drew weekend visitors out of Omaha, it began building point of interest services, more than farm tours, petting zoos, 30-minute tourist flights, but also a theatre, more restaurants, more lodgings, and motels. Then, a spur from Highway 30 to ensure easy freight traffic was built, as the runway was long enough to handle medium freight traffic in and out, though it would have to be made IFR to accommodate real traffic. The locals did not want to become another industrial hub and North Platte didn't want any competition. That reluctance to grow the next step doomed Flyover to a long slide into a not very graceful but languorous decline.

The years wore on, WWII came and went, along with the subsequent times, wars, social change, and the area was still predominantly rural agriculture with North Platte as the nearest industrial and commercial hub. Standard maintained its sign, the tower was maintained as an historic relic by the state, though much of the air traffic had disappeared except for crop dusters, the odd flight service and instructor, and a few farmers that wanted to learn to fly and put runways on their properties. The runway was minimally maintained and most of the hospitality industry businesses had long ago closed up shop, usually back when WWII took a lot of the workers and rationing set in. What hospitality there was at the airport terminal was maintained by Maggie who had inherited the property, the strip, the town, and the tower from her grandfather a few years ago. She spent considerable time and efforts rejuvenating the strip to its current functional level. She still offered homemade sandwiches and soup for the occasional pilot and guests and beers for the crop dusters that had finished for the day. She manned the radio when needed, coordinated the fuel deliveries, booked lessons for the instructors that kept their planes in the hangers, arranged for tourist and exploratory rides for visitors and developers, arranged for maintenance on the tower lights when needed, instigated inspections of the tower and repairs for structural integrity, informed Standard if their signage had difficulties, kept the commissary supplied and fresh, cleaned the terminal, used the street sweeper on the runway when necessary, occasionally painted the runway designations, plowed the runway in the winter when it snowed, maintained the lighting on the strip, and handled the persistent complaints from people who were bothered by the high output of light from the Standard sign. It was often visible on clear nights from highway 30... as that had been the original idea. Quite often she contemplated cursing her grandfather, wondering if this was going to be the rest of her life.

The streets around the airport were still maintained by the county, though not a proper excuse for streets they often were unless Maggie kept calling and complaining every day for at least a week. The housing that was built to shelter the local workers was mostly used by farm workers and itinerant migrants these days, following the crop cycles. The film theatre and petting zoos were long gone, though the old Art Deco Theatre still stood with paint flaking off everything and winter after winter exposing the brick and wood construction outside while the inside was relatively intact, being closed and virtually sealed for decades with both the water and heat shut off.

All-in-all. Flyover was in various stages of urban or airfield denouement, one might say. Then one spring afternoon, Raymond, piloting a twin Beechcraft, flew in... and nothing was the same after that.

Raymond was not intending on doing anything but capturing a glimpse of this historic airfield, refilling his plane, and returning to his jaunt across the US, following his own version of Route 66, the real one being far south of him at this point. He taxied up to the terminal and killed the engines to ask where he might find the AVGAS. Having heard him land, Maggie came out to help as he was climbing out... mostly as they hadn't had a twin in there for yonks.

Now Maggie was a slender but not a thin woman of her late 20's, blue eyes and sagebrush colour hair that ran to uncontrolled curls but she was only about 5'6", evenly constructed, and fair, but never striking enough to be a cheerleader or beauty queen in her earlier years. Her dreams of Sky King coming in and rescuing her from her advancing boredom began to fade five or six years ago and she was entertaining herself lately with online feeds of movies as Flyover didn't have much but it did have excellent internet fibre connections for some strange reason. In fact, because all the local farmers made more money playing the futures market than growing and harvesting their crops, they had demanded high speed big pipe service years ago from the local phone company or threatened to go satellite, creating their own download company and service. The phone company complied, laying miles of very high-speed fibre cables to serve central Nebraska. Thus, streaming services to Flyover are better than those in most major US cities. It may come to pass that this is an important dimension as things develop.

Though he was flying a twin beech rather than a Cessna, Raymond still didn't look like ruggedly handsome Kirby Grant. In fact, he was not that tall, 5"8", and not as lean as he wanted to be, but life on the trading floors and in offices had softened him. But just as Flyover was not prepared for Raymond, he wasn't prepared for Maggie, either.

Raymond jumped down to the tarmac in front of Maggie coming around the wingtip to greet him. He looked up and into her eyes and she into his and they just stared for what felt like minutes until they both blushed and apologised simultaneously for staring. Then they apologised, giggled slightly, and introduced themselves. Maggie asked if she could help Raymond with anything. He was going to say "AVGAS", but changed it to "Where am I, anyway, please?"

Maggie began to explain Flyover to Raymond, but after a few minutes of standing in the warm sun, she invited him in to the terminal cafe for something cool to drink and to sit down.

Maggie got them both soft drinks and they sat at one of the Formica covered 1950's vintage tables, the kind with shiny metal around the edges, fake chrome legs, rubber stoppers on the bottom of the legs, and chairs to match. Raymond noted the period decor quietly. And they talked.

Maggie talked about flyover, the local farmers, the virtual time-warp that the airfield was, the still small rental community that existed there, serving the local farmers and a few families that had been working odd-jobs and crop help for years in the spring, summer, fall and snow shovelling and repair jobs in the winters. The farmers paid the modest rent and utilities for their hands and the families spent Sundays going to church in North Platte and grocery shopping afterward.

Then she talked about her life growing up with her grandfather who had built the original runway, airport, gotten clearance and approvals back in the 1920's, built the houses for farm workers, leased property to the commercial interests that sprang up with the mail route through Flyover and the saving grace agriculture that kept the area viable during the 30's, Standard Oil and their tower, the hard times brought on by the war, and the fight that her grandfather had to keep the airfield small, private, and limited.

Then she talked about her youth and school and having to take over the airfield when her grandfather got sick and eventually died almost 10 years ago, now. She sniffed back the tears and went on about her strange and full time life, just maintaining the airfield, the town, and getting people to maintain the tower... and finally apologising for talking so much.

Raymond just smiled. He liked to hear her talk. He wanted to know more of her. Raymond had more than enough of the spoiled-for-choice urban girls he had known for years who also talk, but only of gym classes, dancing, work colleagues, petty disagreements, fake coffee dilettantes, California whines, zombie music, politics about which none of them can do anything, and everything he had ever imagined made up a life measured out by counting coffee spoons. The genuine, simple, and human qualities that were Maggie impressed him more than he could believe.

By the time Raymond was going to tell a bit about himself, it was late afternoon, sunset imminent and time to check to be sure all the lights were on. Oh, they were all on timers, but just in case Maggie always checked them. While she did that, Raymond closed and locked down his plane, still sitting in front of the terminal. That AVGAS had not happened yet, strangely.

When Maggie came back across the field Raymond asked her if he could take her anywhere for dinner. Maggie laughed, and patted his hand. "Raymond, the only place for dinner here, is here and I'm likely the cook. Might I make you dinner, this evening?" smiled Maggie.

And it was not but simple fare, but Raymond thought it lovely and more than satisfying enough for him. Accompanying the dinner was Raymond's turn to explain a bit about himself. Some of it, like Maggie, was a bit self-pitying and indulgent, but most was mere description of university, work on the trading floor, successes, failures, changes of career, the developed love of flying, dislike of cities, the decision to find a new life which led him here, likes and dislikes, favourite things and the question of how to find the values in life and what he wanted. Because Maggie had never knowingly lived in an urban environment, she did not understand the stresses and pressures of the city. But she could relate to the work burden and constraints as it was up to her alone to maintain the airfield.

Funny, both of them wanted something slightly, but not radically different than what they had known. Both of them understood the value of work and the necessity for it along a number of dimensions. Both of them felt underutilised and more than a bit taken for granted - but was there anyone to blame for that but themselves? Whining was a luxury they could afford to some extent, but not for very long as it only opened up a hole to the abyss of self-pity and degradation.

Maggie was not able to see her way out of the endless trap of the albatross around her neck that looked like an airfield. Raymond could not envision a place where the pressures he had known would not be engaged, at least in the lines of work he knew. Without saying it, they began thinking that the other represented an opportunity to move out of their traps and build something - but what? Without creative investment Flyover was going nowhere but the mind-achingly boring routine of maintaining an asset you can see falling, failing, deteriorating and band-aids of upkeep were not going to make it anything more than a rusting relic of the past.

But the dishes had to be done and after that Maggie offered Raymond one of the R 'n R rooms in the second floor of the terminal, generally used to allow crop dusters to catch a few hours sleep before going back up to spray in prime season...." 'cause if you don't do it, they can just as well call someone who can...". But the rooms had their own en suite facilities and were tastefully appointed in the period style to compete with the motels that used to be in Flyover as Maggie's grandfather had rented them out for a bit of extra money. So Raymond retrieved his modest bag and settled down for the night. The discussion of the futures ahead of each of them had cooled whatever ardour might have been generated earlier that evening, though the mutual attraction was not in any way denied, just being assessed. It was recognised that they understood more of each other than their words said.

Maggie's routine was to get up at dawn and kill the lights across the airfield, check to be sure there were no loose craft sitting around, check to be sure no loose vehicles were abandoned or occupied, and check the security of the buildings and hangers. She often thought it would be nice to have a dog to accompany her both for protection and companionship but never got around to finding one. But this morning she wondered what

Raymond was going to do. There was an old song, "will she stay or will she go..." that kept running through her mind while walking the buildings and strip, then back to the Terminal.

She never did this for herself, but made a small pot of coffee in case Raymond wanted some. He did. He had awakened on hearing her go out and got up, dressed, prepared, and even straightened the bed and towels. He left his bag in the room, not knowing what he was going to do. He came downstairs while the coffee was brewing and, once again, they stood and stared in each other's eyes, not so much searching, but learning and perceiving, until Raymond finally asked what she usually did for breakfast.

"Well, it depends," she smiled, "sometimes I have the time and feel like bacon and eggs and sometimes I have not so much time and have to do with toast and jam. Today I have time. What would you like?"

"I'd like to help you make bacon and eggs and maybe toast to go with it IF and only IF I can be a help and not be an observer."

"Okay, what do you want to do?"

"What if you put on the bacon so we can get some melted fat for the eggs. And I'll cook the eggs while you do the toast as I do not know your kitchen at all," smiled Raymond. And Maggie returned the grin while they moved into the diner style kitchen.

The kitchen had a couple of cook-tops below a rectangular opening behind the service aisle behind the counter that ran the length of the, well, diner, as that was the style. Beneath the cook tops were a couple of ovens. At one end of the cook tops was a butcher block with a sharp looking set of knives. On the back wall were some reach-in chilled storage and two racks of shelving filled with assorted sauté and fry pans, sheet pans, various sized pots, SS bowls, some large pots, and a few oven or roasting pans. Above the cook tops was a shelf with spices, colanders, metal cylinder containers, and hanging down from small hooks under the shelf were all sorts of tools, various sizes of ladles, various whisks, spatulas, dippers, measuring cups, turners, and so on. Not a badly equipped kitchen he thought. She used a sheet pan on which she laid the bacon and put it in a convection oven that was aside the cook tops near the door. He found the eggs in the reach-in and a fry pan on the shelves. Funny, he didn't feel so out of place and she didn't feel he was an interloper.

They cleaned the dishes and pans after they ate and Raymond asked if he could get a tour of Flyover as surely there was more to it than the field. Maggie checked the log and nothing was pending so she led Raymond out the back of the Terminal across the alleyway, in between a couple of houses with weeds overgrowing the gangway, and there they were on Main Street, Flyover, Nebraska.

For reasons Maggie did not know, the vacated buildings, bereft of water, heat, or air conditioning for all the years they had been abandoned, were not really ramshackle as much as slowly deteriorating. They were not falling down, which was probably a testament to her grandfather's determination to build stable buildings and commercial enterprises, not thrown together cheap that would collapse in 10 to 15 years.

There were small, occupied houses and closed-up establishments that gave an eerie feeling to the village, like the live living amongst the dead. But along the street there was a complex of former malt shops, a diner, a small saloon, and a Dry Cleaner / Laundry, shops with the Flyover Kinescope Miracle in the middle of the complex, standing tall like a large cow lick in a greased-down head of hair. Raymond looked at it for a long time, walked around the back of the complex, and around the other side. Across the street were shuttered storefronts of a grocery, a "5 and dime", pharmacy, and a ladies dress shop. But the Theatre interested him the most.

"So, how many people do you have in this area?" he asked while they were standing there.

"Oh, around 50 to 150 farm workers depending on the time of the year and the crop cycles, then another 50 or so farmers and their families - and that is within a 15 minute drive or less. Why?"

"How many planes can we park on the field?"

"Oh, we've had 20-30 if I open up all the hangers and push the parked planes in or to the side and if they are all single engine or twins like yours."

"Hmmm. Do you know what would it cost to make the airfield IFR?"

"It isn't that," she replied, "it is the hike in landing rates we'd have to initiate in order to afford the initial clearance and annual inspections, because it is over $4,500 for the one and over $3,400 each year thereafter. Then, there is the surveyor's report that goes with the submission as precise latitude and longitude, as well as altitude are required, to two significant places, mind you - so determination needs a professional certification sign-off. We're already a 10,000 foot field and we'd never expect anything over 200,000 pounds anyway, so it is more than long enough. And I'm not even mentioning the EPA Environmental Impact Statement, though most of this airfield is grandfathered, anyway. But further fees and requirements are imposed if we wanted to change from the private IFP we could be to a public one... then there are radio, transponder, radar, and personnel resourcing issues that come into play. Personally, we are probably better off being a VFR field with special published rules for night landings or take-offs. We already run the lights for that and have for years because the local crop dusters often don't finish until after sundown in peak season."

"Hmmmm.... can we take a look inside the closed buildings, please?"

"All of them? There are more than just these.
There are old motels and others on the next couple of
streets, a small old Lutheran church, and storefronts."
"No, just these for now, please?"
"What are you thinking, Raymond? I've been trying
to think of a way to attract people here for years. I've even
talked to many of the pilots and farmers, most of them
think there just isn't the mass, the volume of people or a
sufficient attraction to bring them in as it did when the
airfield was running in the 30's, particularly with the
competition from electronic entertainment. And North
Platte's business people are surely not friendly to
competition, so we'd find no support from the nearest
business hub."
"Just let me think and look, please. I'm not at all
certain what I'm thinking would work, but I want to think it
through. Do we have to go back to the terminal to get the
keys?"
"It will just take a sec. You can wait here if you
like..."
"No, I'll come along..."
And in a couple of minutes they were back as the
doors to the theatre.
"I have no idea what it is like in there. It has been
years since I was in there." And with that she unlocked
both locks on the doors and the padlock.
"We'll see," he smiled warmly.
One of the miraculous things about places shielded
from the severe winds of winter, that are not open to the
extreme vacillations of daily weather change, is that they
can virtually desiccate if moisture is not prevalent or in a
humid atmosphere. Those are the kinds of locations where
winter's snow comes down straight and gentle, not blown
by the furious razor winds; where it piles up gracefully, not
in drifts and hip deep accumulations. If the structural and
component integrity of the buildings are solid, there is no

reason to expect the interiors to degrade if the roofs are intact and they are kept moisture free.

The first thing Raymond noticed was that the smell rushing out at them was not exceptionally musty, something like your aged grandmother's house but not similar to the usually damp basement under her farmhouse. Thinking ahead to closing it up at least for parts of the year, Maggie's grandfather put the ticket window inside the vestibule so that the outer doors actually closed everything and sealed the building.

"Do the lights work?" asked Raymond.

"Wellllll, they used to but I haven't been in here for years."

The clearly period style switches were on the left wall inside the entrance. Raymond switched them all on... and the vestibule and lobby lit up like a grand palace. Where they stepped, they kicked up small clouds of dust from the barely light coloured carpet, a carpet that used to have vibrant and broad stripes of multiple colours that were still visible. They led past what used to be a soda fountain and snacks bar that covered the back wall of the lobby, past a lectern where someone used to take tickets, and to swinging doors that led to the theatre. There was also what looked like a coat room over on the left side of the lobby and between that and the doors to the theatre was a door with a porthole window through which one could see stairs behind it, leading to the projection room Raymond surmised. The ceiling was like a reversed layer cake, built out from areas of interest like the snack bar and coat room with three layers, each one higher than the earlier and each with a different colour on its side, colours matching the carpet at one time, perhaps, but mostly faded and flaking off in flaps of colour. But the lights and mirrors lit up everything. The layer of dust was visible on every surface, but loose, not gelatinous as it would have been with moisture present.

Next to the right hand swinging doors into the theatre was the lectern obviously for the ticket taker, and on the wall next to the lectern was a covered panel. When opened it showed two columns of switches with small, faded, yellowed squares of paper next to them that at one time indicated the location of the lights controlled by the switches. Raymond turned on all of them.

"By the way, the electrics and fuses are working in here, aren't they?" Raymond asked.

""We'll find out, won't we," Maggie smiled, looking hopeful. "I've never looked at anything in here since before my grandfather died."

"This place is amazing," Raymond drooled. "It is like a time capsule. I'd bet the wiring is original - which means it would all have to be replaced if we were to do something."

"We?" queried Maggie, looking at him like Tonto and as though he was the Lone Ranger with the massed hostile warriors of five tribes on the parapets above them and the Ranger says "What are we going to do now, Tonto?" and she was Tonto saying "what do you mean 'we', white man?" She had wracked her brain searching for an idea that would bring barnstormers and tourists into Flyover for years and this yahoo waltzes in out of the blue sky and thinks he knows what will do it? She was more than a bit put off by his seemingly arrogant assumptions at that moment.

Raymond, not being entirely emotionally blind, heard the grate of his thoughts on the frustration of her experience and turned to her, "hold on. I just have a vision of what this place could be that I want to relate to you, knowing that you surely ran every possible use for this theatre through your mind in the last 10 years - but you did so without my input, my friends, my connections, my experiences, or a bit of my capital for making changes. Please?" he asked in an importuning manner, looking directly at her and trying to see if he had quenched the fire that had just flared up in her eyes.

"Can we look in the theatre?" he asked while moving toward the doors.

Opening them was like stepping back into an art deco past, flowing and sculpted chandelier-like lighting regularly spotted in a ceiling that, like the lobby, was a layer cake of coloured levels with different light designs at the top of the layers like birthday candles and smaller sconces in the higher layers. Similarly, there was a wooden chair-rail height set of oak panels running around the walls and around the overly large circular columns reaching to the ceiling and above that were wide swathes of colour, matching the ceiling and the lobby scheme. But much of the painted work showed places where it was chipping off or had fallen away, but the wood, though dry looking, was not damaged from what he could see at the entrance. Because there was no mezzanine, the entry was overwhelmingly large, narrowing down to a distinct stage some 15-20 rows forward. However, by opening the doors, the air rushing in set off currents of dust on the carpet and the aisles that was reflected in the lighting, sending a wave down the main aisle to cascade against the front of the stage. The row after row of theatre seats in the traditional shell conformation were all covered with a patina of dust, but looked no worse for all the years they had been setting there.

"Wow, just wow," declared an astonished Raymond.

"Grandfather spared no expense in here. While he built the houses for a moderate square foot cost, he went overboard in here. It is all the finest available in its time. Then again, he was a key stop or at least a favourite one of the mail service when it ran this way and that paid very well he said. The theatre provided some entertainment for the pilots who stayed overnight here on their way across the country.... as well as the passengers of other craft; which is why we had so many motel rooms in the vicinity and why the kitchen in the terminal was set up so well."

"I'll need a dust mask to explore more in here, I'm afraid, but maybe we need to discuss my thinking before we do that."

"Raymond, having spent 10 years looking for ideas and options outside the box in which I feel trapped, I confess to being more than slightly upbraided by your gleeful expression of a future for this archaic trap when I've been so creatively frustrated by the market factors out here in the middle of nowhere."

And they exited the theatre, switched off the lights, and exited the lobby, turning off those lights, closed and locked the doors. They went around the back of the complex that faced the alley behind the Terminal and Raymond asked if she had the keys for the back doors to the Theatre. She did and opened the locks on the one side. They both peered in, Raymond looking for light switches on the immediate wall surfaces. He found them and switched them on. It looked just like the back of a stage set with curtains and many sets of pulleys and racks that used to hold sets and picture screens - and may still have rolled screens for all they could see from the doorway. But the floor of the stage was intact and still bespoke a slight polished sheen under the visible dust.

"Thank you, Maggie. Let's go back to the terminal, have a bit to drink, and let me tell you the workings of my mind." So they closed it up, locked the doors, and walked up the alley to the back of the Terminal.

"Let me go back and see where the back of the Theatre orients on the airstrip, please?"

So, Raymond quickly walked back to the Theatre while Maggie went in and began preparing some coffee for Raymond and tea for herself.

When he came into the Terminal he mentioned that there was this wide gangway between two small hangers opposite the back of the Theatre.

"Yeah, so?" challenged Maggie.

"Well if people want to access the theatre directly from the airstrip, we'll need a paved or raised walkway with lighting for nights that runs in between those hangers, you see?"

"What people, Raymond? For what reason do they want to come here? There is nothing here for them."

"Not yet, but you have a perfect multiuse building there, perfect for this area because it isn't too big, perfect because it can be adapted to a perfect presentation venue, and even more perfect because it can be a remote location without all the folderol travel and urban tense of other venues. Even more, it can be converted over to an entertainment venue so easily," enthused Raymond to a not-thoroughly believing Maggie.

"That is all very nice. I know the capabilities of the theatre. I also know that conversion to anything takes more capital than the airfield is able to generate in its current form and the potential audiences which you are implying come from where?" she asked.

"Initially, Omaha and other university towns, government towns because we have a conference venue or off-site venue they cannot beat. All we need to be operational is a massive cleaning job, a good mass of electronics, renovation of so many of those empty houses, a liquor license and food service support facilities for the theatre, communication and promotion, a removable and elevated floor for the theatre to give an option of theatre or conference centre, renovation of the theatre and cleaning it up, and a resource base that I already think you have in the farm worker wives. There you go, nothing to it."

"And from where does all the money come for this Mr. Developer?" as Maggie was getting quite sarcastic, now.

"Well, most of it I'll finance as I think we can make Flyover a real humming metropolis once again. You see, I have a good bit of capital left over from my days on the trading floor and if I stay here, it just makes sense to invest the money in making Flyover great again."

"Hmm," stalled Maggie, "more coffee?"

"Please."

And as Maggie walked over to get the coffee pot, two gigantic men wearing Nebraska State Police uniforms and one regular looking guy in a suit entered the Terminal and walked into the diner section.

Maggie turned to look at them while Raymond tensed ever so slightly, not at all if you weren't watching out of the corner of your eye. They walked over to Raymond and addressed him, "Raymond Offthecuff?"

Raymond looked up, and up, and up, "Yes, sir?"

"Stand up, please." And Raymond did while Maggie was standing holding the coffee pot near the counter, but not moving.

The suit talked, "Raymond OfftheCuff, also known as Raymond Stroud, Raymond Fisher, Raymond Mechanical, Raymond Ostentatious, Raymond the Fixer, Raymond the Fish, Raymond D. Raymond, Johnson C. Johnson, we are arresting you for interstate fraud, statutory rape, fleeing to avoid prosecution, theft of aircraft, flying without a license, being a public nuisance, wilful theft of affection, loitering, and public littering. You have the right...," as the suit went on through all the legal clearances. And Raymond gave this hurt puppy look to Maggie that would have broken her heart if she had not looked up the aircraft on the net the night before. She found that it had been stolen in Illinois and the name of the suspect was broadcast requesting anyone that saw the plane to call the

local police so they could apprehend the thief. Maggie did.
It took them a while to arrive, but all's well... she thought.

The uniforms cuffed Raymond and led him to the
car while the suit asked about and then retrieved
Raymond's bag from the room. When he got back down to
the diner he opened it and showed Maggie the .357
revolver in there, noting how lucky she was.

It seems that Raymond is a con man, laying out a
story much like the one he spread for Maggie to many
single women, some older, mostly older and some younger
than Maggie. He doesn't even plan these jobs, but chances
upon them and begins to weave his story, leveraging his
listening ability and studied interest to usually seduce and
subsequently extract vast sums from some of his victims.

"Well, he was S-O-L here, she said, "We're just
squeaking by."

"Thank you Ma'am. We appreciate your
observation and conscientiousness. He could have gotten a
lot further away if you hadn't checked the numbers on the
plane."

The cops all left. Raymond was sent back to
Illinois, was tried, convicted, and sentenced to 15 years in
prison, where he was able to meet many of Illinois' past
Governors.

Later that day Maggie broke down and cried for
hours. She thought that she really saw something in
Raymond's eyes and cursed herself for not making it more
obvious. After all, she perceived that he was being straight
with her. She could feel a sincerity that she seldom saw in
other people. She wept off and on for many weeks after
that.

About a year later, a new crop sprayer showed up in
Flyover. Mike Makeover was in his mid-30's, unmarried,
fair and about 5'8" and he and Maggie just meshed for
some reason. They married and had four children, three
boys and a girl. The boys went on to fly for the Air Force

and then airlines while the girl learned to be as good a
keeper of small airfields as her mama.

Raymond did not finish his prison sentence. About
three years in, he just upped and died. There was no
medical condition, no illness, no injury, no stroke or heart
attack, nothing to which the medical examiner could
attribute a cause for death. The few inmates that knew him
said that he died from a broken heart because of some
woman named Maggie.

[That is one of your worst endings, ever. Ed.]

*[[Okay, okay, I'll change it. Auth.]] [[Please, roll back to
the cops entering...]]*

...And as Maggie walked over to get the coffee pot,
two gigantic men wearing Nebraska State Police uniforms
and one regular looking guy in a suit entered the Terminal
and walked into the diner section.

Maggie turned to look at them while Raymond
tensed ever so slightly, not at all if you weren't watching
out of the corner of your eye. They walked over to
Raymond and addressed him, "Raymond McDonalduck?"

Raymond looked up, and up, and up, "Yes, sir?"

"Stand up, please." And Raymond did while
Maggie was standing holding the coffee pot near the
counter, but not moving.

The suit talked, "Raymond McDonalduck, the
people of Illinois want to thank you sincerely for the great
service you performed for them in helping engineer the
uncovering and capture of that band of government

extortionists. We would have officially thanked you back in Illinois but you ducked out before we could."

"Well, of all the people you busted, there were still a few enforcers on the lam and frankly I figured I was a target and people like professional extortionists never forget a slight, so I thought it was best to leave quickly, quietly, and as unobserved as possible," explained Raymond.

"Fair enough, but you did not give us a chance to give you this reward for breaking up that gang - it had been victimising state government for decades under the surface. Actually this is a small compensation compared to the billions they have cost us over the years, but better this than the retribution of the racketeers." And with that the suit handed him an envelope and said, "Thanks again Raymond. Sorry for the wanted notice on your airplane but that is the only way we thought we could find you quickly. We withdrew the notice when we knew where you were. So you're once again clean to fly, sir."

And with that the suit shook his hand, then he and the troopers left; all of them smiling as though they had completed their good deed for the day.

Maggie had placed the coffee pot on the counter while the police were talking. Now that they were leaving she came up to Raymond, threw her arms around his neck, and softly apologised, talking to his neck. He had shoved the envelope in his pocket and now put his arms around her, pulling her closer, and they kissed one of those kisses that lasts for years and years and for now ended up with them together and horizontal in her room after locking down the terminal.

In discussions and planning sessions over the next couple of days, Raymond and Maggie discovered that it wasn't the fact that Flyover was a central and historic airfield that made it special; it was the fact that it operated so that everything currently underway covered all the fixed and variable costs of the existing operations. Anything they might add as entertainment or featured service to generate revenues only had to cover the variable costs entailed with the service. This meant that, for example, the empty but habitable or cozy small houses could be rented out as motel rooms for only the cost of the cleaning services, sheets, towels, personalised toiletries, heat, light, and landscaping services, if any. While the landscaping services would have to be a more generalised fixed cost across many units, it was still a nothing expense and the rooms could be rented so cheaply as to make the roadside cheapies envious. Plus, while many were single bedroom kitchenettes, many were multiple bedroom suites, perfect for families. Now there was some capitalisation needed to bring them up to code, but most of the code changes were grandfathered and they could refrain from costs like the access ramps that were not essential to services in the target markets. However, bringing the electric up to code and installing fire alarms would be real costs they could not avoid.

Target markets? Remember interstate 80 parallels the old route 30, Lincoln Highway, to which there was a spur constructed decades ago and that was still maintained by the county. And what travels on 80? There are lots of tourists and truckers, loads of people needing clean places to stay overnight for cheap halfway through Nebraska. And it is not much used but there was the cloverleaf to the spur developed for Flyover when the original interstate was built.

Then, Maggie and Raymond thought about support services. Truckers. They would need fuel and food facilities, as would the cars. What if Standard would want to fulfil the marketing dream of 80 years ago and put up a food and fuel stop on the north side of the airstrip? Most of the housing was on the south side with not a long walk between them; though a walk over the airstrip would have to be erected. Then, for families, a small basics and ready-to-eat grocery operation could fit into one of the storefronts aside the theatre or across the street, as if you have a kitchenette, you can fix your own food and not have to "eat out", a realistic concern of families who try to find less expensive options for their holidays.

Then the theatre.

The major costs would be bringing the electrics up to code, they thought. Building the false floor over the theatre seating to make a level serving area for the sofa-centred seating. Because Flyover had such superior internet traffic, the idea was to make small entertainment areas with a central console in each and a small table around the console so that customers could order up movies or shows off the net while they sat and ate or drank. Wireless headphones took care of the likely audio interference of neighbours in the booths. The theatre would be a serving salon with food service from the diner next door - obviously there would have to be an opening between one and the other...and possibly traffic moving from the diner to the saloon.

But because the fixed costs of operation of the airfield were already covered by its existing revenue streams, prices for food and drink only had to cover the costs of goods and labour plus a little for the fixed utilities. Where the usual sum of raw goods and labour were factored as 40% of the cost in some food operations, figuring them as 70% of the costs allowed Ray and Maggie to underprice almost every operation in the state and still show a healthy profit...theoretically. The secret was that everything already bringing in revenues was meeting the break even for the operation, so adding any additional products or services only had to cover the variable costs and everything on top of that was pure profit.

Maggie had never looked at her heirloom like this before. She saw the logic and wondered why it had never occurred to her. The only thing left was to bite the bullet and bring in the contractors and services that would need to be employed to determine the capitalisation that was going to be needed and a good handle on the operating costs expected at various volumes. She and Raymond flew to North Platte to meet with various building and electrical contractors to get them to come out to Flyover and prepare their estimates for the work needed to be done. While they were there, they also dropped into the county clerk's office and picked up a marriage license... something they thought might be handy for their future.

Weeks went by waiting for all the contractors to go through the facility and tally up the costs. Maggie had forgotten how many units were actually on the streets beyond the airfield. Sure, many were rented, all the larger ones, but there were so many small units and medium sized ones. She and Ray decided to keep a few as rental units because they would have to hire new resources for all the facilities that would be created. Because they were literally cost-free to them, they could rent the places only for modest profits above the recovery costs for upgrades that would be assessed against each unit IF all the utilities were to be the renter's responsibility.

Raymond constructed spread sheet after spread sheet, one for each of the units and ones for the theatre...oh, now billed as "MaggieRay's Mezzanine", the diner, grocery, and so on as well as the combined project projection.

The interesting thing is that a team of Standard Oil's brand spanking new MBA's came in and negotiated a deal where they were only paying Maggie a fee in the low five figures per month for the facility they would erect, indemnify, advertise, manage, resource, and support. Maggie and Ray just smiled because before they came in Maggie was willing to let them use the property for free just to draw in the traffic if they'd cover all the building/construction costs and indemnification and throw in some advertising. So, since they were so bright, Ray got them to throw in a small percentage of the monthly revenues on top of that fixed fee. Half of the reason was because Ray thought they would be disappointed if they didn't get any push-back since surely they had already put something like that in their plans. Maggie liked that deal and wondered why anyone in their right mind would waste their time getting an MBA if that is an example of their training.

One of the nice things about the Standard Oil youngsters, though, was that they provided a marketing plan with likely traffic numbers. Ray and Maggie used their numbers to set up a business plan that they could use for financing applications if it was needed. Ray got a small seven figures reward from Illinois that he said would be used for the initial capital for the refurbishment of Flyover. With the exceptional job Maggie's grandfather had done and demanded 80 years ago, the total rehab cost was not twice that amount. However, there was also the initial equipment and supplies inventory that had to be invested; so in the end, they went to the banks to fund the entire rehab and kept Ray's money for the initial inventory in the saloon and diner, as well as the sheets, bedding, and housewares for the motel houses.

Ray and Maggie queried many of the farm working families to see if they would be looking for work in the various facilities that were going to open. Except for the families with infants and very small children, they found most of their resourcing needs could be met from the people who were already living in Flyover. This meant, at least initially, that they didn't have to bring in anyone from outside to resource the new facility.

It took almost a year for the full rehabilitation and stocking of the Flyover Country Oasis as well as the construction of the Standard truckers stop to become

operational. One of the first events in the MaggiRay's
Mezzanine was the wedding of Raymond and an obviously
pregnant Maggie. Everyone in the country around was
invited: farmers, fly-boys, farm hands, crop dusters, local
county officials, and even a few Standard Oil suits.

In the weeks after the wedding and as the Mezzie,
as it came to be called, was up and running, Maggie acted
as the hostess, having hired one of the local farmhand sons
who'd rather not work the farms, to manage the Terminal
while she was working. Raymond served tables, helped
seat people, tended bar, retrieved food orders from the
diner, and kissed Maggie when he had a moment.
Honeymoon? Are you kidding? Not in the food business,
maybe later.

The two of them had two children while all this was
going on, growing the business, making it a real Oasis in
the midst of Nebraska. They organised an Antique Airfield
Association that featured events in a virtual string of old
single lane fields across the country. The local farmers
were often grumbling that the Oasis was taking away good
workers that they needed in their fields - but somehow
always found new bodies to come in and replace them,
renting out more of the remaining houses in the Oasis that
Ray and Maggie had not allowed to be part of the motel
operation.

Then the day that Ray and Maggie had been fearing
finally arrived. Five suits from the Hilton Corporation flew
in to talk to them. The Oasis had been in operation for over
five years, now and had long since paid off the small bank
loan. The profitability of the operation was legend and the
suits wanted part of it.

Maggie was pregnant with their third child and,
honestly, not looking forward to working through it as she
had done with the first two. She and Ray had built a
substantial farmhouse on the south end of the property, just
where the shallow valley was beginning to tilt up, and the

two of them were quite comfortable and amazed at such a success in so short a period of time. The suits offered them a number in the low nine figures for the entire operation, buildings, airfield, land, the lot. Maggie turned them down so fast that it almost snapped their necks. They tried again thinking she had not heard them. Same answer.

They tried a number of different approaches but none of them would work. They were not desperate, but hurting. You see, The Oasis hurt their named business and many of their unnamed storefront motel establishments throughout Lincoln County. That put a real dent in their revenues for the rest of the state as only Omaha was unaffected by this operation.

Ray offered to construct a deal he thought his wife might buy if they'd give them a week to work it out. The suits agreed to come back in a week.

Maggie was really not pleased, but Ray asked for her to listen. He would never construct a deal that sold any of it, not a single door or panel or square inch of the property. So Maggie calmed and Raymond explained that he would construct a lease deal for a specified period where they could take over the operation of the hospitality services, everything except the airfield for "x" dollars per month. The lease would not include the Standard Oil lease money or any of the revenues of the airfield, or any of the farm worker rental housing - because they weren't interested in that, anyway. Basically, all Hilton wanted was the motel business, MaggieRay's, and the diner attached to it. And their operation and management would be what Ray would cover in the lease, which, again, would be for a sum less than the suits would expect, so they'd jump on it.

The suits returned in seven days. Ray showed them the deal he was offering. They went into an impromptu conference amongst themselves, made a couple of phone calls. They jumped on it. Ray had his Chicago lawyers draw up the paperwork and the deal was signed in 14 days.

The turnover period was fairly fraught with teaching urbane sophomores how to deal with real people and things in Flyover, but eventually the balance of people and tasks was complete.

Maggie went back to taking care of the Terminal and her beloved airstrip during the day and employing a night manager of sorts to take care of it at night. Given the high speed net, Ray dabbled in the futures market, again, and formed a market strategy action group with the local farmers.

She and Ray had two more children, lived cozily in their farmhouse, and thoroughly enjoyed watching the rest of the world from Flyover Country, don't you know.

Limitations of Brain Research

Perhaps one of the noted limitations that critics might recognise is the author's separation from the profession for a few decades. However, in reviewing a few research papers two years ago, the author observed that excepting more sophisticated measurement at the neuron level, brain research, per se, does not seem to have moved on very far from its earlier strategy of looking at the brain as a mechanic looks at an automobile engine. It is sort of a more highly cultivated phrenology, if you will. One of the more interesting outputs is, the author understands, the idea that because brain researchers cannot find it, we have no consciousness. One wonders when they will declare memories as non-existent as they can't seem to find them, either.

The author believes Newtonian researchers are showing the basic inadequacy of their Empiricist and reductionist roots, a basic Aristotelian fallacy left over from the Antonio Conti snow job imposing Newton on the world of Science as something more than the heretical, plagiarist, Alchemist kook that he was. One of the more dangerous results of this materialist mechanical nonsense is ignoring the very real electro-magnetic (EM) nature of man and the potentially dangerous and / or fatal poisoning of the EM environment over the last 150 years. However, the EM issue is well described by Arthur Firstenberg in his book ("The Invisible Rainbow"), so any treatment here is decidedly off-topic.

The impact of the refutation of anything outside the myopic Empirical shell meant that not only did science

deny everything spiritual, but ignored and declared anything outside their limited metric world impossible. For an example of this mentality, the reader is suggested to view a brief video of Dr. Rupert Sheldrake on the subject of the limitations of science,
https://www.youtube.com/watch?v=JKHUaNAxsTg

The reader is asked to ignore the absence of the usual scientific citation practices, as this is merely an essay and is not being presented as researched truth.

Background

Decades ago, Penfield noticed that when electrically stimulating certain parts of the brain during surgery - often needed to be accomplished while the patient is conscious for certain procedures - that some elicited vivid memories of events and sensory stimuli in the patients. Thus the search for memories in the brain took off like a frenzied application for funding to the National Institute for Health (NIH). However, as noted in the introduction, success in discovering where or how or when they are deposited in the brain is no closer to fruition than the author's attempt to win the lottery, any lottery, any country, any time.

Other researchers concurrently and consistently have shown that the hippocampus, one of the older phylogenetic structures in the brain, is essential for processing information and learning.

The hippocampus is one of a number of structures including the amygdala, pituitary, hypothalamus, pineal gland, and thalamus that have comprised most all identifiable brains including and above the phylogenetic level of bony fishes. Added onto these basic structures is an increasing amount of cerebral tissue as you look at more advanced animals.

One of the key activities of the brain and these structures is the control of basic physiology and endocrine functions for the survival of the animal, including appetite and reproduction. The feedback loops regarding hormonal stimulation and regulation are all under the control of certain brain areas. However, it is not as simplistic as an I/O control, as ACTH (Adrenocorticotropic Hormone), secreted by the hypothalamus and stimulating the adrenal glands to produce adrenalin, when needed, might be thought to merely feed back to the hypothalamus... but Endroczi, et.al. found in 1970 that rats with their hippocampus removed had three times the level of circulating ACTH than normal rats, thus indicating a role of the hippocampus in a more extensive feedback loop than expected.

Humans with severe damage to their hippocampus lose the ability to process new information into memories BUT retain full memories of events and everything prior to their loss of hippocampal function. See the year 2000 movie "Memento" for an excellent treatment of the issue and problems faced, though considerably more dramatically than most.

Studies referenced by Rupert Sheldrake (see video link in the introduction) and reported by him, indicate that animals of the same species who learn a novel task in one location somehow communicate that information to their species peers in another location because that second group seems to learn the new task faster than the first. He goes on to note that a similar phenomenon shows up in crystalising compounds when they've not been crystalised before. The second attempt to crystalise that same compound always takes less time than the first. Similarly, the third is faster than the second, and so on.

It is postulated in a number of religions (which is why the Dead-Souls faction that represents Empiricism would never even think of it) that after one dies G-d reviews every action of one's life with the departed soul. Okay... excepting Sammy in the first story herein, the author is not aware of any verifiable testimony outside of the "white light" returning-from-the-dead experiences related by many but in which there has not been

verification of this activity. Indeed, this may happen after
physical death is ensured which it has not been in those
cases. However, the reason we are writing about this is that
just as current neuroscientists are having trouble finding
memories within living brains, if this procedure was the
case, would it not be even more difficult when one is no
longer alive and able to remember events from one's
childhood through one's passing? Even more, after death
the physical shell is already deteriorating and any memory
in the brain would be in some stage of organic decrement
already. Therefore, would not those memories have to
exist somewhere that was impervious to the vagaries of
physical existence on this mortal plane? This observation
is of no interest to the Empiricist set, but only to those who
know of and believe in Him. And, indeed, the author
recognises that this may not represent an universally shared
perception or belief.

Hypotheses

The author thinks it is reasonable to posit the
following macro-level functions for the human (and most
animal) brains: self-preservation and communication.

Maintenance and welfare of the physical plant, so to
speak, through an interconnected endocrine and
neuroendocrine mechanisms regulating respiration,
metabolism, satiety, rest, reproduction, thermal
homeostasis, protection from danger, and the various
processes required to keep body and soul together, so to
speak. This is, the author thinks, the primary responsibility
of the archicortical system and its interconnected parts.
Tied in with this are all the sensory perceptions required to
support these functions including, but not exclusively,

sight, olfactory, physical sensory, auditory, temperature sensory, taste, and perceptions outside physical manifestations such as the phenomenon that some animals and some people can "sense" when they are being watched. In the video referenced above, Sheldrake posits that such a well-refined sense contributes significantly to animals being able to avoid predators.

Similarly associated with these functions is the key ability of memory both in learning behaviour, learning survival skills, and, in humans, learning information as well as memories of events, people, smalls, tastes, and all the other experiences that can be so classified.

But where are they?

This author posits that such memories are not physically within the brain, but for the sake of convenience, may exist in a place conveniently termed the memory dimension (MD). The function of the hippocampus, then, becomes not just information or sensory integrative but transmission into this dimension. Retrieval may be a hippocampal function, but not solely likely and would then be mediated by a confluence of other archicortical structures.

That, then is the other macro level function of the brain: communication in a dimension and at a level of which we are thoroughly unaware and presently unable to measure BUT surely is integrated with the EM nature of humans, as noted earlier in this essay. Ignoring the faculty of speech, developed as handy in the near environment when mental communication fails, one might wonder how speech is an adjunct to mental communication abilities left undeveloped due to the easier verbal procedure.

At first glance much of this appears to be preposterous. But then such derision is also based in a Newtonian negation of all possible functions outside the determinist materialist mechanics that is the Newtonian universe. To begin to understand the visible cracks and fallacies of this view, outside the obvious reality of individual consciousness and free will, the case files referenced in the previously noted Firstenberg volume explain the real life experiences of people and their more sensitive EM situations in a world increasingly polluted by sensory poisoning effects.

The implication of this is that cerebral networks are organising the location of memories, parts of memories, associated details, and so on, much the way computer memory has to keep track of the various parts of files laid down in it as memory. This means that what Penfield stimulated was not the memories, per se, but the local representations of the locations where they were stored in the MD.

Then, one might ask, where is this MD? The answer is likely all around us, but in a dimension that is not dependent on our physicality. The author defers to a vast other sphere of interests if anyone wants to bring up the idea of an "aura" in this context, ok? The author is not touching it, so to speak.

Now that should be the trigger for another set of derisive snorts.

However, if you have ever heard Dr. Steven Greer talk about "zero-point Energy" fields, he openly says, "It is all around us", a cubic centimetre of space having sufficient energy to fully power your house, car, etc. In that this energy may not be readily available within the four dimensions in which we limited humans normally play, does not mean it is not there. It only means that we do not have the ready ability to access it with our current technology. Similarly it may be so with the MD, though secured with our individual mental signature.

However where our memories may be, as well as our consciousness, it is obvious that they are not within the physical shell we call our bodies and brain. Is it not time to throw off the limitations imposed by an alchemist described political system that has never been able to move us beyond simple four dimensional relationships to discover things that the former ignorance deftly derided as impossible but of and for which we see constant proofs? Better, the null set of results for finding memories within the brain should be sufficient impetus to begin to look elsewhere were it not for the Newtonian limitations of his cold, dark, hand of formalism and creative inhibition.

Consequences of not necessarily the discovery of the MD, but of understanding what it means are manifold. Remembering that Sheldrake talks about intra-species communications and how one group in one location learning a novel task means that another group in another location can master the task in less time, what does this mean for human learning? In the Hebrew's Torah it is inferred that the learning of the Oral Torah by anyone makes it easier for the next and how such learning develops a shared information set readily available to the larger group of those who would learn. The implications of ideas like this foster a shared culture and knowledge base that would imply greater cohesiveness and shared knowledge amongst members of the same culture. Similarly, divisive elements interrupting the contiguous flow of ideas would tend to disrupt and separate members of that culture. One almost verges on the rationale of the tribal social structure and the absolute need for intellectual integrity to maintain cohesiveness following this thought to its logical conclusion, but the author will not go that far. The next point in that set of thoughts is the obvious reason as to why one marries within the belief set culture and not outside it. However, we're not going there.

The author initially excused this brief essay for not having any scientific rigor, so let us extend that posture with an apology should the author's ideas replicate those published elsewhere and with which the author is unfamiliar. Plagiarism is not the author's intent and he asks if he has inadvertently duplicated the thoughts of another already published, that he be excused and informed via the e-mail address published in the Acknowledgements.

Thank you.